Murder from Scratch

Also available by Leslie Karst

Sally Solari Mysteries

Death al Fresco

A Measure of Murder

Dying for a Taste

Murder from Scratch

A SALLY SOLARI MYSTERY

Leslie Karst

CROOKED
LANE

NEW YORK

Published in the United States by Crooked Lane Books, an imprint of The Quick Brown Fox & Company LLC.

Crooked Lane Books and its logo are trademarks of The Quick Brown Fox & Company LLC.

Library of Congress Catalog-in-Publication data available upon request.

ISBN (hardcover): 978-1-68331-953-5
ISBN (ePub): 978-1-68331-954-2
ISBN (ePDF): 978-1-68331-955-9

Cover illustration by Hiro Kimura
Book design by Jennifer Canzone

Printed in the United States.

www.crookedlanebooks.com

Crooked Lane Books
34 West 27th St., 10th Floor
New York, NY 10001

First Edition: April 2019

10 9 8 7 6 5 4 3 2 1

For my cool cat dad, Kenneth L. Karst,
who first played Frank, Ella, and
Mel for me on his hi-fi.

Chapter 1

Something about Brian seemed off. I couldn't tell precisely what—perhaps the angle of his lanky body as he hunched over the counter? Or maybe the erratic way he was chopping shallots for tonight's béarnaise sauce, making a series of slow, methodical slices followed by a barrage of rapid-fire strokes.

Catching my stare, the cook frowned and set down his rosewood-handled knife. Since Gauguin didn't open for another hour, the kitchen was still cool, its ovens and stovetop not yet fired up for dinner. Nevertheless, several beads of sweat had appeared on Brian's forehead. He wiped them away with the sleeve of his chef's jacket, then reached once more for the knife.

"Hey, you okay?" I asked.

"Yeah, I'm fine. I've just been a little under the weather the past few days. I think it must be that crud that's going around town."

Uh-oh. Visions of infectious pathogens being passed to our customers flashed through my brain as he resumed chopping the mound of shallots before him. "You think you should be working if you're sick?"

He waved off my concern. "Don't worry. I've been washing my hands like crazy. And besides, I'm actually way better today."

Studying Brian's pallid complexion, I found it hard to share his confidence. But I also knew there was no way we could get anyone else to come work in his stead on such short notice. Kris was out of town until tomorrow, and even though it was only a Wednesday night, running the kitchen with just Javier and me on the hot line and grill station would be a nightmare.

"Okay," I said. "But I want to see some heavy-duty hand washing by you tonight. Got it?"

"Yeah, yeah," he responded, annoyance creeping into his voice. "I know the drill." With an impatient shake of his close-cropped head, Brian returned to his chopping.

After checking on the *glace de viande* I had reducing on the stove for tonight's filet mignon special, I headed up the stairs behind the reach-in refrigerator and around the corner into the restaurant office. I'd inherited Gauguin only the previous spring, but the warm, comfy room already felt like home.

Javier, my head chef, was seated at the oak desk, peering at his phone.

"Good news, Sally," he said as I took a seat in the pale-green wing chair across from him. "I just heard from the bank. Looks like I should be able to transfer the money by the beginning of next week."

We were in the process of making Javier a half owner of Gauguin, but the sale wouldn't be final until the deposit of funds and signing of the contract.

"Great," I said. "Because as soon as it's official, that means you'll share legal responsibility with me if our customers get sick from eating our food."

In response to his raised eyebrow, I recounted the conversation I'd had down in the kitchen with Brian.

"I'm not so sure it's a flu that's going on with him," Javier said when I'd finished, staring past me at the tall bookshelf jammed with food essays, cookbooks, and travel memoirs.

"What do you mean?"

Lips pursed, he turned his gaze to me. "Haven't you noticed him lately? How he's been acting, I dunno . . . kind of strange?"

"Strange how?"

The wooden chair creaked as Javier shifted position. "Well, like being late to work, for one. And he's been taking more breaks than usual, too." The chef reached for the small carved tiki atop the desk and rubbed its menacing features absently with his thumb. "And haven't you noticed how he's seemed kind of out of it the past few weeks? You know, staring off into space and not listening when you talk to him?"

"Yeah, now that you mention it, I have. And he's been pretty testy, too. Like just now, when I wanted to make sure he was washing his hands, he got all snippy with me."

"There you go." Javier set the tiki back down with a *clunk*. "I was thinking we should keep an eye on Brian, make sure there's nothing going on. It might just be something like girlfriend problems, but if he's getting super stressed by work, it could be bad. This job can really get to you if you're not careful."

I knew this to be true. Being a line cook had never been an easy job, and with the advent of the so-called "food revolution," the combination of long, exhausting hours and the pressure of frequently changing your menu in an attempt to constantly seem new and exciting could be too much for some restaurant workers.

I nodded my understanding. "Right. I can ask Eric what he knows, too. He sings with Brian in the chorus. And maybe he could even do a little snooping around for us."

"That would be great," Javier said, then picked up his phone at the ping of an incoming text.

As I made my way back downstairs, however, I wondered how Eric—my ex-boyfriend/current best pal—would feel about such a request. Because even though he did work as a district attorney, I could well imagine he might not be too thrilled about being asked to spy on a friend and fellow bass singer.

Brian wasn't in the kitchen when I got back down there, but came in from the dry storage room a couple of minutes later. With a smirk, he made a great show of using the handwash station, then set to work prepping the *mise en place* inserts for the hot line—chopping onions and cilantro, filling plastic squirt bottles, and setting out stainless-steel containers of capers, lemon slices, and brandy-soaked apricots.

I monitored him closely that night. But, other than washing his hands so often I feared they'd shrivel up like my *nonna*'s sun-dried tomatoes (the frequency of which was no doubt increased by my constant surveillance), Brian acted completely normal. The same constant banter with the kitchen crew, the same speed and deftness sautéing an order of broccoli rabe with garlic and red pepper flakes and whipping up a new batch of béarnaise sauce.

Watching as he used a squirt bottle to execute perfectly formed swirls of sriracha-mayonnaise atop an order of our spicy fried chicken, I thought about what Javier had said. *He must be wrong. Brian doesn't even seem sick, much less stressed out about anything. Maybe he simply was down with the flu and is better now, just like he claims.*

Once home from work, I plopped down on the sofa to unwind with a bourbon-rocks and some late-night TV streaming. But as I watched a show about the hectic and stressful life of working at celebrity chef Nobu Matsuhisa's restaurant in New York City, my thoughts returned to the cook. Pausing the episode, I sipped from my drink and stroked Buster, who had curled up next to me on the couch. The big brown dog briefly opened his eyes, then let out a squeaky yawn and promptly went back to sleep.

Javier has been in the restaurant business for years, I thought as I gazed at the frozen image of Chef Matsuhisa slicing through a chunk of shiny red tuna. *And in the eight months we've worked together, he's proved to be a reliable judge of our kitchen staff. If anyone would know whether a fellow cook was having some kind of problem, it would be Javier.*

Maybe I should take his concerns about Brian seriously, after all.

* * *

I slept in the next morning until eight thirty, and would have snoozed even longer had Buster not jumped onto the bed to slather my face with "You need to get up *right this instant*" kisses. Delivering an affectionate slap to his dusty brown flank, I shoved the insistent dog away, then threw off the covers and sat up.

"Fine," I said. "But as punishment for interrupting my beauty sleep, you're gonna have to wait till I make coffee before we go outside."

Once the pot was brewing, I opened the front door, and the dog trotted out to sniff along the edge of the sidewalk and add his messages to those that had been delivered overnight. Shivering from the cold, I collected the morning paper from its usual spot under the Mexican sage bush and scanned the sky. Blue as my father's azure eyes, not a wisp of a cloud in sight. And if today was like yesterday, it would warm up to the high sixties by midday.

This wasn't unusual for early December in Northern California, but the rainy season was just around the corner.

Best take the opportunity to go for a bike ride while I still can without getting drenched.

After downing my coffee and taking Buster for a brisk walk down to Lighthouse Field, I changed into my cycling shorts and Tour of California leader's jersey, then wheeled my red-and-white Specialized Roubaix out the front door. A trip to Davenport, the old whaling community ten miles north of Santa Cruz, seemed like the perfect ride for this glorious morning.

The wind was thankfully minimal and traffic light on Highway 1, so I was able to relax as I pedaled up the coast and enjoy the scenery—rows of spiky artichokes, their dull-green leaves glistening from the day's watering; skeletons of old wooden barns, barely able to stand; and the occasional glimpse of the Pacific Ocean flecked with fishing boats on their way back to port with the morning's catch.

Rather than stopping at the bakery in Davenport as was my usual routine, I turned around and headed immediately back to Santa Cruz. My stomach had started to rumble as I'd pumped up the hill out of Liddell Creek, and a vision had come to me of all that panettone sitting in the Solari's freezer, left over from the big sister-cities dinner my dad had hosted back in October. He was offering the eggy cake, studded with pine nuts and dried fruit, as a dessert special on the weekends until it was gone, but I knew he wouldn't begrudge his darling daughter a free slice.

Back in town, I cruised down West Cliff Drive, then bounced along the asphalt-covered planks to the end of the Municipal Wharf, freewheeling up to the back door of my father's Italian seafood restaurant. He and my mother had run the place together until she'd passed away from cancer several years ago. I'd been working as a lawyer at the time but had already become disillusioned with the life of an associate attorney and its constant scramble for billable hours. As a result, it hadn't taken much for Dad to convince me to return to the family fold after Mom's death to run the front of the house at Solari's.

I'd pretty much grown up in the restaurant, so the work wasn't that difficult. But neither was it fulfilling. Then my

Aunt Letta had been murdered last spring, and I'd been astounded to learn I'd inherited her French-Polynesian restaurant. It had taken some doing, but a few months ago I'd finally managed to maneuver my way out of Solari's so I could put all my energy into Gauguin. Though my father did still use "the dad card" to guilt me into working at his place on occasion when he was in a jam.

Luckily, today was not one of those days. After stowing my bike in the tiny Solari's office, I headed for the walk-in freezer, snagged a slice of panettone, then slid it into the microwave in the corner of the kitchen. My dad was at the stove, stirring an enormous pot of red sauce with a long-handled spoon.

"Hi, hon," he said, setting the spoon aside and covering the pot. "What brings you in? I was about to call you, actually."

"Just a post-ride treat," I said. "Couldn't resist a slice of your panettone."

"Ah." He smiled. "It's been so popular, I'm thinking of adding it as a regular dessert."

"Great idea." At the ding of the microwave, I removed the plate and bit into the soft, hot cake. "So what were you going to call me about?" I asked, mouth full.

My father moved forward to allow Emilio to step behind him to the range top, where the line cook set about heating a large sauté pan over a high flame. "You get the paper, right?" Dad asked, and I nodded. "Well, did you happen to see this morning's story about that woman they found yesterday dead at her house?"

I frowned, wondering where this could be going.

"Uh-huh. But they didn't say who it was, pending notification to the family."

My father shook his head. "Yeah, well, the family actually does know. It was her daughter who found her."

"You know who the dead woman is?"

"I do. And she's a relative of ours. By marriage, anyway. Jackie Olivieri." At my questioning look, he went on. "She was married to Richard, my cousin Sophia's son."

"Oh, right." I remembered now. But Richard had died soon after they married, when I was living down south during college. "I know I went to their wedding, but I never really got to know either of them."

"That's 'cause after Richard died, Jackie didn't have a whole lot of contact with our family. I think the last time I saw her was at Alfred's wake." This was Cousin Sophia's husband, Jackie's father-in-law. "But that was almost ten years ago."

"Wait," I said. "Didn't Richard and Jackie have a daughter who was blind?" And then I put my hand to my mouth. "Oh, no. Is that who found her?"

Dad bit his lip. "Uh-huh. Evelyn is her name. I gather she came home after a night away and Jackie was lying there on the living room floor . . ."

"Dead," I finished for him. "How horrible for her." The image of a young, blind girl stumbling over the body of her dead mother caused a wave of nausea to pass over me, and I leaned against the counter behind me for support. "How old is Evelyn?"

"Nineteen or twenty, I think. She's a student at the community college, and I guess she was living with her mom to save money."

"Right," I said, before looking up at my dad. "How come you know so much about it, anyway?"

"Because when the cops came to her house, Evelyn was, as you can imagine, pretty upset, so they asked her who was her closest relation. And I was it," he said, pointing at his chest with his thumb. "Other than her grandmother, Cousin Sophia, who's gotta be at least eighty and is living in assisted care these days. So, long story short, she came to stay with me last night, and that's how I know everything that happened."

"Wow." I watched as Emilio stirred the mound of chopped onions he now had browning in olive oil and garlic in the large pan, then turned back to Dad. "Do they have any idea what happened to Jackie?"

"The cops haven't said anything to Evelyn, but she told me she found some pill containers as well as a liquor bottle by her mom's body. So I'm guessing overdose."

"Accidental or on purpose?" I asked, and Dad shrugged.

"Who knows," he said. "Anyway, here's the thing. Jackie's house has been cordoned off by the police, and Evelyn's way too freaked out to go back home yet, in any case. So, well, she wants to stay with me for a while."

"Uh-huh . . ."

"But the problem is, she has a dog, and you know how allergic I am."

I was indeed well aware of how sensitive my father was to dogs. Soon after my Aunt Letta had rescued Buster from that shelter in Ensenada, she'd brought the puppy over to my dad's house, and within minutes his eyes had been so red and swollen he looked like he'd contracted a severe case

10

of pink eye and simultaneously been stung by a dozen bees. And now that I'd inherited the dog, Dad would sometimes make me leave my sweater or jacket out on his front porch if it had too much Buster hair on it.

Dad cleared his throat as he stared down at his grease-encrusted leather shoes. "Anyway, that's the reason I was going to call you this morning," he said after a moment, still avoiding my gaze. "I was hoping maybe you could take her in."

Chapter 2

"What? No way," I said. "You can't really expect me to baby-sit some kid I've never even met. And, besides, I'm way too busy right now at Gauguin to—"

"First of all, she's not a kid," Dad interrupted, his eyes now hard and focused on mine. "She's a fully mature adult who needs no babysitting, I can assure you. She just needs a place to stay for a couple of weeks."

"A couple of *weeks*?"

"And I hardly think your work at Gauguin is any more time-consuming than mine here at Solari's, especially since you now have Javier to run the place with you."

He had me there. Although Emilio was a great line cook and a tremendous help to Dad, he was no Javier. No one was.

I tried to imagine what Evelyn must be going through right now, having been suddenly orphaned by the unexpected death of her mother. I could relate to some of it, as my own mom had died several years ago. But I'd known it was coming and I'd been thirty-six at the time, not twenty. *Evelyn must feel completely shattered.*

"So," I asked after a moment, "I take it she has no one else to stay with?"

Dad shook his head. "No. And even if she did, it should still be us. Because we're her family."

And that was that. To the Italians in our community, whose forebears had emigrated to Santa Cruz from Liguria over a hundred years ago, nothing trumped *famiglia*.

His face softened at my nod of understanding. "That's my girl. I promise it won't be that hard. I bet you end up really liking having her around. And to sweeten the pot, I'll even forgive your rent while she stays with you."

It was a generous offer. I was living in my Aunt Letta's old house, which Dad had inherited after she'd been killed last spring. And although he didn't charge me anywhere near market value for the place, having it rent-free for even a couple weeks would be a boon to my finances.

"I tell you what," Dad said, unfastening the white apron tied about his black-and-white-checked chef's pants. "Let's go over there right now before the lunch crowd arrives so you can meet Evelyn, and then I can drive both of you and her dog over to your house." He turned back to the stove. "Emilio, be sure to get a pot of water going for that ravioli special. I'll be back by noon, but if there's a rush before then, you can ask Joe to help out."

"No worries; I got it covered." The line cook waved us away and returned to his onions.

*   *   *

The barking of a dog greeted Dad and me as we climbed out of his old Chevy pickup. I lifted my bike from the bed of the truck, and as I wheeled it up the driveway, I could see the dog's dark-brown face at the window of the guest bedroom—my room, growing up—going ballistic the same way Buster does whenever anyone comes to the door. A hand reached out to grasp the dog's snout, and it quieted down.

Dad unlocked the door and stepped inside. "Evelyn?" he called out. "It's me, Mario." I followed him into the living room and leaned the bike against the wall.

The door to my old bedroom opened a crack, and a slight woman slipped out into the hall, shoving the dog's protruding head back inside the room. "Coco, stay," she said. "And hush. Good girl."

Evelyn closed the door and turned to face us, brushing back a lock of light-brown hair. She held what looked like a bundle of rods in one hand. "Hi. I didn't expect you back so soon." Her dark eyes darted about and came to rest—or so it appeared—on me. "Is someone else with you?"

"My daughter, Sally," Dad said. "I wanted to introduce you two."

"Oh, great." Evelyn popped open what I now realized was a collapsible cane and came down the hall toward me. Stopping, she leaned the cane against the wall, and I stepped forward to take her outstretched hand. Her grip was strong but at the same time warm and friendly.

"Nice to meet you," I said. "Though it's too bad it had to be in this situation. I'm so sorry about your mother."

"Thanks. I'm still trying to take it all in." She released my hand to wrap her arms about herself, as if in a reassuring self-hug. The three of us stood there in the hall, no one speaking.

"Uh, why don't we sit for a bit in the kitchen," Dad finally said, breaking the awkward silence. "I can make us some coffee."

Evelyn dropped her arms with a light smile. "Coffee sounds outstanding."

One big point in her favor. "I couldn't agree more," I said.

Dad touched Evelyn on the shoulder and held out an arm for her to take, but she shook her head. "Thanks, but I think I've got it down."

She made her way confidently down the hallway, the cane swinging back and forth before her, tapping both sides of the wall. Then she turned right into the dining room, skirted the large walnut table, and made her way into the sixties-era kitchen with its vinyl flooring, Formica counter-top, and avocado-green appliances.

Evelyn and I pulled out chairs and took a seat at the small, round breakfast table while my father busied him-self with pouring coffee from a can into a filter, filling the carafe with water, and pouring it into the machine.

"Dad says you're a student at Cabrillo College," I said as he fetched spoons, milk, and sugar and set them on the table.

Evelyn folded up her cane, fastened the tubes together with its elastic band, and set it in her lap. "Uh-huh. I'm studying computer science. I only have one more semester till I get my AS degree, and then I'll transfer to a four-year university. Probably San Jose State."

"Is it hard being a student? You know . . ."

"Because I'm blind?" she said with a laugh. "Don't worry, I'm not offended. It's not as if it's something you can ignore. I am in fact most definitely *blind*. And yeah, it is harder for me than for a sighted person, but that's the reason I'm taking computer classes. These days, with so much new technology, it's way better for blind people than it used to be. All the computer programs and phone apps they have now, it's amazing."

"Like Siri and Alexa, you mean?"

"Sure, those are great. But there are all sorts of other things that are specifically designed for the blind as well. Like, check this out." Evelyn pulled an iPhone from the back pocket of her red capris and swiped her index finger over its screen.

I peered over her shoulder and watched as the website for a local Mexican restaurant appeared. A few more swipes and a robotic voice started speaking: "Appetizers. Cheese nachos. Cheddar and jack cheese, beans, and jalapeños. Six dollars. Deluxe nachos. Cheddar and jack cheese, beans, guacamole, sour cream, and jalapeños. Nine dollars. Tortilla chips with guacamole and sals—"

She shut it off.

"Whoa," I said. "That's awesome."

"I know." Evelyn shoved the phone back into her pocket with a grin. "I picked that app to show you because I love food, but now I'm totally starving, thinking about those nachos. I may have to call a Lyft and go have some for lunch."

Three more big points for her. One for loving food, another for pulling up the menu of one of my favorite Mexican joints, and the third for saying Lyft rather than Uber.

"Okay, look," I said as Dad pushed his chair back and stood up at the beeping of the coffee maker. "I know you need a place to stay for a while, and I imagine my father told you about his massive dog allergy."

"Yeah, Mario told me," Evelyn said, nodding thanks as my dad set a cup down before her with a *clunk*. "Plus I could hear him sneezing like crazy this morning when he got up."

"Milk or sugar?" Dad asked.

"No thanks. I don't like to dilute any of the caffeine." Reaching out her hand, she gently swept the space in front of her until her fingers touched the cup, then raised it to her lips. "So, anyway, I've been thinking of places where I could maybe stay until I'm ready to go back home."

"Well, that's why I brought it up," I said. "Because if you'd like to come stay with me, that would be okay. I have a spare bedroom, so there's plenty of space."

"Really?" For the first time since I'd met her, Evelyn smiled with her entire face. "And Coco, too?"

"Sure, that shouldn't be a problem. I also have a dog, Buster, and he loves other dogs. We could introduce them first to make sure it works out, but I'd be surprised if they didn't get along. Is Coco friendly?"

"Very. Too much, maybe. Here, why don't you come meet her now."

"I'll stay here," Dad said, stirring sugar into his coffee. "For obvious reasons."

Evelyn and I made our way back to my old bedroom, and she slowly opened the door. "Hey, Coco," she said as the dog jumped up on her. "Okay, settle down. Show Sally what a good girl you can be."

I knelt and let the big dog—a chocolate Lab, I now saw—come sniff my hands and make sure I was friend rather than foe, then stroked the soft fur behind her ears.

"This breed is used a lot as service dogs, right? Is Coco your guide dog?"

"No, though she actually was in guide dog training for a while as a puppy. But she was way too obsessed with food to follow commands all the time. She'd completely ignore anyone if she found a piece of a sandwich or something on the ground, so she didn't make the grade." Evelyn reached to scratch Coco under the chin. "You're a guide dog drop-out, aren't you, girl?"

"She's super sweet," I said as the dog rolled over to bare her belly for more petting. "I say we let the dogs meet. We can let them decide whether you come stay with me or not."

"Sounds good to me."

*   *   *

Dad drove the two of us to my place, Coco riding cross-tied in the back of the truck along with my bike and the small amount of belongings Evelyn had. After we'd unloaded everything and carried it up to the house, Dad gave me a warm hug.

"Thanks, hon," he said. "This means a lot to me."

As I'd expected, Buster and Coco hit it off immediately. Since adopting my late aunt's dog, I'd seen how easily he made new friends at the dog beach near our house. And, sure enough, after a few cautious nose-to-tail sniffs and several test paws-down, butt-in-the-air feints, the two dogs were chasing each other around the brick patio in my back-yard as if they'd been pals since puppyhood.

"Okay, I guess that's it, then," I said as two brown blurs streaked past us and bounded over the boxwood hedge onto the scraggly lawn beyond. "I don't know if you can tell, but they appear to like each other. A lot."

Evelyn laughed. "Uh, yeah. I can tell, all right. It's like a surround-sound movie, the way they're tearing around the yard."

Stupid. Of course she can tell. It wasn't as if sight was the only way to sense the world around you. "So why don't I show you around the house, then," I said.

"Sure, that would be great."

But when I took her by the arm to lead her inside, she stopped me. "No, it's better if I take *your* arm."

"Oh, sorry . . ."

"No, no, don't be sorry. There's no reason you'd know. It's just that I'm more in control if I hold your arm, rather than you holding mine."

As I gave Evelyn a tour of the house, I could almost see the cogs in her brain turning as she made a mental map of the layout. Once in a while she'd stop and think a moment, as if committing to memory the number of steps from place to place.

"And this will be your room," I said, showing her the double bed, the chest of drawers, and the closet where Dad had deposited her suitcase and day pack. "I used to sleep here in the guest room once in a while when Letta was still alive. The quilt is really warm, and the mattress is nice and hard." With a sigh, I sat on the edge of the bed, and she joined me.

"You two were close, weren't you?" Evelyn said.

"Uh-huh."

"It must have been hard, her dying like that."

"Yeah, it was. And living here, in her house, it's weird. I sometimes forget and expect her to be in the kitchen whipping up a soufflé or a batch of jalapeño corn bread. I don't know if I'll ever get over—" And then I remembered why Evelyn was here at the house. "Oh, lord. I'm so sorry . . ."

I turned toward her, but she was facing the wall, lips tight and jaw set. "So how you holding up, anyway?" I asked in a soft voice.

Evelyn shrugged. "Not great. Big surprise there. But I'll deal." She lay back on the bed, and Coco jumped up next to her. "No, Coco," she said, starting to sit up and push the dog off. "You can't come up here. You'll mess up the quilt."

"No, it's fine," I said. "Dogs are allowed on all the furniture in this house, as long as they don't have muddy paws. And besides, the quilt's already pretty ratty. I think Letta picked it up at some garage sale."

She lay down again and Coco curled up next to her. Neither of us spoke, Evelyn stroking the dog's thick fur, me staring out the window at Buster asleep in a pool of light on the brick patio.

"So, you wanna talk about it?" I asked after a bit. "Your mom?"

"No, I don't think so. Not right now, anyway. All I really want to do is lie here a while and rest, if that's okay."

"Of course." I stood up. "I'll leave you alone. I have to

be at Gauguin around four, but I'll be here till then. When you're feeling up to it, we can talk before I go to work about anything you might need."

Evelyn smiled and closed her eyes. "Thanks, Sally. You don't know how much it means to me to be around family right now."

Yes. *Famiglia.*

Chapter 3

Brian was in the *garde manger*—the cold food and salad prep room at Gauguin—when I got to work that afternoon.

"How you feeling today?" I asked.

He looked up from sorting through a stack of cardoons. "Way better, thanks. I don't know what bug I had, but I'm super glad it's gone." Selecting one of the vegetables—which resembled a cross between an artichoke stalk and celery—he used a paring knife to remove its strings, sliced it lengthwise and then crosswise in three sections, and tossed the pieces into a pot of cold water.

"Yeah, me too. But be sure and take it easy tonight, okay?"

I was trying to decide whether Brian was showing signs of being either sick or stressed out when Javier and Tomás came tramping into the kitchen from the side door, each bearing an overflowing box of produce.

"Look at the beautiful arugula they had this week," Javier said, depositing his cardboard box onto the counter and removing three plastic bags of the leafy greens. "And I got a great deal on leeks, too. Good thing I ran into Tomás. I'd never have been able to carry all of this by myself."

Downtown Santa Cruz hosts a bustling farmers' market every week, just a few blocks from Gauguin. So even though we get most of our produce from deliveries by local farms, Javier loves to wander the stalls of the market, tasting samples of sun-ripened peaches and heirloom tomatoes, inspecting the towers of carrots, turnips, and parsnips, and chatting up purveyors of preserved lemons and fig jam.

As a result, we usually leave at least one veg or other side undecided for the night, which allows Javier to come up with menu items based on what looks good at the market.

"Check this out," he said, rummaging in the box the prep cook had set down next to his and coming up with several bunches of thyme. "I was thinking we could do the leeks roasted with walnut oil, lemon, and thyme." He set the thyme on the counter and headed with the cardboard box for the walk-in fridge.

"Sounds awesome," Brian said. "And it would go really well with that flounder we got in today." Hefting the second box, he followed Javier into the chilly room, where the two began chattering about the night's specials.

Well, if Brian is still acting odd in any way, Javier will certainly notice. I'd let him worry about the cook. With one last glance in their direction, I headed upstairs to change clothes.

* * *

By five thirty we already had six tables seated, most without reservations. It's one of the benefits of being right downtown, especially on farmers' market days, when hungry shoppers—their mouths watering from all the luscious produce, creamy cheeses, tantalizing rotisserie chicken, and fresh-baked breads at the market—often come in for an early dinner.

I was at the grill station, flipping a rack of baby-back ribs glazed in pineapple, garlic, and soy sauce, when through the pass I spied a familiar head of blond hair. It was Eric, headed toward the bar.

Alone?

No, he appeared to be with a woman.

The two of them took the stools at the end of the mahogany bar, and Eric swiveled around to peer into the kitchen. Catching my eye, he smiled and waved, then swung back around.

I studied the woman. She looked to be about Eric's and my age, so fortyish, with a dark suit, shoulder-length dark-brown hair, and a bulging briefcase on the floor beneath her stool. A lawyer, no doubt. Probably one of Eric's DA cohorts.

Once we had a lull in the dinner tickets, I took a break to go over and say hi, and Eric introduced me to his friend. "This is Gayle," he said. "She's a PD."

"Ah, consorting with the enemy, are we?" I responded, and she laughed. It wasn't unheard of for public defenders to hang out with district attorneys, but it wasn't common, either, given their conflicting interests.

"Her client finally accepted my generous offer in a case we both detested," Eric said, "so we're celebrating."

Gayle raised her Martini in a toast. "And thank God he did. Though I still say three months is too harsh."

"A mere slap on the wrist," Eric said, lifting his matching Martini to clink her glass. "Given that the evidence against him was damning, to say the least."

Gayle grinned. "Yeah, my guy was totally guilty. And a complete scumbag to boot."

"What did he do?" I asked.

"Petty theft," Gayle said, and drained her glass. "A bicycle some surfer left unlocked on West Cliff while he went down to check out the waves. Someone else saw the guy do it and chased him down."

"Well, I'm no fan of bike thieves," I said, "but I have to agree with Gayle. Three months in jail does seem a bit harsh for that."

Eric shook his head. "For a first offense, sure. Which is why he got probation two months back for doing the exact same thing. This time around, though, he gets real time. Not that I'd call three months 'real' time," he added with a light jab to Gayle's waist.

She slapped his hand playfully in response, and it hit me that they had to be more than just colleagues out for a post-work drink. The way they kept looking each other in the eye, how close together they'd been sitting before I'd interrupted their conversation . . .

My jocular reply died on my lips, and I smiled numbly as I tried to regain my composure. But the adrenaline now coursing through my body made it difficult. All I wanted to do was get the hell out of there.

I was saved by Brandon coming up from behind with two plates of food. Stepping aside, I let the waiter set them on the bar: the flounder special with roasted leeks for Gayle, and an inch-thick rib eye atop a bed of arugula with a side of julienne French fries for Eric.

"Uh, I guess I should let you eat," I said. "I need to return to the kitchen, anyway."

Back at the grill station, once I had my new batch of tickets taken care of, the steaks and chicken quarters sizzling on the char broiler, I peered out the pass again to watch the duo eat their dinner. They were now on to a bottle of wine—a light red, it looked like—and were laughing and leaning toward each other like a couple out on a romantic night on the town.

Could it be a date? There was no reason it wouldn't be. Eric and I had split up several years earlier, and although he'd recently expressed interest in getting back together, I'd pretty much rebuffed him on that front. Or at least I'd made it clear that if any rekindling of our previous relationship were to happen, it likely wouldn't be anytime soon.

So I certainly couldn't expect the guy to sit around indefinitely and wait for me to decide. And I had no reason to feel anything but happiness for him if he'd found someone he liked, someone willing to return his affections right now in the present.

But the pang in my gut told me otherwise.

* * *

Evelyn was still awake when I got home after work. The TV was on, and Buster and Coco were curled up on either side of her on the sofa. Both dogs commenced barking as soon as I opened the front door, Buster set off by Coco. Only Buster, however, took the trouble to actually get off the comfy couch, and he took his sweet time—stretching first his front, then his back legs—before coming to greet me.

"Lazy bum," I said when he jumped back onto the couch and lay his head down, tail thumping on the aloha-print cushions. "Hey, Evelyn. I didn't expect you to still be up. How are you doing?"

"Okay. I'm watching an old movie with Cary Grant and some woman whose voice I don't recognize. It's got great, fast-paced dialogue."

I dropped my bag on the floor and squeezed into the tiny space the sprawling Buster had left between him and the end of the couch. On the screen, a bunch of guys in fedoras were jabbering into old-fashioned candlestick telephones. "Oh, *His Girl Friday*," I said as a roll-top desk was opened to reveal a pale, scrawny man with a wispy mustache hidden inside. "With Rosalind Russell. I *love* that movie." After kicking off my grease-spattered shoes, I set my tired feet on the coffee table. "I'm impressed you even know who Cary Grant is. Are you a classic film buff?"

"They're not my favorite or anything. I'm more into action movies—you know, stuff like *The Avengers* and *Black Panther*. But when I channel-surfed past this one I had to stop, 'cause it reminded me of my mom." She paused and swallowed. "Mom loved old films," she went on, her voice now low. "That was one of the things we used to do together, make popcorn and watch DVDs of all the old black-and-white movies."

"Ah, right."

Letting out a sigh, Evelyn slumped further down on the couch, and we watched the last ten minutes of the screwball comedy without speaking. As the credits started to roll, accompanied by a snappy big-band tune, she reached for the remote and shut off the television.

I stood up. "Well, I'm going to make myself a nightcap before bed. Can I get you anything, or are you going to hit the hay? It is kind of late for those not in the food-service biz."

"No, I'm actually going to stay up a little longer. I tend to be a bit of a night owl. But I think I'll pass on the night-cap. I'm not much of a drinker."

"Oh, right. You're not even twenty-one yet. Here we are on our first night together and I'm already being a bad influence."

She smiled and shook her head. "I turn twenty-one week after next, so maybe I'll have a drink with you then. Something really sweet and disgusting like a Harvey Wall-banger or a Fuzzy Navel."

"Ha! I can't believe you even know about those. They were already passé when I was a teenager."

"Yeah, well, my mom and her friends used to have par-ties sometimes when they'd make bizarre old drinks. Or, I know, a Pink Squirrel!"

At the sound of this last word, Buster's head popped up, his eyes and ears at immediate attention. "Now you've done it," I said with a laugh. "You can't say the S-Q word in front of Buster without him going nuts. I think we'll have to ban that particular drink from the house, or at least give it a new name."

Once I was settled back on the couch with my bourbon-rocks, I asked Evelyn about what sorts of things she might need while at the house. "Because you should totally make yourself at home while you're here. *Mi casa es tu casa* and all that. Oh, and since you're a fellow coffee aficionado, I'll have to show you where the beans and filters are and how to work the coffee maker before we go to bed."

"That would be great," she said. "With my weird sleep habits, I could easily be up way before you. But as for anything special I'll need, I can't think of anything."

"Well, what about shopping? Would you like me to take you to the grocery store tomorrow to stock up on stuff you like to eat?"

"Yeah, that would be awesome, actually. I can shop on my own, but it's way easier—and faster—if I go with someone else. Oh, and I guess it would be good to get a tour at some point of where you keep stuff in the kitchen. You know, your pots, pans, measuring cups, knives."

"So you're also a cook?" It hadn't occurred to me that she would actually be making meals from scratch. I'd assumed that the extent of her food preparation would be to open boxes of cereal and heat premade entrées from Trader Joe's in the microwave. "That's totally cool! I guess it must run in our family."

"Yeah, I make something most nights. I really enjoy it. Though I'm pretty slow and I can sometimes make kind of a mess," she added with a giggle. "And you're right, it definitely does run in the family. My mom was a chef like you and your dad, so she thought it was important that I learn my way around the kitchen from a young age. She taught me to cook when I was like ten years old . . ."

Evelyn trailed off. She'd been sitting cross-legged on the sofa, facing me as she spoke, but now closed her eyes and turned away. Shoving Buster off the sofa, I scooted over and touched her lightly on the shoulder. "Here. I think maybe you need a hug right about now."

She turned back and took me in her arms, her body shaking in silent sobs. After about a minute they subsided and she sat up, swinging her legs back down onto the floor. "Thanks," she said. "I guess I haven't really had a chance to let it all out." Evelyn wiped her cheeks, then reached out to stroke Coco, who had started panting in agitation during our emotional embrace.

I took a sip of my drink, letting her have a moment. If she wanted to talk about it, I was more than willing to lend a sympathetic ear. But if not, I wasn't going to push her.

Evelyn let off petting the dog and unzipped her red fleece sweater. "My mom had actually been pretty on edge the past few months," she said in a voice so soft I could barely hear her.

"Oh?"

"Yeah." She cleared her throat, then exhaled slowly. "She had a lot of stuff going on in her life. I don't know how much you know about her—"

"Pretty much nothing," I said. "My father says she had almost no contact with our family after your dad died."

"I know, and that's a shame. I guess I could have contacted you myself, but I never felt, I dunno . . ."

"It's okay," I said. "Family stuff can be hard."

She refastened the zipper of her sweater, then ran it up and down several times. "Well, anyway, my mom used to be a cook at this restaurant called Tamarind, but the kitchen there was totally macho. You know, all these guys constantly swearing and being super competitive and stuff."

I hadn't met any of the kitchen staff at Tamarind, a trendy Southeast Asian place over on the East Side, but this sort of male-dominated, back-of-the-house culture is familiar to any woman who's ever wielded a restaurant sauté pan. It's only because Gauguin was started by my Aunt Letta, and then later owned by me, that our kitchen has always been a relatively civil place to work. "Ugh," was all I had to say to Evelyn's description.

"So she quit and started her own place. A pop-up downtown called The Curry Leaf."

"Oh, wow, that was hers? They have great food. I love their samosas with peanut sauce."

"Yeah, though I don't imagine it will stay open, now that . . ." Evelyn bit her lip and slumped down on the couch. "The thing is," she went on after a moment, "I could tell Mom was stressed the past couple months. Partly from the new restaurant, but also because she left her old place, Tamarind, on really bad terms with the owner, and she hated stuff like that."

Evelyn blinked a few times, then coughed and cleared her throat again.

"Would you like a drink of water?" I asked.

"Yes, please. Thanks."

I brought her one, and she drank it down immediately. Reaching out for the coffee table, she located it with her left hand, then set the glass down with the other. A single tear was making its way down her right cheek.

After a moment, she went on. "Mom had told me all about what was going on with Tamarind, and I knew how hard she was working at the pop-up. But I was so busy at school that I just . . . I don't know, pretended everything was fine. But now we know it wasn't. Fine."

She wiped the tear away, but it was immediately replaced by several more. "I can't help thinking that if only I'd been there that night, I could have prevented it somehow."

"No," I said. "Don't go there. No one can ever know what might have happened if they'd taken some different action at any given time. Second-guessing will only make you crazy."

Evelyn nodded, but I could tell she wasn't convinced.

"And besides," I went on, "you couldn't be expected to be your mom's sole emotional caretaker, in any case. She must have had other people to confide in. A best friend, family?"

"She did have people she hung out with, but I don't think you could call any of them a 'best friend.' And as for family . . ." She shrugged. "Not much. None of her family lives around here, and as you know, she pretty much cut off contact with your side of the family after Dad died. She and my Nonna Sophie kept in contact, but they were never that close. So she really didn't have anyone to talk to but me."

Evelyn sat motionless on the sofa, head in her hands.

"Do you think she might have done it on purpose?" I asked in a soft voice. "That it wasn't an accident?"

"No!" Her head popped back up, eyes glassy with tears.

"Mom always promised she'd be there for me. No way would she leave me all alone like this on purpose."

As more tears streaked down her cheeks, I took Evelyn once more in my arms. "You're not alone," I said. "I'm your family."

Chapter 4

I woke to the glorious smell of coffee.

Normally, I laze about for a few minutes after coming fully to consciousness in the morning, but the aroma was so enticing that I popped immediately out of bed, startling the still-snoozing Buster, and headed for the kitchen.

The last time I'd awakened to an already-brewed pot of coffee in my own home had been back when Eric and I still lived together. He was a good guy that way, making the morning joe, bringing in the newspaper, even preparing us both sandwiches for work on occasion. And, I have to admit, I missed it—and not just the coffee.

Evelyn was at the red Formica kitchen table, a steaming mug before her, with Coco lying at her feet. She had her phone in her hands and was swiping it in rapid strokes.

"Good morning," I said. Evelyn didn't respond or make any sign she realized I'd entered the room, though the dog raised its head. Then I noticed the tiny earbuds. "Good morning!" I repeated, louder this time.

"Oh." Startled, she turned to face me. "Hold on a sec." She swiped at the phone again and removed the earbuds. "I was just reading all the emails and texts I've gotten since last night."

"No worries. And thanks for making the coffee, by the way. Looks like you were able to find everything I showed you last night."

"Uh-huh. Though I may have missed cleaning up some of the grounds. Sorry about that."

"Looks about the same as when I do it, actually." I grabbed a sponge to wipe up the few black grounds scattered across the counter, then helped myself from the pot, added a healthy slug of half-and-half, and took a seat across the table from her. "I don't want to keep you from checking your messages, if you want."

She tapped a finger rhythmically on her phone several times, then shoved it away. "No, that's okay," she said. "There's a ton, mostly about my mom. I can only take them in small doses."

"Yeah, that must be hard."

"Oh, and Mario left a message about my mom's memorial service. He offered to make all the arrangements so I wouldn't have to. It's going to be tomorrow."

"Really?" I said. "That seems awfully soon."

"I guess it was the only Saturday afternoon the place had available for the next month. Mom didn't belong to any church, so we're using this rent-a-chapel Mario found. And he just sent a text saying he was able to get a notice in the newspaper starting this morning, so people will know about it."

"Oh, that reminds me." Evelyn reached for her phone and clicked it to life. "I got a voicemail from the police. They'd like to interview me again about my mom. We talked the day I found her, but I guess there's more they want to ask. I was pretty freaked out at the time, so I bet I wasn't all that coherent."

She swiped, then tapped the screen, and a familiar voice started speaking: "Hello, Ms. Olivieri. This is Detective Vargas from the Santa Cruz Police Department. I was wondering if you'd be willing to talk to me again sometime, you know, about your mother? You could either stop by the station or, if it's easier, I could come by your place . . . or, uh . . . wherever you're staying right now. I should be in the office all day today, if that would work for you. Okay, well, thanks. I appreciate it. Talk to you soon."

Evelyn set the phone back on the table and reached for her coffee.

"Detective Vargas," I said. "I know him. He's a good guy."

"Really? Would you be willing to be there when I talked to him?"

"Sure, no problem. But it's not like we're great friends or anything. He was the lead detective on my aunt's murder case, and then I got to know him a little better when . . ."

"When you helped them solve those other cases," she finished for me. "I read about them in the paper. And I gotta say, even though I never contacted you like I should have, I was super proud to have such an amazing sleuth as a—what are we, cousins, right?"

"Yeah, second cousins once removed," I said. "I'm pretty sure, anyway."

Evelyn got up to help herself to more coffee. "So you think I should have the detective come here to the house, or should we go down to the station?" she asked.

"Uh, maybe I should drive you down there. We could do it on our way home from the store."

Vargas and I had gotten off to a rocky start after he'd taken a dim view of what he saw as my "interference" with their investigation into my Aunt Letta's stabbing. Since then, however, our relationship had significantly improved, and he'd even recently joked that one day I might make a good detective if I ever decided to change careers.

But that didn't mean I wanted the guy at my own home.

*　*　*

Three hours later, I pulled my '57 Thunderbird into the police station parking lot, its tiny trunk jammed with bags of groceries. Since I'd inherited the classic convertible from my Aunt Letta the previous spring, Evelyn had been the only passenger not to slaver over its creamy-yellow color and Jetsons-style tail fins. But she did razz me about the smelly dog cushion on the passenger side—which she shoved onto the floor at her feet, there being no back seat in the car—as well as the T-Bird's clunky engine noise and obvious need for a tune-up.

Shopping with Evelyn had proved to be an enlightening event. Not only did it make me appreciate how easy I had it with regard to the day-to-day tasks of life, but it also opened my eyes to the astounding adaptive technology out there these days for the blind. Evelyn showed me an app on her phone, for instance, that is a bar code reader and tells her in a robotic voice whether the can she's holding contains sliced beets or petit pois peas. Pretty awesome.

We extricated ourselves from the T-Bird's bucket seats,

then made our way across the parking lot and up the stairs into the police station. She was using her cane, tapping it back and forth in front of her as we walked, but she'd also taken my arm to help her navigate the unfamiliar route.

After announcing ourselves to the receptionist, we took a seat on one of the wooden benches in the lobby. Evelyn folded up her cane and snapped the elastic loop about its metal tubes. Her right knee was bouncing up and down in a severe case of the jimmy leg.

"Nervous?" I asked.

She stilled her leg. "What makes you think that?" she said with a short laugh, then sighed. "I guess a little. But mostly I'm afraid I won't be able to hold it together, that I'll completely lose it in front of the detective."

"Yeah, totally understandable. But even if you do break down in front of Detective Vargas, it'll be okay. I've been known to do it and he was totally cool. Oh, speak of the—"

"Ms. Solari." A beefy man in brown slacks and a light-pink Oxford cloth shirt strode across the lobby. "I didn't expect to see you here," he said, shaking my hand. Evelyn had stood at the sound of his approach, and the detective turned to take her outstretched hand as well. "Good to see you again, Ms. Olivieri. I'm so glad you were able to stop by. Would you like to come upstairs where we can talk in private?"

"Sure, but can my cousin Sally come along, too?"

A frown momentarily creased Vargas's brow, but he quickly nodded. "I see no reason why not." We followed him through the door from which he'd emerged and then up the stairs, Evelyn gripping her cane in one hand and taking hold of my forearm with the other.

"So you two are cousins?" the detective asked as we entered the investigation department's interview room, a place I'd visited on several previous occasions. "Please, sit," he said, motioning for us to sit on the small couch, then took the chair across from us.

"Uh-huh. Second cousins once removed, actually."

"Ah." Vargas leaned back and clasped his hands behind his shaved head. "Are you staying with your cousin, then, Ms. Olivieri?"

"Evelyn, please. And yes. Sally was generous enough to take me in for a while."

He dropped his arms onto his legs and smiled. "Well, I do have some good news. The investigation at the house has been completed. Oh, and by the way," Vargas said, turning toward Evelyn. "We couldn't locate your mom's phone or her computer. They weren't at the house or at her restaurant. Did she have a laptop?"

"Uh-huh. A Mac Air."

"Well, if you happen to find it—or her phone—I'd appreciate it if you'd let me know. In any case, we finished up at the house this morning, so you're free to go back whenever you want."

Evelyn bit her lower lip but didn't respond.

"It's okay," I said. "You can stay with me as long as you like."

"Thanks. It's just that the memory of coming home and tripping over her like that . . ." The jimmy leg had now returned. "I think it's going to take a while before I'm ready to sleep there again."

"Of course. I completely understand." Vargas cleared

his throat. "Since we're on the subject of your finding your mother like that, I was wondering if you'd be willing to describe for me exactly what happened that day when you came home."

"All right." Evelyn swallowed, then sat up straighter on the couch. "I'd spent that Monday night at a friend's house—Lucy. She's a student with me at Cabrillo, and we'd both turned in our last papers for the semester that day, so we decided to hang out together and celebrate."

"What time did you leave the house?" Vargas asked.

"Around six, I think. Maybe seven at the latest." She frowned. "Do they know what time Mom died?"

"The coroner says at least twelve hours before she was found, probably more. Which would place the time somewhere between when you left and midnight." Vargas jotted a note in the file, then set down his pen. "So, you were talking about what happened when you came home that day . . ."

"Right. I didn't get back till a little before noon, and when I came in the door, Coco—that's our dog—was acting really weird, pacing and panting and stuff. I sat on the sofa to comfort her and try to figure out why she was so agitated, and when I called out for my mom, she didn't answer, so I just assumed she'd gone out."

Evelyn paused, twisting the cane's elastic loop about her fingers. Neither Vargas nor I spoke, letting her take her time. "After a couple minutes, Coco seemed to have calmed down, and I started across the living room to take my overnight bag upstairs to my bedroom. That's when I discovered her. At first I thought it was a seat cushion or something on the floor that I'd walked into, but when I knelt down to move it out of the way, I realized . . . what it really was."

I reached out to lay a palm on her knee, and Evelyn took my hand in hers.

"I knew right away it was Mom," she went on. "From the shoes she was wearing—these short leather boots with buckles on the side. But I went ahead and felt her face to make absolutely sure . . ." The grip on my hand tightened. "Her skin was clammy and cold, so I knew there was probably nothing I could do at that point. And then as I crawled over to get my phone out of my bag to call 911, I knocked into the bottles. A couple of pill containers and some kind of alcohol. Vodka, I think."

"That's right," Vargas said. "But how did you know?"

"From the smell. Vodka is really medicinal, almost like rubbing alcohol. Plus, it's what my mom liked to drink." She lifted her head, which had gradually drooped down as she spoke, to face the detective. "Can you tell me, were there other fingerprints on the bottles besides my mom's?"

The detective shook his head, then, realizing she wouldn't notice this response, said, "No, there weren't any but hers."

"On the vodka bottle, too?"

"That's correct. Hers were the only prints on all three of the bottles. Why? Do you think that's odd?"

"Not for the pill bottles," Evelyn said. "But it is a little surprising for the vodka, since I know she'd have friends over for drinks."

"Well, there was still a fair amount left in the bottle, so perhaps it hadn't been opened until that night."

Evelyn thought a moment. "So what was in the two pill bottles?"

"Percocet and Ambien," he answered. "And they both were prescribed to your mother. Do you know why she'd gotten a prescription for Percocet?"

"It was when she had oral surgery a few months ago—two really badly impacted wisdom teeth. But she only took one or two, 'cause she didn't like how they made her feel. How many were left in the bottle?"

"None," Vargas said with a frown. "Which means she must have taken at least four that day, based on what you say, since the prescription was for six."

Evelyn bit her lip again and slumped back down into the couch, letting go of my hand. I wanted to take it back, to squeeze it hard and let her know I was there for her, but resisted the impulse. "How about the other bottle?" she asked quietly. "The Ambien."

"It was a prescription for thirty and there were fifteen left. Did she take it very often, do you know?"

"Not every night, but maybe a couple times a week, I think. Mom had been having a hard time sleeping for the past few months, so she finally went to the doctor and got the Ambien to help with her insomnia."

Vargas picked up a file that sat on the low table between us and consulted the report inside. "So if she was taking two a week," he said, tapping his finger on the page, "given the date of the prescription, that means she must have taken about four or five the night she died."

"Would that have been enough to . . . ?" Evelyn asked.

"The forensic pathologist at the coroner's office says yes,

that about four of each—the Percocet and the Ambien—along with several strong drinks could be enough to cause a fatal overdose for someone of her weight."

"Really?" I sat up straighter. "That doesn't sound like a whole lot."

"Yeah, well, that's one of the dangers with opioids. It doesn't take very much, especially when they're mixed with other drugs. You fall asleep and slip into a coma, essentially, from the buildup of excess CO_2, and when your brain tells you to take a deep breath, you're so sedated that you can't."

"So she suffocated," Evelyn said, wrapping her arms about herself.

"Probably. I'm truly sorry."

No one spoke, and the only sound was that of Vargas tapping the typed label affixed to the front of the case file.

Although it was somewhat chilly in the small interview room, I felt the heat rise within me and shrugged out of my wool blazer. I'd come to learn that the annoying hot flashes I'd been experiencing over the past year could occur at any moment, but times of stress or high emotion were especially likely to trigger them.

After a moment, Evelyn shook her head. "But I just don't understand how she could have taken that many pills by accident," she said. "Are you sure there weren't any on the floor you might have missed?"

"No, there weren't any other pills that we found. And you should know that it seems pretty clear it wasn't an accident." Vargas glanced in my direction before continuing. "Because, well, there was a note."

Evelyn flinched as if she'd been struck by an actual blow

to the face. "No," she said. "That's not possible. She would never have done it on purpose."

Vargas removed a sheet of plain white paper from the file and handed it to me. Two short sentences were hand-printed on the page in blue ink. "We found this next to her body," he said.

"What's it say?" Evelyn asked.

The combination of hurt and fear in her eyes made it difficult for me to speak. "It says," I answered, my voice catching. "I'm sorry, Evelyn. I love you."

I'd expected her to slump, or cry out, or react in some obvious way, but she didn't move—except for a slow furrowing of the brow. After a moment she swallowed, then turned to face Detective Vargas.

"It's not from her," Evelyn said.

He shifted in his chair, then glanced my way once more. "Um, well, we did have our handwriting guy examine the note, and he says that although he can't be absolutely certain, it does match her writing pretty well."

"But you don't understand," Evelyn said, leaning forward. "My mom never called me that. She always called me Evie, or sometimes Ev. But she never *ever* called me Evelyn."

Vargas frowned and scratched his ear. "Never? Not even when she was angry or upset?"

Evelyn was shaking her head vehemently. "No, never. She's called me Evie since I was a baby. So don't you see? She can't have written that note. It had to be somebody else."

Chapter 5

Once Evelyn and I had put away the groceries, I rustled up some leftover rigatoni with fennel and Italian sausage for lunch, and we sat at the kitchen table to eat. Buster and Coco crouched expectantly on either side of us, hoping for a dropped morsel or handout.

Since leaving the police station, Evelyn hadn't mentioned her mom or the note they'd found beside her body, so I let the subject be. She could bring it up again when she was ready.

"You have any plans for this afternoon?" I asked.

"Not much." Evelyn poked a fork at her mound of pasta and came up with several tubes. "I guess I should answer all those texts and emails I've gotten in the past few days," she said, sounding anything but enthusiastic about the chore. "How about you?"

"I have to go down to Gauguin after lunch. I left my laptop there last night, and since I'm not working tonight, I need to swing by and pick it up."

"Could I come with you? I've never been to Gauguin."

"Sure," I said. "I'd be happy to give you a quick tour of the place."

Evelyn helped with the dishes, washing and rinsing them in the sink and handing them to me to dry and put away. Then, after taking the dogs for a walk down to the ocean and back, Evelyn and I climbed into the T-Bird and headed downtown.

Javier's car was parked in the small lot alongside the restaurant. Not finding the chef in the kitchen, I took Evelyn upstairs to the office, where he sat at the desk, a pad of inventory sheets before him.

"You're here early," I said.

"Getting a head start on the weekend ordering," he replied. "And this must be Evelyn, no?" I'd told Javier about my new, temporary housemate, and given the white-and-red cane she held, it didn't take a mastermind to realize this was she.

"Hi." Evelyn extended her hand, and Javier stood and reached across the desk to take it in his.

"Pleased to meet you," he said. "Would you care to sit?"

I got Evelyn situated in the wing chair and, since there were no other seats in the office, made do with leaning against the bookshelf.

After expressing his condolences to Evelyn about her mother, Javier turned to me. "You have a minute to talk about tonight's specials?"

"Sure."

"So, a buddy of mine brought me a couple bags of chanterelles this morning," he said, "which would be perfect for a risotto with butter and shallots. And we could use up the rest of that Grana Padano cheese we got in last week."

Evelyn sat up in her chair. "Oh, wow," she said. "That sounds delicious. My *nonna* made great risotto, but I've never had it with fresh chanterelles."

"Evelyn's grandmother is a wonderful cook," I told Javier. "I remember she used to make this amazing fresh pasta. She didn't use a machine, but rolled it out and cut it by hand. Does she still do that?"

"Not since she moved into that assisted-care place," Evelyn said. "But I do."

"Really?" Javier and I said simultaneously.

"Yeah, Nonna taught me years ago."

She smiled at the memory, then slapped her hand on the armrest. "Hey, how 'bout I make fresh pasta for you sometime, Sally? I could use some kind of extracurricular activity now that school's out. Maybe I could even cook a whole dinner for you, as a way to thank you for letting me stay at your house. I know some amazing recipes for fettuccine my *nonna* taught me."

Javier smacked his lips theatrically. "Oooh, sounds delicious. So how do I finagle an invitation to that dinner?"

I was so taken aback by the fact that the Michoacán native had the word *finagle* in his vocabulary that I almost missed the spark in his eyes as he watched Evelyn's laughing response.

* * *

Javier and I had been swapping Friday nights off of late, in an effort for each of us to have at least some semblance of a normal social life. Tonight was my free night, so I called Eric to see if he wanted to meet someplace for dinner.

"Uh, sorry, Sal, but no can do. I've got other plans." He didn't elaborate and I didn't ask, but I figured it was Gayle, the public defender he'd brought to Gauguin the other night.

"That's cool," I said, hoping he wouldn't sense my disappointment. "It is kind of late notice, and I'm sure you're in very high demand." *Oops.* So much for hiding my feelings.

But Eric merely chuckled, taking it as simple joke. "So what's new with you, anyway?" he asked. "We didn't really get to talk when I saw you last night, since you were working."

And you were flirting.

No, I wasn't going to let myself go there. I'd been the one to push him away, after all.

"Oh, lord," I said. "You haven't heard the latest. First off, Javier is worried that Brian—our new cook and your fellow bass singer—is having some kind of stress-related meltdown."

"Really? How so?"

"Well, he has seemed kind of distracted at work, not as focused as he usually is. And he's been a lot more testy of late than usual."

"It might be simply a case of fatigue," Eric said. "We did have our marathon of chorus concerts last weekend, preceded by a pretty intense week of rehearsals. Maybe he's just exhausted."

"So you haven't noticed him acting weird or anything?"

"Not that I can think of. No, wait. He missed a rehearsal last week, but said it was 'cause he'd been sick. That must be what's been going on with him. So, anyway, what was the other news you had?"

"I have a new roommate."

There was a sputtering sound, as if he'd choked on his morning Starbucks. "No way."

"Way." I told him about Evelyn—how we were related, what had happened to her mom, and how my father had asked me to take her in for a few weeks.

"Huh," he said, then, "Hold on a sec." I could hear a woman's voice murmuring in the background, to which Eric responded with something about a pretrial hearing. He came back on the line. "I'm really sorry, Sal, but I gotta go and help put out a fire. I'll talk to you soon, okay?"

After we hung up, I tried my buddy Allison as well, but she and her husband Greg were going to a party up on the university campus hosted by the provost of her college. "I'd actually rather go out with you tonight," she said, "but duty calls. The provost was, after all, one of my biggest supporters when I was up for tenure, so the least I can do is attend her end-of-the-semester shindig."

Oh, well. Maybe it'll be good for me to just stay in tonight and relax.

Setting my phone on the kitchen table, I spied Evelyn through the window. She was out in the backyard, throwing a pair of balls for Buster and Coco. My dog was not being cooperative. As I watched, he ran after the ball, but then lay down where he was to chew on it its ratty felt. Coco, however, brought her tennis ball promptly back and dropped it at Evelyn's feet so she could pick it up and throw it again.

I headed out the back door and plopped down at the wooden picnic table set up in the middle of the brick patio. There was a chill to the air, accompanied by the faint bite of a neighbor's wood-burning stove. A cluster of gray clouds chased across the sky, likely the advance guard of the storm predicted in this morning's paper. "Buster's not much of a retriever," I said, buttoning up my blue flannel shirt.

Evelyn grinned. "Well, Coco has it in her genes. She's obsessed. Mom and I had to make a no-balls-in-the-house rule."

But as she said this, the smile faded. *How long does it take*, I wondered, *before you get over the death of someone you love?* I still felt a pang of hurt every time someone mentioned my Aunt Letta's name, and she'd been gone eight months now.

Evelyn picked up the slobbery green ball and tossed it again, but with less enthusiasm than before.

"I was thinking," I said, "that maybe we could go out to dinner tonight. My treat."

The smile returned. "That would be awesome. Thanks. Where should we go?"

"Someplace fun," I said, "and I know the perfect spot."

*   *   *

The bar area at Kalo's that night was packed, as usual, but Evelyn and I were able to get a table in the dining room after only a five-minute wait. I'd started frequenting this Hawaiian-themed restaurant the previous summer when I'd sung the Mozart *Requiem* with Eric's chorus, since it was the group's preferred post-rehearsal watering hole. As a seasonal touch, Christmas lights in the shape of tikis and pineapples were now strung from the ceiling, and slack-key Christmas music was playing over the stereo system.

"You want me to read you the menu?" I asked Evelyn.

"Sure. That would be easier. It's hard to hear my app when it's crowded like this."

Once we'd placed our dinner orders—kalua pork with coleslaw, sticky rice, and a tunafish-spiked mac salad for me, a burger and sweet potato fries for Evelyn—we sat back to sip our drinks. I'd branched out from my usual bourbon-rocks to try the dark rum and fresh lime juice special I'd seen posted on the board, and Evelyn had opted for an iced tea.

"You don't worry the caffeine will keep you awake?"

"That's actually why I ordered it," she said, "since I'm feeling a little sleepy right now. But then, of course, around midnight when I want to go to sleep, I won't be able to." Her lips formed a smile, but it was a moment before the rest of her face caught up with it.

"Sounds like me," I said. "I'll be standing at the line flipping medallions of pork when all of a sudden I feel like I'm about to nod off. But then once I'm home in bed, I'm wide awake, as if my body's been shot up with speed or something."

"My mom used to say the same thing." Evelyn reached out for her glass, but instead of taking a drink, she turned it slowly around on the polished wood tabletop.

"How long was she a cook?" I asked. "Was it something she'd done for a while?"

"Well, when I was little, she worked as an administrative assistant for this tech firm that made some kind of computer hardware. She hated it, but it paid really well. Stan, my stepdad, was in nursing school at the time, so he wasn't making any money."

"You have a stepdad?"

"Uh-huh. Though he and my mom got divorced about five years ago." This last bit was accompanied by a sneer.

"I take it you weren't terribly heartbroken by the split?"

She snorted. "Not hardly. He basically used my mom to support him while he was in school, then dumped her once he graduated and found a younger woman. I haven't seen him much since he got remarried."

"Ah, got it."

"Anyway, after he left, Mom quit that job and started cooking, which is what she'd wanted to do all along. And she really loved it. Until she ended up at Tamarind."

The server approached our table bearing two large plates. "Oh, good, here's our food," I said, and Evelyn leaned back and let the gal set them down. She reached out for the plate to touch the hamburger and then the fries, popping one of the hot, crispy sticks into her mouth. "Is there mayo on the burger?" she asked the waitress.

"It's here on the table," the server said, and placed the caddy with mayo, mustard, and ketchup in front of Evelyn.

She busied herself with dressing her burger while I tasted my pork. Sweet, smoky, and fall-off-the-bone tender (though there was of course no bone, this being pulled pork). *Yum*.

"What restaurants had your mom worked at before Tamarind?" I asked between bites.

"She started out at IHOP, and then moved on to a California cuisine–type place. But she was super happy when she got the job at Tamarind. She really wanted to learn to cook Southeast Asian food."

"But then she ended up hating the kitchen culture there."

"Right." Evelyn licked a gob of mayonnaise off her thumb, then dunked a fry into the ketchup she'd squirted onto her plate. "But at around the same time she was trying to decide whether to stick it out or quit, she heard that this pop-up space downtown was about to open and was looking for tenants. Since they supplied all the equipment and Mom would just have to pay a nightly fee for use of the space, she realized it was something she could probably afford. And she figured it would be a good way to see if her idea for The Curry Leaf was popular. She was hoping she could maybe eventually open an actual restaurant of her own."

"But from what you said before, it ended up being pretty stressful, even though it was just a few nights a week."

"Uh-huh."

I poured a glug of soy sauce onto my rice. "She wasn't running it all alone, was she?"

"No way. She had three other people working for her." Evelyn took a bite of burger, raising her finger to indicate a further thought.

"And that's another thing that was stressing Mom out, actually," she went on after swallowing. "The woman who was the other main cook quit a few weeks ago after some big argument, and Mom hadn't found anyone yet to replace her."

"Ugh. So she was having to do that job as well as her own." I was well acquainted with the situation from years of working in the restaurant business and having to cover for absent employees. "No fun, that. You know what their argument was about?"

"Not really. But I do know Mom was pretty upset by the whole thing. They'd been friends before she even started The Curry Leaf, so that was hard." Evelyn set her hamburger on her plate and wiped her hands on the napkin in her lap, smearing red ketchup all over the white cloth. "I guess if I'd been a better daughter, I would have talked to her more about it, and maybe . . ." She shook her head, as if trying to free the memory from her brain.

"Look, Evelyn, you really shouldn't—"

"I know, I know. I shouldn't blame myself. Mom's the one who chose to do this to herself." She picked up the burger again and took an angry bite, but almost right away her jaw stopped moving. She set the burger back down.

"Buh whah if," she started, then finished chewing before going on. "What if there was somebody else there that night? Somebody who wrote that note."

"Wait, what do you mean?"

"I mean that I think someone must have forged it. Or forced Mom to write it. Ohmygod," she said with an intake of breath. "Maybe she even wrote *Evelyn* on purpose, as a clue so I'd know it wasn't really from her." Realizing how loud her voice had become, Evelyn stopped and cleared her throat. "Because," she went on more quietly, leaning across the table so I could hear her, "there's no way Mom would have committed suicide."

"You realize what you're saying, right?"

She nodded.

Neither of us spoke. A falsetto voice coming over the

speakers was singing "Winter Wonderland," accompanied by an ukulele and slack-key guitar, but I barely noticed when the song came to an end.

"Detective Vargas did look concerned when you said that about your mom never calling you Evelyn," I said after a bit. "And I saw him write a note in the file about it, too. But if you're right—and that's one hell of an *if*—an even bigger question remains. Who would want to kill your mother, and why?"

Evelyn shook her head. "I have no idea."

Chapter 6

The next morning, the pungent aroma of coffee once more filled the house. *I could get used to this*, I thought as I made my way down the hallway to the kitchen. Evelyn stood at the counter spreading butter onto a piece of whole-wheat bread, with Buster and Coco sitting expectantly at her feet.

At my approach, she turned. "Good morning. Want some toast?" She held out the plate, and all four canine eyes tracked its path like a hypnotist's patient following the swing of a pocket watch.

"Sure, that sounds perfect." I accepted the plate and set it on the table, then made a beeline for the coffee maker. "How'd you sleep?"

Evelyn popped another slice of bread into the toaster. "Not great," she said with a shrug.

"Insomnia?"

"Uh-huh. I tossed for at least an hour after I went to bed, but then finally fell asleep."

"Do you think it might be hereditary?" I asked as I poured half-and-half into my mug. "You told Detective Vargas yesterday about your mom suffering from insomnia."

"Doubtful." Evelyn took a sip of coffee as she waited for her bread to toast. "Mine isn't so much insomnia as this thing called non-twenty-four."

"Nine twenty-four?"

"*Non*-twenty-four, a sleep disorder some blind people get, especially if they have no sensitivity to light, like me. It's kind of complicated, but basically what happens is that since we can't detect the light of the sun, our internal body clocks get out of sync, and we can end up not being able to sleep at night and then feel sleepy a lot during the day. It's kind of like having jet lag all the time."

I winced in sympathy. "That sucks."

"No kidding." Evelyn buttered her toast and brought it and her coffee to the table. "Speaking of sleeping—or rather the lack thereof—I was thinking that maybe this morning before the memorial service we could stop by my house to pick up my pillow, since the detective said it was okay to go back there now. I forgot to bring it when I left in such a hurry the other day. I'm kind of a princess and the pea when it comes to having the one I'm used to. Would that be okay?"

"Of course, no problem."

She reached out a hand and I took it in mine. "Thanks, Sally. It really means a lot, having your support right now."

After finishing our breakfast, we took the dogs for a walk, then headed over to the house Evelyn had shared with her mother out near Branciforte Avenue.

I pulled into the driveway behind a Subaru hatchback with a BUY LOCAL bumper sticker on the rear window. Jackie's car. Or rather, Evelyn's now, no doubt. There had been no talk by anybody of a will or trust, but even if Jackie had died without one, her only daughter would inherit her estate.

Evelyn walked quickly up the brick pathway to the front porch. "Nice place," I said, trotting behind her. And it was indeed nice, much bigger than I would have expected for a single mom who ran a part-time pop-up restaurant.

She unlocked the door, then hesitated on the threshold. I waited, watching the emotions play across her face: fear, apprehension, sadness, then finally, determination. Jaw clenched, she stepped inside, and I followed her into the dimly lit room.

Only three days had passed since the house had been closed up, during which time various police personnel had been in and out of the place. Nevertheless, it smelled musty—and of stale dog. The drapes were drawn shut, left as they must have been the night Jackie had died. I resisted the urge to fling them open. It wasn't my place to change anything. Besides, we were going to be there only a few minutes.

The living room was large, though sparsely furnished. A wall-mounted TV and a newish-looking couch upholstered in brown fabric dominated the center of the room, and the corner near the fireplace had been set up as a reading area. It was a cozy nook, with a well-worn recliner, floor lamp, and side table stacked with paperback books.

Evelyn started across the room but suddenly stopped, then skirted a spot on the beige carpet. *Where she found her mother.*

Following after her, I studied the carpet for any signs that might remain of the death and was taken aback to see distinct blotches of color. I crouched down to get a better look. It appeared that someone had tried to clean them but had done a poor job of it, for the carpet still bore several pale-purple stains.

Could it be blood? But then I immediately realized, no, it was the wrong color. Dried blood had more of a brown, rusty hue. And, besides, Vargas would surely have mentioned it if the police had found blood at the scene.

I scurried to catch up to Evelyn, who was heading up the stairway. "This is my room," she said, opening the first of two doors off the upstairs hallway. The shades were open in here, and it took a moment for my eyes to adjust to the bright light.

Evelyn went to the closet and began running her fingers over the tops, skirts, and pants hanging inside. "I might as well get some more clothes while I'm here, too," she said.

While she decided what she wanted and laid them out on the bed, I took in the room's contents. Several plush dog toys, their stuffing poking out of rips in the fabric, were on the floor, as well as a denim jacket that lay crumpled in the corner by the closet.

The covers of the single bed had been drawn up in a halfhearted attempt to make it neat, and a pair of faded jeans, as well as some sort of boxy electronic device, lay on its wrinkled, blue bedspread. Next to me stood an antique-looking dresser with an open jewelry box on top. Several bracelets and earrings were scattered across its oak surface, along with three bottles of perfume, a carved sculpture of a rearing horse, and a bowl of highly polished stones. Beside the dresser sat a tall, wooden floor lamp.

A small desk had been squeezed between the bed and the dresser, its surface cluttered with a docking station and several more electronic devices I didn't recognize. Above it hung a shelf lined with large, thick books.

"What color is this shirt?" Evelyn asked, holding up a V-neck top.

"Hot pink," I said with a laugh. "Very bright."

"Yeah, that's the one I want. I have it in yellow too, so I wanted to make sure. This'll go better with the black leggings."

She set the shirt on the bed and headed for the dresser, and as she rummaged through the items wadded up inside, I studied the wall hanging tacked above the bed. It was made of several different fabrics, and a variety of crocheted designs poked out from its surface. Reaching out to touch it, I was surprised by the softness of the yarn used to create the three-dimensional effect.

Once she'd finished choosing her clothes, Evelyn collected her pillow—as well the machine on the bed (a digital book player, she told me) and a stack of blue plastic boxes (book cartridges for the player)—and I helped her carry everything downstairs. Turning the corner into the living room, I noticed a shelf of vinyl LPs tucked away behind the stairwell that I'd missed before. An old-school turntable and pair of speakers sat next to them atop a low table.

"Oh, wow, look at all the records!" I laid the clothes I held on the back of the couch and knelt to scan their titles. It was hard to read in the dark room, but they looked like mostly jazz and jazz vocals.

"Yeah, those were my granddad's. He was really into

jazz. When I was little, he used to play his records for me all the time, and we'd dance together in their living room. So when he died, Nonna Sophia gave his collection to me. You like jazz?"

"I do," I said. "I'm not an expert or anything—I'm more into new wave and Italian opera—but my mom used to play it a lot when I was growing up, and I do have a decent collection of jazz CDs. Nothing like what you've got here, though."

Evelyn came to sit next to me, ran her fingers down the line of records, and pulled one out—*Ella Fitzgerald Sings the Johnny Mercer Songbook*. "Here, you gotta listen to this. No one sings like this anymore."

She opened the lid of the record player, then removed the disk from its dust cover, placed it on the turntable, and set the tone arm carefully onto the vinyl. "You're just too marvelous, too marvelous for words," she sang along with Ella's smooth, silky voice.

"How'd you know that was the right one?" I asked. "That's amazing."

Evelyn grinned. "I've got them all alphabetically arranged, and I also have these tabs every so often, separating the different sections and artists. Like there's one here"—she touched a piece of cardboard sticking out slightly from the row of tattered record jackets—"where the Ella section starts. There's a ton of those, 'cause Grandpa *loved* her. And I just learn where they all are."

"I'm still impressed," I said. "If nothing else, just by how organized you have to be to keep a system like that working."

"Yeah, I am pretty organized. Especially for a Sagittarius," she added with a laugh, then shut off the stereo and returned the record to its place. "Oh, that reminds me. I think I know where Mom's computer is."

Evelyn trotted up the stairs once again, me following after, and headed into the second door off the hallway. Reaching under the mattress of her mother's queen-size bed, she extracted a thin, silver MacBook Air with a white Food Not Bombs sticker affixed to its lid.

"Voilà," she said. "This is Mom's not-very-original hiding place for her laptop whenever she goes out. She's kind of paranoid about it being stolen. Or . . . used to be," Evelyn added, sitting down on the bed with a sigh.

I sat next to her and put my arm around her shoulders. "I'm sorry," I said. "I know this must be incredibly hard for you."

"Yeah," she whispered. Wiping her eyes, she sat up and opened the laptop. "We might as well see if there's anything important on it," she said. "Here, can you open her Gmail?"

I took the computer and tapped the space bar to bring it to life. The log-in screen for Jackie's profile popped up. "Uh, what's her password?" I asked.

Evelyn shook her head. "I have no idea. Try *Coco*." When neither that nor *Evelyn*, nor *Evie*, nor *Jackie*, nor any names of past pets worked, we gave up.

"Well, I bet the tech person at the police station will be able to unlock it," I said, setting the laptop next to me on the bed. I stood up. "So, I don't want to be too morbid or anything, but do you know if your mom had a will? Because if so, we should probably look for that as well."

"I guess you're right," Evelyn said, then bit her lip. "She never mentioned anything about it to me, but if there is one, it's probably in that chest of drawers over there."

I walked over to where she was pointing and pulled open the top drawer. "This one's full of jewelry and knick-knacks," I said.

"Try the middle one."

It was full of files and paperwork. "Bingo! Let's see. Car insurance stuff, bank statements, utilities . . . Aha! Found it."

I removed a large white envelope with the words WILL OF JACQUELINE OLIVIERI typed on its front. Inside was a standard printed will, with the name of an attorney whose name seemed vaguely familiar at the top of the first page.

"What's it say?" Evelyn asked.

Holding the pages under the light of the bedside lamp, I read the will's provisions aloud: "I, JACQUELINE OLIVIERI, RESIDENT OF SANTA CRUZ, CALIFORNIA, DECLARE THAT THIS IS MY WILL AND THAT ALL PREVIOUS WILLS AND CODICILS ARE HEREBY REVOKED. Next there's a bunch of boilerplate. Blah, blah, blah . . . Okay, here's the important bit: I LEAVE MY ENTIRE ESTATE TO EVELYN JOAN OLIVIERI." Flipping to the last page, I checked that the document was properly executed and witnessed. "It's dated March of last year and has all the necessary signatures. I never did much probate when I worked as an attorney, but it looks valid to me."

"Well, that's good, I guess." Evelyn blinked, then let out a slow breath. "If she was going to have to die, I mean . . ."

I studied the will for any other relevant provisions. It didn't designate the property that comprised Jackie's estate, but Evelyn was clearly the sole beneficiary of whatever that property was. "I suppose you might want to contact the attorney who drafted this will," I said. "To help with the transfer of things like the house and the car."

Evelyn nodded. "Would you be willing to call them?" she asked in a soft voice. "Since you know about that kind of stuff."

"Sure, I'd be happy to." I returned the sheets to the envelope and set it on top of the dresser next to a worn copy of *The Art of Eating* by M. F. K. Fisher. "Oh, cool, I love this book," I said, picking up the volume to flip through its yellowed pages. And then I noticed what looked to be a bank check stuck into the middle of the volume. I pulled out the check and examined its bold, sweeping script. "Huh, this is interesting," I said, coming to sit once more next to Evelyn, who had lain back on the bed.

She sat up. "What?"

"A check I just found. It's from Stanley Kruger and made out to your mom. And it's for a fair amount of money—thirty-two hundred dollars."

"Really?"

"Wait, there's something written in the memo part of the check. It's hard to read . . . *Spowel*? No . . . *spousal* support. Right, you said your stepdad was named Stan." I turned to face her. "Did you know he was paying your mom spousal support?"

"No. She never mentioned anything about that to me. Though it would explain how Mom was able to quit her job as secretary and start working as a cook. I always kind of wondered how she was able to do that, since I'm sure it didn't pay nearly as much." Evelyn chewed her lip. "But it's weird she never told me."

"Maybe she was worried how you'd feel. You know, living off his money, given how you felt about him."

"Maybe," Evelyn said. She slid off the bed and started for the hallway. "I guess we should get going, so we have time to get ready for the memorial service. But before we leave, I want to check the fridge to make sure there's nothing that'll go bad while I'm gone."

"Good idea."

I followed her downstairs and into the kitchen, where Evelyn opened the gleaming stainless-steel refrigerator. "You want something to drink? I'm gonna have a little cranberry juice." She reached into the bottom shelf, then frowned. "That's weird."

"What?" I came to stand next to her and peered into the fridge. "Here it is," I said, taking the bottle from next to the meat-and-cheese drawer on the top shelf and handing it to her.

"Where was it?" Evelyn asked, and I told her. "But that's not where it goes," she said, continuing to frown.

"Maybe your mom just forgot to put it back in its normal place."

She shook her head emphatically. "No. She wouldn't do that. We have a system, and the bottom shelf is where all my food goes, so I always know where things are. We've used it my entire life. She would never put my stuff on the wrong shelf."

"Well, we do know your mom had to have been pretty out of it that night, so maybe she just spaced out and put it in the wrong place. Or one of the cops could have moved it."

"But why would the police be moving things around in the fridge? No, it had to be someone who was here with Mom the night she died."

Realization spread across her face, and Evelyn turned to me, eyes wide. "The same person who forged that suicide note."

Chapter 7

Back at my house, Evelyn couldn't sit still. It was only an hour till Jackie's memorial service, and I assumed her keyed-up state was in anticipation of what would no doubt be a difficult afternoon. A heavy rain had begun to fall, preventing us from taking the dogs for a walk, as had been our plan, so we were hanging out in the living room, listening to the rhythmic patter on the windowpanes.

Coco was trying to engage Evelyn in a game of tug-of-war, but her human partner had little patience for the activity. Each time the dog brought her the ratty stuffed animal—which looked as if it might at one time have resembled an ostrich—Evelyn would give a halfhearted tug, then drop the toy and stand up to pace from the sofa to the front door and back again.

"Look," I said, picking up the bird and holding it out for Coco. "I know this memorial is going to be hard for you, but it'll also be good in a lot of ways. I didn't even want to go to my mother's service, but it actually ended up being really cathartic."

Evelyn returned to the couch and plopped down next to

me. "I know," she said. "But that's only part of what has me so on edge. I just can't stop thinking about who might have been with my mom the night she died. You know, whoever moved the juice—and wrote that note to make her death look like a suicide." She exhaled loudly, clenching and unclenching her fists. "And the more I think about it, the more I'm convinced it must have been Stan."

"Whoa. You think your stepdad might have killed your mom?"

"C'mon, think about it. He's apparently been paying her tons of money for the past few years, so there's a classic motive. And who would know better than a nurse how to kill someone with drugs like that?"

I considered what she was saying. If someone other than Jackie had indeed written that note—or forced her to write it—then the death couldn't have been a suicide. And the presence of the note also ruled out a simple overdose.

Which left only murder as the likely cause.

"Well," I said, "it is most often the current or ex-partner who . . ."

"Exactly!" Evelyn jumped off the couch once again, startling Coco, who was now methodically pulling the toy's stuffing out of the hole where its eye had once been.

"But what would Stan have been doing at your mom's house in the first place?" I asked. "Would she have even let him come over?"

"Maybe. There was a long period when Mom didn't talk to him at all, but they'd started getting along a little better over the past few months. I know they talked on the phone once in a while. But she knew how I felt about him."

She fingered the buttons on the pale-blue blouse she'd changed into for the memorial service. "So I guess she might have had him over, but if she did, I bet she would have made sure it was when I wasn't around." And then she put her hand to her mouth.

"Like the night she died," I filled in, and she nodded.

*　　*　　*

We left early for Jackie's memorial because of the rain and got to the rent-a-chapel twenty minutes before the service. Two of Evelyn's friends had already arrived, so we took seats next to them, near the front of the pews.

"Oh, Ev," the taller of the two said. "I can't believe it about your mom. I am so sorry." They embraced, and after the second gal had given Evelyn a hug as well, she introduced me to Molly and Anne.

"We met in high school English class," Evelyn said, "and bonded over our love of *The Handmaid's Tale*."

"And Mr. Walton," Anne added with an exaggerated swoon, causing the three women to giggle. Anne touched Evelyn on the arm. "So how are you doing?" she asked.

While the three friends leaned in close to talk, I turned to examine the decor of the rent-a-chapel. It wasn't bad, actually—subdued and comforting. The walls were painted a pale salmon with ornate, cream-colored molding, and although the "chapel" contained no religious symbols or icons, it still managed to convey an air of nonsectarian reverence.

"Oh, look, here's Lucy and Sharon," Molly said, and I turned to see another pair of young women coming toward us, using canes to make their way up the aisle. Evelyn introduced me to the two new arrivals, who took the bench behind us. Lucy, she announced, was a fellow computer science student at the college, and Sharon was studying political science.

Ah, the Lucy whose house Evelyn was staying at the night her mom died.

Spying my dad coming through the wide wooden doors at the back of the hall with Sophia, I waved him over, and he escorted his elderly cousin to the row of seats in front of us.

Sophia swiveled around to give her granddaughter a hug and a kiss on the cheek, and the two spoke in low voices. This was the first time they'd seen each other since Jackie's death, so the older woman was offering her sympathy to Evelyn. But from Sophia's manner—consoling but not what I'd call mournful—I could tell it was true that she hadn't been all that close to her daughter-in-law.

After they'd finished talking, Sophia squeezed Evelyn's shoulder, then turned back to my dad. "This feels like a fake church," she said, making *tsk*ing noises just like my *nonna* would do.

"That's because it isn't a church," Dad replied. "You know Jackie wasn't Catholic, so it wouldn't have been appropriate to have it at the parish church."

I glanced over to see how Evelyn was taking this little exchange and was relieved to see she wore an amused expression.

As more attendees streamed in, I tried to discern who in Jackie's life they might have been. Two twenty-something guys, both with tattoos decorating their forearms, had to be cooks. But the woman with salt-and-pepper hair pulled back in a scrunchie, I wasn't so sure about. A relative, perhaps?

"Are there any relations of yours coming today besides your *nonna*?" I asked Evelyn in a low voice.

"Not likely," she said. "My grandparents on Mom's side are both dead, and her brother lives in Vietnam. Or is it Thailand? They didn't talk very often. And since she's originally from back East, all her cousins and other relations are pretty far away. I doubt any of them would come."

"That's too bad. But at least you have our side of the family, now."

She smiled and patted my knee.

Glancing at my phone, I saw there were only five minutes till the service was due to start. About twenty people were now in attendance, but folks continued to straggle in. As I watched, a sinewy man came through the doors, then stopped. He was balding, with one of those trendy goatees that every other guy seems to sport these days, and stood at the door squinting, as if looking for someone.

Recognition flashed across his face, and he started down the aisle. I turned back around to face forward, not wanting to appear nosy, and was startled when he stopped at our row and leaned over. *Do I know this guy?*

"Hello, Evelyn," he said, and she started at the voice.

"Stan?"

Ah, her stepdad.

"Yeah. I thought I should come and pay my respects." He cleared his throat. "Listen, hon," he said, "I just want you to know how sorry I am. About everything."

"Hon," just like my dad calls me. So he must feel close to her.

71

But from Evelyn's lips—curled back as if she'd just had a sip of sour milk—it was obvious she didn't share the feeling.

"If you need anything, a place to stay, or . . ."

"Thanks, but I'm staying with my cousin Sally for a while," was all Evelyn said, not even turning her head in response.

Stan hesitated a moment. "Well, okay then," he finally murmured, and started to leave.

"Wait," Evelyn said, and he turned back. "I wanted to ask something: were you by any chance at our house recently?"

"Why would you ask that?" He swallowed and glanced about him, as if worried that others were listening in on the conversation.

"Uh, just wondering if you'd seen Mom recently is all."

"No, I haven't seen her in months," Stan said with a frown, then made his way to a seat several rows behind us.

"How did he look while we were talking?" Evelyn asked in a whisper after he'd gone. "You notice he didn't answer the question whether he'd actually been at the house recently."

"He seemed nervous. Or maybe just embarrassed or confused. But don't you think it might be a little unwise to be asking something like that? Because if he did in fact"—I lowered my voice—"hurt your mom, he may well now suspect that we're on to him."

"Yeah, you're right," Evelyn said, shaking her head. "That was stupid."

Our conversation was cut short by the quieting of the crowd as a woman in the front row stood and turned to face us. Swiveling in my seat, I looked to see how big a crowd had turned up and was surprised to spot Detective Vargas in one of the back rows. *Huh.* Had he decided that Jackie's death was suspicious after all?

The service was short and impersonal. I got the impression the woman officiating had never even met Jackie and was merely recounting stories someone else—perhaps my father—had told her. She'd probably come with the rent-a-chapel, along with the flowers and the tea and cookies to follow.

I was getting increasingly morose as the officiant started winding up her spiel, and nervous for Evelyn's sake that when the time came to ask attendees to stand up and say something nice about the deceased, she'd be met with dead silence. So I was relieved when two women near the front immediately jumped up and took the microphone to speak.

"We worked with Jackie back when she still flipped eggs at the IHOP," the first one said. "Before she moved on to become a local celebrity chef," she added with a chuckle.

Celebrity chef? I'd have to rib Javier about that, because if Jackie constituted a celebrity chef, then he'd be up there with Bobby Flay and Gordon Ramsay.

The second woman grabbed the mic and told a story about the three of them taking a trip to Las Vegas several years back. They'd eaten at fancy restaurants each day, and on the last night Jackie had wangled a tour of the kitchen at Picasso, the French-Spanish fusion place at Bellagio with original canvases by the famous artist hanging on its dining room walls.

Relinquishing the microphone, the two women—who appeared to have fortified themselves with a few pre-memorial service drinks—sat back down.

Next to speak was a man named Max, who said he'd worked with Jackie at Tamarind. This got my attention. Was he one of the jerks whose male posturing had driven Jackie from the restaurant?

But no, probably not, I realized as he went on. He and Jackie had known each other before her time at Tamarind, and, he told us, he'd gotten her the gig cooking there.

"I loved having Jackie at the restaurant," he said. "She was a great cook and a pleasure to work with, and I sure missed her when she left." He glanced in the direction of the two young guys with tattoos. *Aha.* I must have been right about them being the Tamarind cooks.

He paused to take a handkerchief from the pocket of his black slacks and wipe his aquiline nose, and when he looked up, there were tears in his eyes. "She was a special woman," he said. "I can't believe she's gone." For a moment it looked as if he was going to say something else, but then, with a quick shake of his curly, black hair, he handed the microphone back to the officiant and returned to his seat.

"Do you know that guy?" I asked Evelyn as a young woman made her way to the front to speak.

"Yeah," she said. "Mom used to hang out with Max sometimes. And he was really nice to her after she quit Tamarind."

Evelyn hushed as the next person started to speak.

"Hi, my name is Maya, and I worked with Jackie at The Curry Leaf," she said, raising pitch at the end of the sentence as if it were a question. "I only knew Jackie for a while, but I had to come up and say something because she was such an awesome boss." Maya toyed nervously with the Indian prayer beads she wore on her left wrist, then cleared her throat. "Like, when I asked to take off for a whole week to go to the Rainbow Gathering, she was totally cool about it. And even though I wasn't a cook, she paid me the same as them, and we shared all the tips totally equally."

She went on more about why Jackie had been "such an amazing lady," and as she spoke I thought about the woman Evelyn had told me about who'd quit working at the pop-up. Why, I wondered, if Jackie was such a great boss, had that other employee quit like she had? What could their argument have been about?

After the hippie gal finished talking, two more people stood up to speak—a friend of Jackie's from college who'd recently moved to Santa Cruz and a bartender from the place where she'd cooked before Tamarind. Neither seemed to have been particularly close to her, but perhaps they were simply conscious of how few people were standing up to talk about the deceased and decided to add a few kind words.

Stan did not speak. Of course, even if he'd planned on doing so, Evelyn's cold reception of her ex-stepfather could easily have put the kibosh on any such idea.

After a brief closing by the officiator and the compulsory rendition of "Amazing Grace" (by a pianist in an ill-fitting suit who, I suspected, also came with the rental), we were directed to a reception hall next door. A large table running down the middle of the room had been set with stainless-steel urns of coffee and tea, pitchers of lemonade, and platters of store-bought cookies and "freshly cut" ham and turkey sandwiches. Not the sort of repast to best honor a chef, but having had no breakfast, I dug right in.

My dad joined us at the table and piled a sandwich and

three chocolate-chunk cookies onto his plate. "I'm really sorry," he said, "but I can't stay for the reception. Sophia's tired and wants to go home. She's waiting for me back in the chapel, but she did tell me to say goodbye and to give you a pair of *baci*."

"That's okay, Mario," Evelyn said, accepting the proffered kisses to her cheeks. "I understand. Tell Nonna I really appreciate her coming. And you, too."

Evelyn and I took our plates to the chairs that had been placed along the wall, finding two spots next to Molly and Anne. As I ate, I studied the crowd, and my attention was drawn to three women standing apart from all the others, glancing our way. The gal who'd talked during the service about Jackie being an "awesome boss" was nodding at something the tallest of the group was saying. The tall woman then shook her head with a frown and made her way to the food table. After conferring for a moment, the other two women came over to where Evelyn and I were camped out along the wall.

"Hi, Evelyn," one of the women said. "We just want to say how sorry we are about Jackie."

"It was such a shock," the other put in. Then, noticing me for the first time, she held out her hand to shake. "Hi, I'm Sarah," she said. "And this is Maya. We worked with Evelyn's mom at The Curry Leaf, her pop-up."

"Good to meet you. I'm Sally Solari, Evelyn's cousin."

Sarah's polite expression changed to one of pronounced interest as she took my hand in a strong grip. "Really? You're the one who owns Gauguin, right?"

"Yeah, that's me."

"Oh, I love that place," Sarah said. "I mean, I've only eaten there once, since it's kind of pricey for someone on my budget, but I thought the food was amazing!" She glanced at Maya, then back at me. "Um, I know you might think this is a little weird, given the occasion and all, but I was wondering—any chance you might be looking for a new cook right about now? 'Cause, you know . . ." She inclined her head in the direction of the chapel.

"Maybe," I said. "We don't have any positions open on the line, but we're always on the lookout for good prep cooks these days."

"That's okay. I don't really have enough experience to be a line cook at a place like Gauguin, anyway." Sarah stuffed her hands into the pockets of her black jeans and laughed.

"So you're not going to keep The Curry Leaf going?" I asked.

"I don't see how we could. Neither of us has the money to do it, and even if I could afford it, there's no way I'd want to run my own restaurant. It's way too much work."

Amen to that, I thought.

"And also, Jackie and Rachel—until she left, that is—" Sarah nodded in the direction of the woman who'd extricated herself from their group and was now standing by the sandwiches looking our way. "They did all the creative part of the cooking. I'd come in and basically just fry and reheat things and plate them up."

"Besides," Maya added, "it was Jackie's business, not ours. It wouldn't feel right reopening the place now that she's gone."

A large guy who'd just filled a plate with sandwiches

overheard this last comment and strode our way. He had on a shiny black-and-orange Giants baseball jacket and an expensive-looking straw fedora with a black-and-white-striped hatband.

"You'd better not reopen," he growled. "If you do, you can be sure I'll sue your ass."

He took a step toward the two women, and I was trying to decide whether or not to intervene when someone else stepped between the two of them, placing his hand on the big guy's chest. It was Max, the man who'd spoken during the memorial service.

"Hold on, Al," he said, pushing him backward. "This is neither the time nor place." Max took the man by the arm and steered him away, talking him down as they moved off.

"What was that about?" Maya asked.

Sarah shook her shaggy blond hair and exhaled, allowing her shoulders to relax. "I have no idea," she said. "I don't even know who that guy is."

"It's my mom's ex-boss, from Tamarind," Evelyn said.

"So what the hell was he going on about?" Sarah turned to look at the two men, who were standing near the refreshment table, talking in hushed but animated voices.

Evelyn shook her head. "Nothing," she said. "He's just a jerk. And it doesn't matter anymore, anyway."

Vargas joined us at this point. "You ladies all right?" he asked with a nod toward Al, who was still staring at us with a scowl.

"We're fine," I said. "Jackie's ex-boss just seems to have some kind of a chip on his shoulder, is all. Which brings me to the next question: what are you doing here today?" I moved closer to him and lowered my voice. "Have you decided that Jackie's death might not be a suicide after all?"

"Just covering all my bases," he answered noncommittally, then, at the sound of his phone, pulled it from the pocket of his khaki slacks. He took a few steps away and spoke quietly for a minute. "Gotta go," he said, returning to our foursome. "Something's come up."

"Wait." I put a hand on his forearm. "Before you leave, I wanted to let you know that Evelyn found Jackie's laptop at the house."

"Really? Where? Because my officers searched the entire premises."

"In her secret hiding place under the mattress," Evelyn said with a smile, prompting the detective to slap his forehead in frustration.

"Did you find her phone too?" Vargas asked.

"No, just the computer," I said. "It's actually in my car, if you want me to run out and get it for you."

"No, that's okay. I really have to get going. But could you bring it to the station Monday morning? The tech guy won't be in till then, anyway."

"Sure thing."

We shook hands goodbye, and when I turned back to our group, both Maya and Sarah were eyeing me curiously.

Chapter 8

It was still raining as we left the memorial service reception, so I had Evelyn wait under cover of the hall's entryway while I dashed out to the parking lot to fetch the car.

Folding my lanky body into the driver's seat, I started up the rattly engine, then used the side towel I keep to wipe down the inside of the windshield. The T-Bird was a supercool car, and I the envy of folks who'd watch me cruise down the street in the creamy-yellow convertible, but I did sometimes miss the luxury of electric windows and a windshield that didn't completely fog up every time it rained.

"So what the heck was that guy Al going on about back there?" I asked once Evelyn had gotten settled into the passenger's bucket seat. "Why would he want to sue Sarah and Maya for continuing your mom's pop-up?"

She waved her hand. "Oh, he's got it in his head that Mom stole some of the Tamarind recipes when she quit, and that because of that he's been losing customers over the past couple months to her pop-up. It's another reason she was so stressed the past few months."

"Huh." I wondered if any of it was true. Restaurant

owners have little legal recourse against ex-employees who take recipes with them when they leave. Nevertheless, it's considered very bad form for departing chefs to co-opt a recipe for their new place, especially if they didn't create the dish. And it's even more of a no-no if they start competing with the same dish in the very same town, which is what Al had apparently been accusing Jackie of doing.

"But Mom swore she didn't take any recipes," Evelyn went on. "She said Al was just mad at her for quitting, and for telling people that the guys had been harassing her in the kitchen."

I downshifted to slow for a truck that had lurched out in front of me. "Well, even if she didn't use any of their recipes at The Curry Leaf, if it's true that Tamarind did start losing money right after she opened the pop-up . . ." I glanced at Evelyn, who was chewing her lip.

"You're right," she said. "It sure does give Al reason to be mad at my mom. But mad enough to want to kill her?"

I had no answer for this.

We rode the rest of the way in silence, Evelyn tapping her fingers against the aluminum rods of her cane, me trying to wrap my mind around the fact that I seemed to be getting myself mixed up in yet another murder investigation.

By the time we got home, it was pouring down buckets, which—due to the vicious wind that had come up as well— managed to drench the both of us in the time it took to get from the garage to the front door. We shook the rain off our jackets and hung them to dry, then greeted the two dogs, who were acting as if we'd been gone for three days as opposed to three hours.

Evelyn retired to her room to rest, pleading sleepiness brought on by her non-twenty-four condition. But I suspected she was also emotionally drained from the afternoon's activity. From experience, I knew it wasn't easy having to attend a memorial service for your own mother.

"No worries," I said. "Have a good rest. I have to be at work in a little bit, so I'll see you when I get back tonight if you're up. And if you're hungry later on, don't forget the leftovers from last night's dinner are in the fridge."

An hour later, I parked the T-Bird in the Gauguin parking lot and let myself through the side door into the *garde manger*. Tomás was at the counter, dicing a mirepoix of carrots, celery, and onions for the stock pot.

"Hey, Tomás," I said. "*¿Qué pasa?*"

"Not much," he replied with a shrug.

I leaned against the sink and watched as he returned to his chopping. His strokes were sure and fast, and the dices— though it hardly mattered for a stock—were evenly matched in size. After a moment he set the knife down and sighed.

"Sorry if I seem grumpy. It's just that I heard a buddy of mine got caught up last night in an ICE bust at that taqueria down the street. He didn't have his papers with him, so they carted him off to jail."

"Oh, man. I'm so sorry, Tomás. But if he does in fact have the right papers, he should be released really soon."

"I guess." He didn't seem very convinced.

"And if not, maybe I could ask my friend Nichole to help out. She's an immigration attorney up in San Francisco."

"Thanks, Sally," he said, smiling now. "I'll let you know if that's necessary."

Heading upstairs, I took the stairs two at a time, and as I turned the corner into the office I almost collided with Brian. The cook mumbled a curt "Sorry," then hurried past me down the narrow hallway.

"What's up with him?" I asked Javier.

He looked up from the ledger he was studying and waved his hand. "He's just mad because I asked him, instead of Kris, to switch nights with me next weekend so I can go to a friend's wedding up in the City. I tried to explain that it was because he's the more experienced cook, but he just stormed off without letting me finish. For some reason he's got it in his head that I've been favoring her over him."

"Did he at least agree to swap nights?"

"Yeah, though I doubt I've heard the last of his bitching about it."

* * *

We had a full house that evening. Saturdays are always a big day for Gauguin, but ever since a rave review in the local newspaper several months back, our weekends had been consistently crazy busy, even on rainy nights like this.

We'd been open for about an hour and I was at the grill station, searing a pair of plump fillets for two orders of salmon with habanero-lime butter, when a burst of shrieks emanated from the dining room. I looked out through the pass window just in time to see three of our card-stock menus fly off the reception desk, one coming dangerously close to poking a customer in the eye at table two. A gust of wind had blown open the front door, lifting the menus into the air. Before Gloria, the Gauguin hostess, had time to rush over to close the door, I had a glimpse of the sheets of rain streaming down the sides of the awning onto the restaurant's front porch.

The shrieks in the dining room turned to laughter as a boom of thunder was followed by the flickering of lights.

"Great," I said to no one in particular. "That's all we need—a power outage."

I glanced over at the line, where Javier and Brian were scurrying about tending saucepots and sauté pans. If they'd noticed the lights going off and on, they showed no signs of it.

By a quarter to nine, most of the remaining grill and hot-line orders had been sent out to the dining room, and the restaurant was beginning to clear out. "Fire table four!" Brandon shouted at me through the pass, and I threw two New York steaks and a salmon fillet on the charbroiler. Only four more grill tickets left, thank goodness.

I was brushing the steaks with a mixture of olive oil, black pepper, and chopped garlic when the lights went off again. *Damn.* After what seemed like forever, they came back on and I let out the breath I hadn't even realized I'd been holding.

Flipping the two steaks, I reached for the brush to baste their other side, and then the kitchen went dark once more. I counted out the seconds, waiting for them to flicker back to life. When I got to fifteen, I set down the brush. The only illumination in the kitchen was from the propane flames of the charbroiler and the blue-white gas flames at the Wolf range.

Brandon was at the pass window. "What do we do know?" he asked in a panicked voice.

Having the power go out during winter storms is nothing new in Santa Cruz, and I'd worked several shifts at Solari's when it had happened, so I knew the drill.

"Tell the customers to stay put," I said, "and go grab the battery-powered table lights from the storage closet and get them set up. Anyone who already has their food is free to stay and finish it, and we'll send out any orders that are already cooked."

"What about the tickets?" the waiter asked. "The POS isn't gonna be working."

"Well, they've all been printed out, so if people don't have cash to pay, we can use the credit card reader and restaurant cell phone. They're in the top drawer of the hostess stand."

"Got it." Brandon turned to confer with the other waitstaff, who'd come up behind him while I spoke.

Javier finished plating up two orders of Coq au Vin au Gauguin and set them on the pass. "Order up!" he hollered over the din of chattering customers that now filled the dining room. Nothing like a minor emergency to get folks animated. "I'm gonna go check on the generator for the freezer and walk-in," the chef said. "It's supposed to go on automatically when the electricity goes out, but I better make sure it's working. This might last a while and I sure don't want to lose any food."

"Can't we use the generator to get the lights back on?" Brian asked, turning a pork chop that he had searing in a pan.

"It's only hooked up to the refrigeration units," Javier said. "Those ones that power the whole restaurant are way too expensive. Oh, and you might as well toss that pork chop. We can't do any more cooking, since the hood isn't working."

Brian frowned. "Oh, c'mon, man," he said. "It's almost done. It'd be stupid to waste it."

"No." Javier reached for the knob and turned off the gas under Brian's sauté pan. "I'm not going to risk the buildup of toxic fumes in my kitchen."

Brian slammed the pan down on the stove. In the dim light coming from the battery-powered lights in the dining room, I could see the sweat on his brow and the hardness in his eyes.

"*Your* kitchen. Right." He stared at Javier for a moment, his chest rising and falling with his rapid breaths. Then, raising his arms with palms spread in an I-give-up gesture, he flashed a humorless smile. "Fine. I'll leave you to *your* kitchen." And with that, he untied his apron and dropped it to the floor, pushed past Javier and me, and headed for the *garde manger*.

Tomás came running into the kitchen from the cold food prep area. "What the hell's wrong with Brian?" he said. "He just about knocked me down, he was in such a hurry to get outside."

"I don't know for sure," Javier replied. "But what I do know is it looks like you've just been promoted to line cook for the rest of the shift."

I ran after Brian. Javier might have been willing to let him take off in a rage, but I thought it better to try to talk him down. No matter what issues the guy might have been going through of late, Brian was a terrific cook, and I didn't want to lose him merely because of some fit of male pique.

The streetlights were all off, and with the rain spilling down my face and into my eyes, it was difficult to make out anything in the dark parking lot other than the vague shapes of cars. "Brian!" I called out. "Wait!"

A car door slammed and its headlights flashed on, casting an eerie, rain-filled beam of light across the restaurant's orange stucco wall and pale-violet trim. I dashed toward Brian's VW Beetle, shouting for him to stop, but he either didn't notice or simply chose to ignore my plea.

He backed quickly out of his spot, and as I watched the black Bug speed toward the street, its headlights lit up my T-Bird, parked on the other side of the lot.

Wait, is that someone standing there, hunched over, next to my car?

The figure, caught in the headlights, froze. "Hey, what are you doing?" I yelled. With a glance in my direction, the person pulled the hood of their sweatshirt down over their face and took off running.

Before I even reached my car, I could see the long gash in its creamy-white ragtop. *Great. Not only will that cost a bundle to fix, but everything inside is gonna get soaked.*

And then I remembered: I'd left Jackie's laptop in the car. I'd meant to bring it into the house when I'd gotten home from the memorial service, but had spaced it out. And, I realized with dismay, it had been in plain sight on the passenger seat—easy pickings for anyone who might want to swipe an expensive MacBook Air.

Switching on my phone's flashlight app, I shined it inside the T-Bird. Yep, the computer was gone. *Damn.* I unlocked the door and dropped heavily into the bucket seat, oblivious to the water streaming from my clothes and hair onto the leather upholstery.

What was I going to tell Detective Vargas?

I shined my phone once more around the car's interior, hoping I'd simply missed seeing the laptop, that perhaps it was on the floor. But no, the only item in the car besides Buster's cushion was my wallet, which must have fallen out of my bag without me noticing.

But why, I wondered with an intake of breath, *would a thief take the computer and not the wallet?* It was lying on the passenger seat, right next to where the computer had been, so it would have been hard to miss.

Because it wasn't a simple theft, was the obvious answer. *They wanted that specific laptop and weren't interested in anything else. So whoever took it must have known it was Jackie's. But how . . . ?*

My mind went back to the reception after the memorial service, when I'd told Detective Vargas about finding the computer. Yes, I'd definitely mentioned that I'd left it in my car. So who could have heard me?

Maya and Sarah had been nearby at the time. But, I realized with a sigh, I hadn't been paying attention to where anyone else was, which meant that pretty much anybody in attendance could have heard me say that Jackie's laptop was sitting in my car.

A car that was about as distinctive as any in the whole of Santa Cruz.

Chapter 9

Javier was right about one thing. The power was still out over much of Santa Cruz the next morning, including my neighborhood on the West Side and the downtown area where Gauguin is located. I called the chef to see if he'd been down to the restaurant, and he said no, agreeing to meet me there at ten thirty.

Although the rain had subsided for the time being, it was still windy, and driving down to Gauguin I had to dodge an array of branches, overturned recycling bins, and bottles and cans that littered the streets. Not only that, but the wind was whistling through the slash in the T-Bird's ragtop. I'd need to do a temporary fix with duct tape till I could figure out how to do a real patch job.

The building looked fine from the outside. Water was pooled up along the edge of the parking lot and we had some cleaning up to do of leaves and other debris, but no roof shingles appeared to have come loose, which had been my main concern. The two of us walked around back to check on the generator, and as soon as we rounded the corner of the building, we heard the reassuring roar of its natural gas–powered motor.

Javier unlocked the side door and let us into the *garde manger*. "Let's check the temp in the refrigeration units," I said, and he followed me into the walk-in. The wall thermometer read thirty-eight degrees. "Good. And the fans seem to be working, too."

After confirming that the freezer was also at the proper temperature, we headed to the kitchen. Enough sunlight streamed through the two windows for us to see that, although our cleanup job the night before hadn't been perfect, we'd done a pretty good job of it, given that the only light had been from the dim, battery-operated lamps.

"Have you heard anything about when the power's supposed to come back on?" Javier asked. He took a side towel from the stack on the counter and wiped a spot of gunk from the stainless-steel table running down the middle of the kitchen.

"I checked this morning, and they're saying a bunch of lines were knocked down. They're not expecting to have them all back up till late tonight at the earliest. And if this wind keeps up, it could be even longer."

"Bummer."

"Yeah." I pulled my phone from my jeans pocket. "So I guess that means we all have the night off. Better get busy calling folks to let them know. You wanna take the kitchen staff and I'll call everyone else?"

"Sounds good."

Javier retreated to the office to make his calls while I sat in the dining room and phoned the hostess as well as all the servers and bussers scheduled for tonight. Gauguin was closed on Mondays anyway, so even if the electricity wasn't restored until tomorrow night, we'd lose only one day's business.

That done, I headed upstairs to the office, where Javier was leaving a message for Kris. "Any news on the money transfer for Gauguin?" I asked once he'd punched off his phone.

"I was hoping for tomorrow," he said, "but it got delayed a day because of the power outage, so now they're saying Tuesday."

"Well, I've got the papers all drawn up and ready to go. Maybe we can have a signing celebration that night at the restaurant, to celebrate your new status as co-owner. Oh, that reminds me, did you decide on the specials for Tuesday?"

After conferring with Javier about Dungeness crab, Asian pears, and rainbow chard, I took off back home. Evelyn was in the living room, with the battery-powered transistor radio I'd unearthed that morning tuned to the 49ers-Seahawks game. Both dogs were snuggled on the couch with her, but Buster jumped down and came trotting over to greet me as I opened the door.

"Who's winning?" I asked through slobbery dog kisses.

"Seattle fourteen, Niners zip," she said, "with seventeen seconds left in the second quarter. But we've got a first-and-goal, so hopefully we'll score at least three points before the half. How's the restaurant?"

"Fine. But it doesn't look like the power will be restored in time for us to open tonight." I stood up and shook the dog hair from my pants. "I'm gonna go call my dad to see about Sunday dinner."

"Oh, you going over to his house tonight since Gauguin will be closed?"

"No," I said with a chuckle. "It's a lunchtime dinner thing my family's done since I was a baby. My *nonna* makes this braised meat dish—the Sunday gravy—and pasta, and so much other food that only an Italian grandmother could imagine you'd possibly be able to consume it all in one sitting. But I'm guessing with the power out, it's not happening today. Too bad, 'cause the gravy's delicious and I was hoping you could try it out today. But hey, there's always next Sunday."

I left her as the tinny radio crowd groaned in unison, indicating the kicker had missed his field goal. *So much for scoring at least three points.*

Dad picked up after the first ring. "Hi, hon. How you doing this blustery morning?"

"Not bad. And you? You didn't open today, did you?"

"No way. Back in the day, you can bet I would've. But nowadys with all the damn rules and regulations they have, no can do. So instead I'm taking the opportunity to organize my tackle box. Only four months till the opening of salmon season, after all, and it may take that long for me to untangle this mess of lures and lines I seem to have."

"I'm guessing Sunday dinner isn't happening."

"Nope. I stopped by to see how Nonna's doing, and she's got half the parish over there. She told everyone to come by after mass this morning, 'cause she's worried all the food in her freezer will spoil and wants to give it away." He snorted. "I tried to tell her the food would be fine as long as she didn't keep opening the freezer door, but she wouldn't listen to me, of course."

"C'mon, what do you expect?" I said. "It's not as if you ever listen to my advice, either. Parents are stubborn that way. Anyway, at least we both have a full day off for a change. You got any plans?"

Dad didn't answer right away. "Uh, yeah, I do," he finally said. "I have . . ." A pause, then, "Someone coming over."

"Someone? Do tell."

"Just this woman I met. She moved here from LA last summer and doesn't know many people in Santa Cruz yet, so . . ." He trailed off.

"How'd you meet her?"

"Uh, well, actually, it was on one of those computer sites where you meet people."

"No way, Dad! You signed up for an online dating site?"

"Yeah, well, I didn't want to tell you about it yet, because I thought you might be mad. You know, that you might think I was trying to replace your mother or something."

"I'm not mad, Dad. But I gotta say, I am surprised. So what's she like? What's her name?"

"Abby. She's a real estate agent. In fact, she was salesperson-of-the-month for November at her agency, so I'd say she must be pretty good." *Did my dad just giggle?* "And she's really into food and wine and stuff, so I'm sure you're gonna like her."

He wants us to meet? How serious is this?

"Uh, sure, Dad," I finally managed to say. "I'd love to meet her. Maybe next week at Sunday dinner. I was thinking of bringing Evelyn, too, if you don't think Nonna would mind that many people."

"I doubt she'd mind," Dad said. "But I'm not sure

I want to subject Abby to Nonna just yet. She's about as opposite from Italian as you can get."

I laughed. My grandmother could be pretty hard on people outside her insular little group of parishioners and the Italian American community here in Santa Cruz, especially if they were dating one of her own. I remembered how hard she'd been on Eric when I'd first brought him to Sunday dinner, making cracks about his blond hair and fair complexion and how she should have prepared potatoes instead of pasta for the meal.

"Well, I think you should bring her. If you're at all serious about her, she'll have to face Nonna at some point. And besides, *I'd* like to meet her."

"We'll see," was all he said.

After hanging up, I stared out the window at the liquid-ambar tree across the street, its gray branches, now bare of their glorious fall color, whipping about in the wind. *I should call that attorney who drafted Jackie's will.* I fetched the file from the kitchen counter and punched in the number at the top of the document, only to have the call go straight to voicemail—not surprising, given it was Sunday.

Using my best lawyerly voice and somewhat rusty attorney vocabulary, I left a message saying I was calling on behalf of Jackie's daughter "in regards to her mother's recent death and the provisions of her will" and asking him to please return my call "at your earliest convenience."

I didn't go so far as to claim I was "representing" Evelyn or that she was my "client." That would have been unethical, since as an inactive member of the California bar, I was prohibited from engaging in the practice of law. But if he merely assumed I was an attorney, perhaps he'd call me back that little bit faster. That done, I turned my thoughts to lunch.

Evelyn helped me rustle up a can of bean-with-bacon soup and a pair of grilled-cheese sandwiches made with Gouda, horseradish, arugula, and thinly sliced apple. As I rinsed the salad greens and then shook them dry in a colander, I watched her deftly core and slice the Fuji apple for our sandwiches. "By the way," I said, "I have some bad news."

"Oh?" She set down the paring knife and turned my way.

"Yeah. Your mom's laptop was stolen from my car last night." I told her about the person running away from the T-Bird and how I'd found my wallet on the seat. "So my guess is the thief was someone who was at Jackie's memorial service and overheard what I said to Detective Vargas about her computer being in my car."

Evelyn sucked in her breath. "If that's the case, then there's a good chance whoever stole it was Mom's killer."

"I know. Super creepy." I shivered, then gave an angry shake to the colander. "And now I also have to break the news to Vargas, how I managed to lose a valuable piece of evidence in the case."

Evelyn picked the knife up again, brow furrowed, and I finished drying the greens and then set to work buttering the bread and slicing cheese. Neither of us spoke as she continued cutting up her apples and I got the bread grilling in a cast-iron skillet.

"Hey," Evelyn said after a bit, scraping the apple pieces into a small bowl, "I have an idea. Since you're not working tonight, how about I cook that dinner for you I talked about? After all, it won't make any difference to me that there's no lights." Evelyn grinned as she wiped the paring knife clean with a dish towel.

"Sure, that sounds fun."

"But would it be okay if we did it at my house? It'll be way easier for me to cook there, since I know where everything is."

"You don't mind hanging out there that long?" I asked.

She shrugged. "It should be okay, especially since you'll be there, too. And I think it'd be good to see how I feel being at the place for more than just a short time. You know, to try to work my way up to being able to spend the night there, and move back in one of these days."

"I think that's a great idea. So it's a date, then—assuming there's a gas range."

"Yep. And a gas oven, too. And candles, for you poor sighted folks who can't live a single second in the dark."

"Thanks," I said with a laugh. "Will you make your famous pasta from scratch that you were telling me and Javier about?"

"Absolutely." Evelyn carried the bowl of apples over to the stove and, lightly touching the buttered bread browning in the skillet, began arranging the slices on top of the cheese I'd placed on the bread. "Do you happen to have any porcini mushrooms?" she asked. "For the dinner tonight?"

"I do, actually. My dad and I hosted this huge banquet a couple months back and we got about twenty pounds from the Santa Cruz Fungus Federation—way more than we needed. So Dad dried the ones we ended up not using.

Here." I pulled a plastic bag full of the dried bolete mushrooms from the cupboard above me and opened it, then held the bag under Evelyn's nose. "He gave me some. Smell."

"Ahhhh, yes!" she said. "Let's get some of these soaking right away. I know you have garlic, onions, and Parmigiano cheese, but I don't suppose you also have any peas, do you?"

"Just the frozen variety. It's not really pea season."

"That'll work. Not quite like fresh, but way better than canned. So you're in luck. I'm going to make you Nonna Sophia's fettuccine with mushrooms and peas. It was my father's favorite when he was growing up, according to Nonna, anyway.

"Oh, man. Sounds incredible."

* * *

After lunch, I finally got up the nerve to call Detective Vargas. *It is Sunday afternoon*, I thought, *so maybe he won't pick up and I can just leave a message.* But no, he was apparently one of those always-on-the-job types.

"Vargas here," his deep voice answered before the second ring.

"Oh hi, it's Sally Solari. I, uh . . . have some bad news."

From the groans and exaggerated sighs coming over the line, I could tell he was not at all happy about the laptop, but he did let me recount my story without interruption. "So it seems to me it must have been someone at the memorial service who stole it," I finished.

"Given what you said about your wallet being there in plain sight, I have to say—much as it pains me to do so— that you may very well be right." Another audible sigh.

I laughed. "Well, that's something, anyway. Which means we need to figure out who was there who could have overheard us talking, and which of them would have any reason to want Jackie's computer—or to want her dead."

"Hold on," Vargas said. "Just because someone may have wanted her computer doesn't mean they murdered her. I'm still not convinced it wasn't a suicide."

"But what about what Evelyn said, about how her mom never called her by that name? And don't you think it's a little suspicious that the computer was stolen just days after Jackie died? Oh, and there's another thing." I told him about finding the bottle of cranberry juice in the wrong place in the refrigerator. "Would the police who searched the house have moved things around in the fridge?"

"I doubt it," he said. "But I don't see how that proves much. Jackie could have moved the bottle that night. Given all the alcohol and drugs she'd ingested, she could easily have neglected to put it back in its right place."

Exactly what I'd said to Evelyn.

"Back to the memorial service," Vargas went on. "Why don't you give me a list of all the people you can remember who were there."

"Okay. Lemme think . . ." I ticked off the names for the detective: Stan, Max, Sarah, Maya, Rachel, Al, the two women who'd worked with Jackie at IHOP, the two Tamarind cooks, Evelyn's four friends, my dad, and his Cousin Sophia.

"And then, of course, you, me, and Evelyn," I added. "Oh, and the gal who led the service and the guy who played the piano. There were other people there too, but those are the only ones I know anything about."

"And out of those people, are there any you have reason to believe might have wanted to steal Jackie's computer?"

"Well, I don't know exactly why this might make him want her computer, but Evelyn and I did just find out that Stan, her ex-stepdad, had been paying spousal support to Jackie. And then there's Al, the guy you saw get all weird with those two women at the reception. He's Jackie's old boss and apparently thinks she stole recipes from him when she left Tamarind."

I closed my eyes, trying to remember the people I'd seen at the memorial service. "Oh, and I almost forgot. This woman, Rachel, who recently quit working for Jackie's pop-up restaurant—apparently over some argument they had or something—she was at the memorial, too. So that makes three suspects we have at this point."

"Okay, thanks," Vargas said with a chuckle. "That's a start. And on the subject of *suspects*, I think it goes without saying—"

"But you're going to anyway," I cut in.

Vargas ignored my interruption. "That you should let us do our job without any interference on your part. But if you do happen to come across any other evidence relevant to the case, I'm assuming you'll be a little more careful with it, yes?"

"Absolutely," I said. "I promise."

Chapter 10

Evelyn's house was not only dark but also cold and damp when we got there at six o'clock that evening, and the first thing I did while she went in search of candles was locate the thermostat. *Yes.* It was an old-style gas heater that didn't require electricity. I cranked the knob up to eighty degrees. Once the place warmed up a bit, I could turn it down.

"Look what I found," Evelyn said, emerging from the hall closet. She held up an object that, when I shined my phone's light on it, proved to be a large camping lantern. "Let's see if the battery's still good." She flipped the switch and brightness filled the room.

"It works!" I said. "Awesome."

"And I found a bunch of candles, too. But since I never use them, I'm not sure where Mom kept the matches or candle holders."

"That's okay. We can use the flame from the stove to light them." I followed Evelyn into the kitchen, and after setting up the lantern and lighting several candles and placing them on saucers, we set about organizing all the food we'd brought over for the meal: the rehydrated porcini mushrooms, a chunk of Parmigiano cheese, the packet of frozen peas, an onion and head of garlic, three eggs, and half a baguette I'd discovered in my freezer. "Okay," she said. "I should get the pasta going first. It needs to rest for a while before I can roll it out."

Evelyn pulled a dry measuring cup from a drawer, then lifted the lid off a 1950s-era metal canister on the counter with FLOUR written on its side in elaborate script. She filled the cup from the canister, scraped across its top with the flat edge of a butter knife, and dumped the flour onto a large cutting board. After adding a second cup to the mound, she used her knuckles to make a well in the flour, then cracked the eggs into its center.

"Grab a fork for me from the drawer, would ya? It's to the right of the sink."

I handed her the fork and she began to beat the eggs, using her other hand to keep propping up the flour wall. "You have to be really careful at this point," she said, "or else you'll punch a hole in the thing and end up with egg all over the counter and floor."

As I watched, she slowly incorporated the flour into the eggs, touching the mixture with a forefinger every once in a while to gauge its consistency. Once the eggs and flour had turned into a thick batter, she brought the flour walls down upon it, then quickly mixed it all together with her hands until the mass became a ragged, sticky lump.

"Kind of a messy process," I said as flour and bits of dough flew onto the floor.

"Uh-huh." Gathering the dough together in a rough ball, she wrapped it in a sheet of plastic wrap, then washed the mess off her hands at the sink. Once she'd scraped the cutting board clean with a bench knife—getting even more flour and bits of dough on the counter and floor— she unwrapped the sticky ball.

"This is the hard part," she said. "You gotta knead it for at least ten minutes. But it does build up your upper-body strength."

"Well, I'm happy to lend a hand, if you want."

We took turns working the dough, adding a dusting of flour as needed, until Evelyn deemed it ready. "See? Feel this. Soft and silky as a baby's butt, Nonna Sophia always says." She wrapped the ball in a new sheet of plastic and set it on the counter. "Okay, that has to rest now for a half hour. Time to make the sauce."

* * *

An hour later we sat down to one of the best dinners I've ever had, the dramatic candlelit table and the gorgeous Limoges china Evelyn had insisted we use adding an even more sublime tone to the meal. The flavors of the peas and porcini blended beautifully, and the sharp, tangy cheese added the perfect contrast to the earthy flavors of the vegetables. But the fettuccine was the star of the show. It had a delicate, eggy flavor and a melt-in-your-mouth texture I'd never before experienced with pasta—not even my *nonna*'s.

"Ohmygod, how'd you get it so tender?" I asked, a long strand dangling from my mouth.

"It's all in the rolling," Evelyn said with a smile. "You have to do it quickly without overworking the dough. That's why most people use a machine. But I think the hand-rolled kind is way better."

"No kidding, it is," I said, slurping up the errant pasta. "If we could make this at Gauguin, it'd be a best seller. You think there's any way you could teach Javier how to do it? He already has a great touch with pastry dough, so I bet he'd be a natural for fresh pasta."

"Sure, I could try. I'm on break from school till early January, so I have lots of free time right now."

Evelyn and I ate in silence for a bit, and I watched as she speared strands of fettuccine, swirled them around her fork, and raised the pasta to her mouth. *What would it be like to live your life in total darkness*, I wondered, *no hint of light penetrating your senses?*

"Could I ask you something?" I said. "It's about being blind."

Evelyn smiled as she reached for her glass of iced tea. "You can ask me anything you want."

"Okay." I took a sip of water as I pondered my question. "It's just that I'm curious about colors. Since you've never actually seen the color green, or red or blue, what do you imagine when people talk about them? Does the concept of colors even mean anything to you?"

"Sure, absolutely they do. I've heard people talk about colors my entire life, so even though I can't actually see them, I have a pretty good idea in my head of what they mean. Red and orange and yellow are warm—you know, like a fire, or the sun, or the blood in our veins. And they're also the colors of passion and excitement. And then blue and green are cool colors, like the ocean, or the lawn in our backyard which I'd lie on in the summer, smelling the freshly cut grass."

"Huh. Well, I guess that makes sense. And I bet your other senses are way more heightened than mine."

"Maybe not taste, 'cause I happen to know you're pretty good in that department. But for sure hearing and touch. They're how I get by in the world. And maybe even smell, too. Like, I can often tell where I am on campus by the smells around me: paint and turpentine at the art studios, musty paper in the library, gas fumes in the parking lots. And of course it's super easy knowing when I'm anywhere near the cafeteria from the smell. But pretty much anyone would notice that."

"Yep," I said with a laugh. "I'm pretty much always attuned to the smell of food."

* * *

After dinner, we retired to the living room to digest our meal. I hadn't been able to resist having seconds, which I'd then proceeded to mop up with several slices of crusty baguette, so I was feeling more than a little stuffed.

"I saw a bottle of Cognac in the cupboard," I said as I plopped down on the couch next to Evelyn. "Would it be okay if I had a glass—you know, as a digestif to help process that mass of delicious pasta I just consumed?"

"Sure, help yourself," she said.

"Can I get you anything?"

"Some herbal tea would be nice. There's a box of peppermint next to the Cognac."

I was poking around the cupboard, using the flashlight on my phone to search for the tea, when a blinding light filled the room. "Whoa!" I shouted, covering my eyes with my hand.

"What happened?" Evelyn jumped up from the couch, ready to dash into the kitchen to my aid. "Are you okay?"

"I'm fine," I said, blinking and rubbing my eyes. "The power just came back on is all, and boy are those kitchen lights *bright*. I don't know why they were even on." Looking around for the light switch, I located it against the wall next to the fridge. "Aha, mystery solved. The switch is on the wall where I was leaning while I watched you roll out the pasta. I must have turned it on by accident."

At the sound of the whistling kettle, I poured hot water into a mug for Evelyn's tea, then helped myself to two fingers of Cognac. "Hey, wait," I said as I brought the drinks into the living room. "That reading lamp was on a timer, so why'd it turn back on now?"

When we'd come to pick up Evelyn's pillow and clothes, I'd seen a timer on the floor by the lamp and had suggested we plug it in so the house wouldn't look unoccupied while Evelyn was staying with me. But because the power had been out since last night, the timing on the mechanism should have been thrown off.

"Oh right," I realized. "It's been almost exactly twenty-four hours, so it's on the same schedule I set it at." I sat back down on the couch with my drink. "It's a gorgeous lamp. The colors coming through the cut glass make for lovely mood lighting."

"Hey, speaking of mood," Evelyn said, "why don't I play

you some of my granddad's records, now that we have power again." She stood and walked to the corner where the stereo was, flipped through several albums at the far right of the shelf, and selected one. "Okay, get ready to listen to the smoothest male voice in jazz."

It was too dim in the room for me to see who the artist was, so I waited with interest to see what she'd chosen to play. After a moment I heard the scratch of the needle on vinyl and then the opening strains of the song.

"Oh," I said. "I know that one! It's Frank Sinatra, singing 'I've Got You Under My Skin.' Side B, track one of *Songs for Swingin' Lovers*," I added. "My mom used to play that album all the time."

I swiveled around to see if I'd impressed her with my knowledge of 1950s jazz vocals, but instead of smiling as I would have expected, Evelyn wore a frown. "What's wrong?" I asked.

She was clutching the record jacket tightly, and if I hadn't known better I would have said she was staring at the clean-cut couple locked in a youthful embrace on its cover. "This isn't the one I meant to put on," she said, shaking her head. "I don't understand . . ."

"Well, you can't always bat a thousand. And it's a great album, so I don't mind."

"Someone's been messing with my records," she said quietly, and set the jacket down. "I played it the night before Mom died, the one I was just looking for—Mel Tormé and Artie Shaw."

I joined her by the shelf and knelt to examine the spines

of the record jackets. "Here it is," I said, pulling out an LP. *"Mel Tormé With the Meltones and Artie Shaw."*

"That's the one. Where was it?"

I squinted in the dim light at the row of albums. "Right between George Shearing and Sarah Vaughan. Which is where it should be, right? *T* comes between *S* and *V.*"

"No." She took the Mel Tormé record from me and hugged it to her breast, her breath coming quickly now, as if she'd been running. "Because the Sinatra record was the second one from the end just now. Where *this one* should have been." She shook the record in her hands.

"I know *I* didn't misfile the album," she said. "And Mom never touches my records. She doesn't even like jazz all that much, and if she had played it, she would have put it back where it belongs. She *knows* how organized I am about . . ." Evelyn stopped and bit her lip, which I could see had started to tremble.

Neither of us spoke. Frank was now on to the second track, "I Thought About You," and I was tempted to pick up the needle lest the lyrics upset Evelyn further. But she made no sign that she even noticed that the song was playing.

After a few moments, she exhaled and turned to face me. "This absolutely proves it," she said, jaw set. "Someone was *definitely* here with Mom the night she died. And whoever played my records that night had to be the same person who killed Mom and wrote that note to make it look like a suicide."

I nodded, staring blankly at the floor. And then my eyes were drawn to the purple-red stain on the carpet. "And they were drinking that cranberry juice out here," I said, "because there's a new-looking stain that someone clearly tried to clean up but did a bad job of it. Given what we know about the juice in the fridge being moved that same night, it had to be the same person."

I returned to the couch and took a sip of my drink, a Rémy Martin VSOP. It was smooth and balanced, with hints of fig and leather. Jackie had not skimped on her choice of Cognac.

"Does Stan like jazz?" I asked after a bit. "Or cranberry juice?"

Evelyn set the record she'd been clutching onto the shelf next to the turntable and came to sit next to me. "I have no idea what he likes to drink. And as for jazz, I can't remember for sure. He used to play lots of kinds of music around the house."

"Well, was he into vinyl records? Did he ever ask to play yours?"

She shook her head. "He'd already moved out by the time Nonna gave me Grandpa's records, so no. But that doesn't rule him out."

"No," I agreed, "he's definitely a prime suspect. But let's assume for the moment it wasn't Stan who was here that night. Who else could it have been?"

"Lots of people. Mom was always having friends over to hang out and eat and drink, watch movies. She was pretty social."

"Like who in particular?"

Evelyn leaned back on the couch, and her eyes darted about as she thought. "Mostly restaurant people, 'cause that was pretty much her whole life of late. People she knew from the places she used to work at, the women from the pop-up and the owners of the place that hosts it, and a few old friends, too."

"So really," I said, "there are lots of possible suspects."

She chewed her lip a moment, then turned to me. "You think we should give those records to Detective Vargas to test for fingerprints? And the juice bottle too?"

"I don't know." I finished off my Cognac and set the glass back down on the coffee table.

"But you're the one who said he seemed interested in what I said about my mom never calling me Evelyn. And he did show up at the memorial service."

"True. But it might be better to wait. I already told him about the juice being moved, and he didn't seem to think it was all that important. But maybe if we had a little more evidence, then he'd take us seriously."

Evelyn sat bolt upright, shoulders back and chin high. "Okay, then. Let's get that evidence."

Chapter 11

I woke up the next morning to a text from Eric: U FREE
TONIGHT?

SURE, I wrote back. DINNER?

SOUNDS GOOD. U PICK PLACE AND TIME.

I thought a moment, then looked up a website on my
phone before replying: TAMARIND AT 6.

I'd been wanting to try their Southeast Asian menu for
some time now, and, their website had confirmed, they
were open on Mondays—a night many restaurants (including Gauguin) are closed. But more importantly, if Evelyn
and I were going to gather more evidence regarding Jackie's
death, it seemed like as good a place to start as any.

Evelyn hadn't yet emerged from her bedroom by the time
I wandered into the kitchen wearing my cycling gear. I let
Buster out the back door. It was a gray day and the thermometer out on the patio read a frigid thirty-nine degrees, but at
least it wasn't raining. This time of year you had to take your
cycling opportunities when you could, cold or not.

Nevertheless, I'd keep the ride short—out to Wilder
Ranch, down to the Boardwalk, then back home. Bundled up

in leggings, a long-sleeved jacket, and fleece-lined gloves, I clipped into my pedals and headed down to West Cliff Drive.

The weather had not frightened off the sea life. Brown pelicans soared above me in ragged *V*s as I pedaled up the coast, and I spotted several sea lions close to shore, diving for fish in the steel-gray water. A few hardy humans besides me were also out this morning, walking dogs or jogging along the twisty path that hugs the cliffs.

It hadn't seemed windy on the ride down to the ocean, but as soon as I turned north, I was hit with what felt like an arctic blast. *Yes, definitely a short ride this morning.* Some cyclists claim the wind is their friend, helping with training. But the idea of voluntarily subjecting myself to a gale such as this on any regular basis seemed crazy to me.

Once I reached the old dairy at Wilder Ranch State Park and turned back south, however, the ride was far more pleasant, with the wind at my back instead of buffeting me head on. (Okay, so maybe the wind is sometimes my friend.) And as I cruised along the eucalyptus-lined bike path, past stables and fields of brussels sprouts and artichokes, my thoughts turned to the day ahead.

Hot coffee and a hot shower were first on the agenda. Then a walk for Buster and Coco, after which I wanted to work on the front-of-the-house scheduling for Gauguin over the next few weeks. Our head waiter, Brandon, as well as the hostess, Gloria, and several other servers, had all asked for time off around the holidays, and the gymnastics required to make the schedule work was going to be a nightmare. At least I didn't have to deal with the kitchen staff, too; that was Javier's unhappy task.

Once home, coffee mug in hand, I sat on the living room couch with my phone to check my email and do a quick scan of Facebook. As I was watching a video on how to make a batch of cardiac arrest–inducing sliders stuffed with cheese sauce and French fries, the device buzzed.

The screen displayed a number I didn't recognize, but since it was our local 831 area code, I went ahead and answered it. "Sally here."

"Good morning, Ms. Solari. This is Adam Scurich. You called me yesterday about a will?"

"Oh, right. Hi. Thanks so much for calling back."

"Sure, no problem," he said. "You may not remember me, but we were opposing counsel years ago on a land condemnation case. I worked for the city attorney's office back then."

"Aha! I thought your name sounded familiar."

"So you said you were representing Jackie Olivieri's estate? I've been out of town for a week and only got back in last night, so I didn't hear about her death till then. I'm so sorry."

"Uh, thanks," I mumbled, trying to decide how unethical it would be not to correct his assumption that I was acting as an attorney with regard to the matter. "Well, Jackie's daughter Evelyn and I found her will that had your name on it, and I wondered if I could ask a couple questions."

"Sure, go ahead. I pulled the file, so I have it right here in front of me. What do you want to know?"

"First off, is any of the estate in a trust?"

"None was at the time she executed the will," he said. "I advised her to do a trust, but she said she didn't want to bother. Of course, she might have had a change of heart since then and created one, but if so, she didn't use me."

"I know she owns a house here in town," I said, reaching for a pen and a piece of junk mail on the side table to take notes on. "Can you tell me if she had any other properties or assets of value?"

I could hear the rustling of papers as he looked through the file. "I asked her about that in regards to a possible trust, and it looks like the house—which still has a mortgage— and a car, as well as a savings account with Wells Fargo, are the only things besides personal items. And you should know," he added, "that she owned the house as a tenant in common with . . ." He paused as he searched for the name. "Stanley Kruger, her ex-husband. It had been a joint tenancy while they were married, but they changed it to a tenancy in common once the divorce proceedings were initiated."

Huh. This was news. I'd assumed Jackie was the sole owner. I wondered if Evelyn knew that her stepdad owned half the house. *Probably not, or she would surely have mentioned it to me.*

"So that means Evelyn will inherit Jackie's share," I said, "but that Stan—the ex—could force a sale if he wanted to cash out his half."

"Yes to the inheritance part, but no as for the other. It says here in the copy of the divorce settlement I have that there can be no forced sale of the property until Ms. Olivieri's daughter turns twenty-five. I seem to remember the reason being that she has some sort of disability."

"Evelyn's blind," I said. "She was living at home when her mom died."

"Right. So the court must have determined that she required that security until she'd be able to go out on her own. The settlement also states that the parties are to share the mortgage payments equally, but that the ex-husband is to pay spousal support until, let's see . . . two years from now."

"But the obligation to pay spousal support would end with the death of the ex-wife."

"That is correct," he said.

Neither of us spoke. Jackie had obviously been using the spousal support to pay her share of the mortgage, as well as to get The Curry Leaf up and running. But how on earth would Evelyn be able to make her share of the mortgage without the alimony payments?

She wouldn't.

"Okay, one more question," I said. "Even though the divorce settlement mandates that neither party can force the other to sell until Evelyn turns twenty-five, there's nothing to prevent a *voluntary* sale by both parties, right?"

He immediately clued in to where I was going with this. "Right. Now that she's on the hook for half the mortgage payment—which I assume she has no way of making—she'll probably want to sell her share. And as long as they both agree, the sale would not run afoul of the settlement."

That certainly looked to be Evelyn's only option at this point. So not only did Stan no longer have to fork out over three grand a month in alimony, but there was a good chance he'd get to cash out his half of the house two years ahead of schedule.

Jackie's death had been quite the boon to his pocketbook.

*   *   *

Evelyn came into the room a few minutes later. She was still wearing her bathrobe and slippers and had a bleary look in her eyes.

"Morning," I said. "You look like you could use some coffee. Bad night?"

She plopped down next to me on the couch. "Bad morning, more like. I woke up at around three and didn't get back to sleep till at least seven."

"Man, that non-twenty-four thing really sucks."

Evelyn only nodded absently, more of a "Whatever you say" kind of response than one of agreement.

"Oh," I went on, "it's something else, isn't it? Your mom?"

This time the nod was again slow, but sincere. "Uh-huh. That's what kept me up," she said, her eyes shining with tears. "Thinking about her."

I put an arm around her shoulders to pull her toward me as she cried, chest jerking with sporadic shudders.

Her body grew still, and she sat back and wiped her eyes. "I just can't stop thinking about it," she said, voice trembling. "That someone would murder her like that—forcing her to overdose." Evelyn straightened up and balled her fists. "We really do need to get more evidence. Figure out who was there that night. I don't know if I'll ever be able to sleep again until Mom's killer is in jail."

"Well," I said, "I actually just got some news that could be relevant to that. The attorney who drafted your mom's will called me back a few minutes ago."

"Oh, yeah? What'd he say?"

"Some of it's not great, I'm afraid."

I told her about the house being held in a tenancy in common with Stan, which meant that although she would inherit her mother's half of the property, her stepfather owned the other half.

"Wow. I wonder why Mom never told me the place was half his."

"Maybe because she knew how much you disliked him? And also, well, it does seem like she kept pretty much everything about Stan from you. You know, like the alimony payments."

But I had to agree it did seem odd for Jackie not to have told her daughter about the house. "And the other bad news," I said, "is that not only does he own half the house, but you're now on the hook for your mom's half of the mortgage payment."

"How much is it?" Evelyn asked.

"I imagine it's gotta be at least a thousand or two a month, but we can find out easily enough."

She slumped over. "It doesn't really matter. Even if it were only a few hundred dollars, I'd have no way to pay it. I have no job, and have to pay my student fees and for books . . ."

"Yeah, I know," I said, tapping my fingers on my coffee mug. Evelyn crossed her arms over her chest. "It seems like it would make more sense to sell the house so I can get my half and use it to live off of. But could we even do that?"

"The agreement just says neither owner can *force* the

other to sell, so I see no reason you couldn't if you both wanted to." I leaned back and thought a moment. "But given what we now know—how much Stan has benefited financially from your mom dying—it seems to me what we really need to do right now is talk to the guy to see if we can find out anything connecting him to the death."

"Could you do that without me?" she asked, scrunching up her face. "I'm sure he knows how much I dislike him, so he's way more likely to talk to you."

"Sure, I guess so. Do you know anything about his habits? Like, where he shops, or goes jogging or something?"

"Not a lot," she said. "Except . . . Yes." She sat up. "He has a dog, or at least used to, anyway. A big black Standard Poodle named Harry. And he used to walk him early every morning on West Cliff. If he still has the dog, I bet he still does it. He was always super regular about his routines."

"How early?" I asked.

"Like seven or eight. But it would depend on his work schedule at the clinic."

"He's a high-paid nurse, you said, right? You know what kind, exactly?"

Evelyn nodded. "Yeah, he assists anesthesiologists in surgery. I think it's called a nurse anesthetist."

"So he'd certainly know a lot about drugs," I said. "Including what would work to kill someone. I definitely need to talk to him." I finished my coffee and stood. "Guess I'll go shower. Oh, by the way, you should know I'm working on another angle of the case, too. I'm going to Tamarind tonight, with a friend."

Was that what Eric was now? Just a friend?

"Oh, good." Evelyn smiled for the first time that morning. "Do you have a plan of action?"

"God, no," I said with a short laugh. "I'm just going to play it by ear."

Chapter 12

Pacific Avenue, the main shopping street in Santa Cruz, was bustling with people that evening. It was twenty to six, and thus already dark on this chilly, early December evening, and the white fairy lights strung along the ornamental cherry trees downtown added a heightened level of gaiety to the already-festive pre-Christmas atmosphere.

I was on my way back to my car after making the Gauguin bank deposit, and had stopped to admire a window display at one of the trendy clothing stores along the outdoor mall. A mannequin Santa, sporting gold hoop earrings and a snug red suit, sat astride a fat-tired bicycle with a surfboard tucked under one arm. Santa Cruzin' Santa! the hand-lettered sign behind him read.

A woman came to stand next to me and laughed. "Did you see last year's window?" she said. "It was good too, but the Santa was far more risqué."

I turned, recognizing the voice. "Oh, hi . . ."

"Sarah," she filled in. "We met at Jackie's memorial the other day. I worked with her at The Curry Leaf."

"Ah, right."

"How's Evelyn doing?" she asked.

"Okay, I guess, all things considered. She's been staying at my place for a while, till she's ready to go back home." I nodded at the large brown bag Sarah carried. "You been doing some Christmas shopping?"

"Uh-huh, for my girlfriend." She hoisted the bag, from which a large, colorfully wrapped package protruded.

"Looks heavy," I observed.

"A set a knives—Henckels."

"Nice. She must really be into cooking, to merit knives like that."

"She is." Sarah paused. "She used to cook at The Curry Leaf, actually, until she, uh . . . left."

"Rachel? She's your girlfriend?"

"Well, we only just got together pretty recently, but yeah. Christmas day will be our three-month anniversary. Hence the nice present," she added. "We met when I started at The Curry Leaf, but Rachel didn't want to tell Jackie about us, 'cause she was worried she wouldn't like the idea of a couple working for her. And then after Rachel quit, there was no real reason to tell her, so she never knew."

"Huh." Hadn't Evelyn said that Jackie and Rachel had been friends since before she'd started The Curry Leaf? So why wouldn't Rachel have been honest with her friend about her romance with Sarah?

My interest in Jackie's ex-cook had just jumped up a notch.

"Oh, and I should tell you also," Sarah said, setting her bag down on the sidewalk. "It looks like I won't be looking for a job as prep cook after all. Rachel's opening a pop-up restaurant downtown and has asked me and Maya to come work for her. It's gonna be at the same place as The Curry Leaf, starting this Wednesday."

Sarah was staring at the surfer Santa in the window, so she failed to notice my interested expression and continued on excitedly, "I really like the idea of only working part-time so I can concentrate on the group I play bass with. And this pop-up Rachel's doing is only gonna be open a few days a week, so it's perfect for me."

"Uh-huh," I said, letting her chatter on.

"Yeah, and it's gonna be basically the same as The Curry Leaf, actually. You know, using a lot of the same recipes, but with a different name, of course. So it'll be easy for me to learn the menu."

Make that two notches.

*   *   *

Although the conversation with Sarah made me ten minutes late for my dinner with Eric, I still beat him to Tamarind. No big surprise there; Eric is chronically late.

I'd asked Evelyn if she'd like to join us, but she'd declined, saying she actually preferred to stay home by herself. Which I understood. I could see how she wouldn't want to spend an evening right now at the restaurant that had caused her mom so much grief.

After giving my name, I was shown to a table near the back, not far from the restrooms. I would have been annoyed by the location except for the fact that almost every seat in the house was filled and I'd made the reservation only this afternoon. I figured I was lucky to have gotten a table at all.

The maître d' handed me a menu and asked if I'd like anything from the bar while I waited for my "other party." He returned four minutes later with my Maker's Mark, and I was savoring those luscious first few sips while my palate was still fresh, humming along to a breathy woman singing "Night and Day," when Eric strode across the room.

"Hey, Sal," he said, leaning over to give me a kiss on the cheek. "Sorry I'm late."

"No, you're not. But I appreciate the fact that you acknowledge your tardiness." I consulted my phone. "Fifteen minutes, to be exact." No way was I going to give him the satisfaction of knowing I'd been late as well.

Our waiter—a skinny guy with a dirty-blond man-bun held in place by a pair of ebony chopsticks—appeared at the table to ask if Eric would like something to drink before ordering.

"No thanks," he said. "I think I'll stick with some wine or beer with dinner. I already had a Martini before I came here," he added once the server had disappeared. "That's why I'm late, actually."

"Oh? Do tell."

"It's just that I ran into Gayle at the courthouse this afternoon as her trial was getting out, so we went to Kalo's for a quick drink. You know, that PD who—"

"Yeah, I know who she is."

He gave me a questioning look, and I realized my comment had come out rather curtly. "The woman who chose the light over the dark side," I added with a forced smile, "and works for the public defender instead of the evil DA's office."

"Very funny. Yes, that's the one." He picked up his menu and studied the handwritten page with today's specials.

"I liked her," I said. "She's clearly smart, and it seems like she has a snarky sense of humor." This wasn't a lie. I *had* liked Gayle, even if I didn't love the idea of her and Eric together.

Eric looked up from the menu and grinned. "Yeah, she is pretty great. She told me today that she has a degree from Vassar in French literature. But she decided she didn't want to teach, so she went to law school instead. Stanford."

"Rich parents?" I asked. No way would a public defender's salary be high enough to pay off the student loans from both those institutions.

"I gather. She grew up in Atherton, so . . ."

"Say no more." That residential community at the northern end of Silicon Valley is so expensive that even wealthy techies have a hard time affording its real estate.

"But she's not snobby at all," Eric went on. "She's really down to earth and wants to give back to society—help people that didn't have the opportunities she did. She can't help it that she grew up rich." He stopped, perhaps aware how defensive he was beginning to sound on her behalf.

I said nothing, instead sipping from my drink as I perused the menu.

Eric waved his hand. "Anyway, who cares if she's a trust fund baby or not. I don't even know why we're spending so much time talking about her. I mean, it's not like we're dating or anything. We're just friends."

Not dating? Right. So it's some hard-core pre-dating, then.

"Speaking of dating. Okay, *not* dating, in your case," I amended, provoking an eye roll from Eric. "It looks like my dad might be doing just that—dating."

"No way."

"Well, he seems pretty besotted with the woman."

I recounted what I knew about Abby. "Of course, that's only what Dad's told me. She could be a complete lunatic, for all I know."

"You jealous?" Eric asked. "Or at least, you know, upset that your dad's dating someone who's not your mom?"

"No, I don't think so. I doubt Mom would have wanted him to be alone forever after she died. But it'll depend on what I think of this Abby woman when we meet. If I feel like she's not good enough for Dad, or taking advantage of him, I sure won't be happy."

"I can't see anyone taking advantage of Mario," Eric said with a chuckle. "He's pretty capable of fending for himself."

"Yeah, well, you don't know him as well as I do. I'd say he's plenty capable of succumbing to the wiles of a seductive woman." *As are most men I know*, I thought to myself, *including you, my unwary friend.*

Our waiter arrived to take our orders, with apologies for not returning sooner. "That's okay," I said. "It looks like you're really slammed tonight, especially for a Monday."

"Yeah." He reached up to adjust one of the sticks protruding from his bun. "We've been super busy the last few months, even recently, when it's usually slow after the tourists have disappeared. So have you decided what you'd like?"

Eric ordered the Penang Beef, a hanger steak simmered

in coconut curry sauce, and I went for the Singapore Noodles with Roast Pork and Broccolini.

"Oh, and throw in an order of spring rolls, too," Eric said. "And I'll have a Tiger beer."

"Make that two beers." I waited for the server to finish scribbling down our order, then handed him my menu. "It's weird the place is so crowded," I said to Eric once he'd headed off to place our order.

"Yeah, for a Monday night."

"No, it's not just that. It's something Evelyn told me."

"Evelyn? Oh, right, your cousin."

"Right. This is where her mom, Jackie, worked as a cook before quitting to start her pop-up restaurant. And apparently, the owner of Tamarind was accusing Jackie of stealing recipes from here to use at her new place, and saying he'd been losing money because of her stealing away his customers."

"This doesn't look at all like a place that's losing money," Eric said, swiveling in his chair to take in the bustling dining room. "Or customers."

"No, it doesn't," I agreed.

Eric turned back around and reached for his water glass. Before taking a sip, however, he put it back down. "Oh, no," he said.

"What?"

"Your expression. I can tell."

"What?" I repeated.

"That you're at it again. This is about Jackie's mom, isn't it? Her death." Eric sat back in his chair with a knowing smile. "The great master sleuth of Santa Cruz has uncovered yet another suspicious death. Could it be murder?" Chuckling to himself, he finally took his drink of water.

I was trying to come up with a witty reply when the waiter set an order of golden-brown spring rolls between us. Next to the platter, he placed a small bowl of creamy dipping sauce, topped with a scattering of chopped green onions.

That did the trick. Food is the one sure way to distract Eric when you need to. "Ah," he said, eyes bright. "The famous Tamarind peanut sauce."

"Indeed." The server placed his hands together as if in prayer. "Our best seller. And since you are clearly a fan, you're in luck. We're going to be selling bottles of our peanut sauce starting in a week or so."

"Nice!" Eric picked up one of the rolls, dunked it in the sauce, and bit into its crispy wrapper. "Mmmm," he intoned, bobbing his head in approval.

The waiter smiled. "I'll be right back with your beers."

"Okay, let's taste this famous sauce," I said, blowing on the hot spring roll before taking a tentative bite. "Not bad."

"C'mon, it's way better than *not bad*." Eric popped the rest of his roll into his mouth, then nodded an enthusiastic thank-you to the waiter, who had returned to set down our bottles of beer.

"You've never met a peanut sauce you didn't love," I said. "But I've had better."

"Where?" he asked, selecting another crispy roll from the plate.

"At The Curry Leaf, for one. Jackie's pop-up."

He arched an eyebrow but didn't say anything. Most

likely only because his mouth was full of spring roll slathered in peanut sauce.

"Though I do have to say the two are similar," I continued. "Very similar, in fact." I dipped my spoon into the sauce and took another taste. "This one has more chili, I'd say, and more soy sauce. So it's saltier and has more of a kick, but it lacks the complexity of Jackie's recipe. I think hers must have had more ginger and lime than this one."

I was gazing out toward the bar area, contemplating the ingredients of the two sauces, when a man sitting at one of the barstools turned to speak to his neighbor and his profile caught my attention. Beaked nose and short, curly black hair. *Right.* It was the guy who worked here who'd spoken at Jackie's memorial service. The one who'd interceded when her old boss had been about to get into it with Sarah.

As if detecting my stare, he looked in my direction. I returned his gaze with a flirtatious smile, hoping he'd be prompted to come over and chat, and was pleased to see him take the bait. After saying something to his friend, he stood and walked my way.

"Oh, hi," Eric said, as the man came to stand at our table.

"Hi," he replied. "I'm Max." He turned to face me. "I recognized you from the other day, at Jackie's service, and wanted to come over and apologize on behalf of my employer."

"Right, you work here."

"Uh-huh. I manage the front of the house, though I'm not actually working tonight. I just came in with a friend for a drink. But when I saw you sitting here, it took me a minute to remember where I recognized you from."

"Yeah, me too," I said, even though I'd recognized him right off the bat.

"Anyway, once I remembered where I'd seen you, I realized I should apologize for Al. He can be a bit of a . . ."

"Jerk?" I offered.

"I was about to say hothead, but *jerk* certainly describes how he was on Saturday. He's actually a good guy in general, but his behavior was way out of line."

"Well, I appreciate the apology and will tell Evelyn. You know, Jackie's daughter."

He nodded, indicating he knew who she was.

"And Sarah and Maya, if I see them again. Sarah's the one Al confronted. But it would be a better apology if he made it, don't you think?"

"It would. But he's not working tonight, so all you get is me." His quick smile revealed several misaligned teeth in his lower jaw.

Max continued to hover as I sipped from my beer. "What was that all about, anyway?" I asked. "Al seemed pretty pissed off about Jackie's pop-up." Even though I was fairly sure I knew exactly what he'd been upset about, I was curious what Max would say.

He shifted his weight and scratched his nose, then looked over his shoulder. "Okay," he said, "I guess I owe you that, anyway. And you're a chef, so you'd understand."

So he knew who I was. Had he been into Gauguin? "I wouldn't call myself a chef," I said. "Javier's the head of our kitchen. I'm more just a line cook there."

"Well, you're the owner and have say over what happens

at the restaurant, so I'd call that being a chef." He held my eyes a moment longer than called for, his crooked smile exuding familiarity.

It was obvious the charm he was laying on was purely of the salesman variety, but I didn't care. What with Eric going on about Gayle and my dad gushing about his new flame, it felt good to have someone flirt with me.

I returned his smile, and it was all I could do not to bat my eyelashes at the man, as our little routine seemed to require. Eric, I noted with some satisfaction, was doing his best to avoid watching us, instead feigning intense interest in the goings-on across the room, where a party of eight was being noisily seated at a long table near the kitchen.

Max leaned in closer to our table. "Anyway, here's the thing. I think Al was jealous of Jackie. Of her cooking ability and her creativity. He fancies himself a great chef, but he's really more of a magpie than an innovator—you know, someone who takes ideas from other people and puts them together and then calls the dish new."

"Isn't that what all great chefs do?" Eric said, having been sucked back into the conversation. "Riff on what others have done to make it new, their own?"

"Sure. But some do more ripping off than riffing on, if you know what I mean."

Eric laughed. "Touché," he said.

Max glanced around again before continuing. "Al and Jackie had collaborated on some of the dishes here that ended up being our best sellers. And I think the reason he went so ballistic when she quit was that it meant she wouldn't be coming up with recipes for *him* anymore—they'd be for her new place. And then when The Curry Leaf started getting good reviews, it added fuel to his fire."

"But that doesn't explain why he was going on like that at the memorial, though," I said. "About suing Sarah and Maya if they reopened The Curry Leaf."

"Yeah, well, he'd started telling people after Jackie quit that she'd taken *his* recipes to use at her new place. And I think he retold the story so many times that maybe he started to believe it himself." With a shrug, Max straightened up.

"Some of the dishes do seem kind of similar," I said, indicating the peanut sauce on our table.

"Yeah, but you can't own a recipe like that. And Al never had anyone sign a noncompete agreement. Though he's thinking of starting to now," he added with a snort. "But I think the hardest part for Jackie was how unsympathetic he was about the guys in the kitchen. Al went around telling everyone after she left that 'she just couldn't take the heat,' that she needed everyone to be super easy on her."

Max's body slumped and his face fell along with it. "But maybe he was partly right. If it's true what people are saying about how she died. That she . . . took . . ." He swallowed, then pinched his nose as if the incomplete thought had made him slightly ill.

"Her own life?" I said softly.

He nodded. "That's what they're saying around here, anyway. And if that's true, maybe it was in fact too much, the long hours, the macho atmosphere. I guess I feel like I'm partly to blame since I got her the job here, and then tried to convince her to stay. I know how those guys in our kitchen can be, so I just wish I'd been a little more supportive." His face had taken on a hangdog look, but then he seemed to shake it off. "Oh, well. If all the wishes were fishes . . ."

"We'd all be castanets," Eric finished with a jaunty snap of the fingers.

"I am curious," I said, after giving Eric a swat on the arm. "Assuming Jackie did use the recipes at her pop-up, why would Al have been so upset about it? You think there's any way The Curry Leaf could have been affecting business here at Tamarind?"

"I suppose it's possible," Max said, then waved a hand over the bustling dining room. "But we still seem to be doing pretty well."

Our waiter arrived with our entrées. "Hey, Max," he said as he set down the plates. "I didn't know you all were friends."

I knew what was really going on in the server's mind: *Should I be more attentive to this table, since they're pals with the dining room manager?*

"We actually just met," Max said. "But I wouldn't mind becoming friends." This last with a furtive grin in my direction. *Oh, boy.* Had he figured out that Eric and I were not an item, or did he simply not care?

"Well, I'll leave you to eat," he said. "But if you ever need a table at the last minute, or any other special service," he added with a wink, "here's my business card." I accepted the proffered card with a polite smile, and Max headed back to the bar. Would he say anything about me to his buddy who'd been waiting there for him? If he did, it wasn't obvious. Neither of them glanced my way, in any case.

I turned my attention to the waiter, who was giving a detailed description of our dishes—de rigueur these days in upscale restaurants (though we leave our guests to figure it out on their own at Gauguin). My noodles, I learned, had been pan-fried in toasted sesame oil with roast pork, broccolini, and onions, then finished with a glaze of brown sugar, black beans, oyster sauce, and black pepper.

Might as well just hand me the recipe on a card, I thought. It did smell mighty tasty, though.

Eric's beef, he recited, palms once more together, was "a traditional Thai curry, simmered in coconut milk and our house-made Panang curry paste, a combination of three different chilis, lemongrass, peanuts, galangal, kaffir lime leaves, shallots, garlic, and cumin." If I'd been taking notes, I could easily have stolen the recipes myself.

I'd tried the Singapore noodles Jackie had served at The Curry Leaf and was curious to see if her version—like the peanut sauce—was better than what they served here at Tamarind. Taking up the bamboo chopsticks at my place, I slurped down a strand of egg noodle coated in thick, brown sauce.

"How is it?" asked Eric, slicing a chunk of hanger steak and dunking it into his creamy red sauce.

I chewed my noodle slowly, savoring the combination of salt, sweet, and umami. "Good," I said.

Eric looked up from his curry. "You don't like it."

He knew me well. My tone of voice had indeed been less than exuberant. "No, it's fine. It's just not quite as good as the noodles at The Curry Leaf, is all."

"Which goes to show that what that guy said must be

right." Eric jabbed his fork in the direction of the bar, where Max still sat with his friend. "That Jackie was the better cook. But I gotta say, this curry is great."

I watched as he spooned a dab of green-tomato chutney onto his sauce, then stirred the mixture into the mound of jasmine rice that had come with his beef. *Just how angry had Al been about Jackie leaving?* I wondered. Even if it hadn't affected the business here, if he'd known she was the better cook, the fact that she'd opened her own place serving the same dishes must have truly rankled.

But could it have angered him enough to provoke him to do something about it?

Chapter 13

The house was silent when I returned that night. I'd gotten used to coming home to Evelyn hanging out in the living room, watching a movie or listening to music, but tonight the room was empty and dark. Not even Buster was there to greet me as I let myself in through the front door.

I switched on the lights, dropped my bag and keys on the coffee table, and headed down the hallway in search of any signs of life in the building. Evelyn's door was closed, but I could hear her talking on the phone to someone—a friend, I guessed, based on the laughter on her end.

Buster looked up from where he lay sprawled on the bed, tail thumping, as I came into my room. "Caught you napping, did I?" I plopped down and scratched the coarse hair along his backbone. "Did ya miss me?" The dog responded with a kiss to my cheek, then let his head fall back onto the green-and-white afghan that Nonna had made for me years ago. Within thirty seconds he was asleep, nose and ears twitching as he fell into some sort of doggy dream. "Some company you are," I said, standing back up.

I wasn't yet tired, so I headed for the study, sat down at

the large oak desk, and opened my laptop. After answering a few emails, I wasted twenty minutes on Facebook, watching baby goats cavort in pajamas, penguins waddle and slip across a sheet of ice, and children dressed as angels screech out a painful rendition of "O Holy Night."

Before logging off, I decided to check my go-to restaurant review sites to see if anything new had been posted about Gauguin. There were three new reviews—one so-so ("okay, but not as great as all the hype") and two enthusiastic ("the best duck confit I've ever had" and "still dreaming about that asparagus with béarnaise sauce"). Not bad, given I'd checked just three nights earlier. They say you should never read your own reviews, but I seem to lack the willpower to follow such sage advice.

I was about to close the computer when I remembered what Max had said about his boss Al being so upset when The Curry Leaf had started getting good reviews. Curious to see what they'd said, I typed CURRY LEAF SANTA CRUZ REVIEW into the search box. A list of several articles came up, the first from our local weekly entertainment newspaper, dated three months back. I clicked on the link, and a photograph of Jackie, holding up a plate of crispy samosas nestled between ramekins of chutney and peanut sauce, appeared on the screen.

They'd given her four and a half stars out of five, and the praise lavished on the place made me slightly jealous of what she'd managed to accomplish with a tiny, three-night-a-week restaurant. "Specializing in Indian and Southeast Asian street food, this magnificent new addition to the Santa Cruz culinary scene will transport you to the bustling marketplaces of Singapore and Delhi, and have you coming back again and again." The Curry Leaf was sure to become the "next big thing" downtown, the reviewer predicted, going on to rave about the tender Tandoori chicken, fragrant basmati rice with saffron and butter, and "best I've ever tasted" peanut sauce.

Then, near the end of the article, I came to a paragraph that made me stop and read it again:

Jackie Olivieri last worked at Tamarind, where she was a cook for only half a year before branching out on her own to open The Curry Leaf. But she was clearly the star of her old kitchen, as the samosas, noodles, curries and chutneys at her new pop-up are as tasty and innovative as anything I've ever had at Tamarind—if not more so. Check out this gem soon, before it's so crowded you can't get in the door.

Oh boy, I thought, scrolling back up and staring at the photo of Jackie and her platter of triangular delicacies. *I wonder how many stars the reviewer gave Tamarind.* I did another search and found she'd awarded them only three and a half stars for her most recent review, just a month after her gush-fest over The Curry Leaf.

Closing my laptop, I stared at the calendar of Hawaiian scenes tacked to the wall above the desk, left over from my Aunt Letta. December featured a black sand beach with baby sea turtles making tracks down to a turquoise-blue sea.

How would I feel, I wondered, if Brian or Kris quit Gauguin only to open a new restaurant in town featuring our recipes for Coq au Vin and Duck à la Lilikoi? And what if, in addition, that new place were to garner better reviews than Gauguin, with a simultaneous snub to Javier and me?

Not good, was the answer. Not good at all.

* * *

When my alarm went off at seven the next morning, it woke me from a dream about being at a dinner party with Julia Child, George Clooney, and Michelle Obama. I was tempted to throw the phone across the room. Now I'd never get to taste that perfectly puffed cheese soufflé George had just set down before me, nor ever get to ask Julia that burning question I'd had—which of course had flown out of my head as soon as I'd come fully awake.

But then I remembered why I'd set the alarm: I had a suspect to track down. Throwing back the covers, I set my feet on the chilly hardwood floor. I generally turned the furnace off at night to save money, but on this particular morning I wished I'd been a little less stingy and had left it set at at least sixty degrees.

I dashed to the dresser to find a pair of wool socks, then changed from my flannel pj's into a pair of jeans and a long-sleeved T-shirt topped by my fleece sweatshirt. *Ah, much better.* Now I could face the day.

Twenty minutes later, I was cruising down West Cliff Drive in the T-Bird, Buster hanging his head out the window as I scouted the walking path for signs of a man with a big black poodle. I'd just passed Woodrow Avenue and was coming up the hill toward Mitchell's Cove when I spotted a familiar form.

Was that *Eric*? *Jogging*? I slowed down to get a better look. It sure looked like him, with that shaggy blond hair flying in the wind. And those black-and-white-checkered sneakers were just like the ones he owned, though they seemed far more appropriate for skateboarding than for running any distance.

He was with a woman. Yep, it was Gayle. She had on one of those Santa Cruz public defender T-shirts with the great slogan A REASONABLE DOUBT AT A REASONABLE PRICE. Hoping they hadn't spotted me spying on them, I let out the clutch and sped forward.

Eric never jogged. At least as far as I knew. He'd always made fun of people who jogged, calling them *juppies*, with their fancy outfits and big-wheeled baby strollers. So the fact that he'd been willing to go running with Gayle this morning spoke volumes—and I'm talking those enormous legal casebook–sized volumes—about his feelings for her.

Trying not to think about Eric and Gayle, I drove on, scanning the people walking along the cliffs. Near the end of the twisty road, my pulse quickened at the sight of a man with a large black dog, but as I passed by I saw that it was in fact a tall, slender woman walking some sort of black setter.

Shoot. I turned the car around at the Natural Bridges lookout, then headed back down West Cliff toward home. *Maybe he's not out walking this morning, or maybe he doesn't even have the dog anymore.*

And then I spotted him. The same lanky build, balding head, and goatee I'd seen at the memorial service. And he was walking an immaculately groomed black Standard Poodle.

I drove a block more, parked around the corner, and hustled Buster out of the car. "C'mon, we're going for a walk."

Feigning disinterest in Stan himself, I gazed at his poodle as Buster and I approached. Then, looking up at the human with the dog, I graced Stan with a broad smile.

He smiled back, as I'd known he would. People always love it when you love their dog.

"What a beauty," I said, as the poodle and Buster touched noses, then walked in a circle as they went for sniffs of each other's nether ends. "Do you show him?" *Oops, I'm not supposed to know the dog's sex.* "Or her?"

"Oh, no. Harry's just a pampered pet." He bent to scratch his dog behind the ear, then gave me a second look. "Have we met somewhere before? You look familiar."

"Uh, I don't think so," I lied. "But now that you mention it, you do kind of look familiar. Wait, I think I remember. It was at Jackie Olivieri's memorial service last weekend. You stopped to pay your respects to Evelyn."

"Oh, right." Stan let off scratching the dog and straightened up. "And you are . . . ?"

"I'm Evelyn's cousin, Sally. How about you? Are you a friend of Jackie's from the restaurant business?" This subterfuge game came so very easily when you just let yourself go.

He shifted his feet, turning to watch a pair of pelicans as they glided up the coast. "Uh, I'm actually Evelyn's stepdad. Ex-stepdad, I guess you'd say. Jackie and I have been divorced about five years."

"Ah. That explains it."

"Explains what?" He glanced my way, then returned his attention to the soaring birds.

"How Evelyn was when you spoke to her at the memorial. She seemed kind of cold, if you ask me."

Stan shrugged, as if he really wanted not to be having this conversation. But I wasn't yet ready to let him go.

"I think I might know why she's upset with you," I said.

"Oh, yeah?" A flicker of the eyes in my direction. He was interested, whether he wanted to admit it or not.

"She told me she overheard you and Jackie on the phone arguing. About the money." Now this, of course, was purely conjecture on my part. But it finally got his attention. He dropped his gaze from the pelicans, then slowly turned back to face me. From the deflation of his upper body, I guessed I'd hit the mark.

"I saw the spousal support check you'd written to Jackie," I said. "Was that it? Were you trying to get out of paying her alimony?"

Harry pulled on his leash, anxious to get moving. "No," Stan said, telling him to sit and be still. "Okay, look." This was directed at me, but from the stern tone of voice, he might as well have been speaking to his dog. "Not that it's any of your business, but you can tell this to Evelyn. I've been paying Jackie a hefty sum every single month since the divorce. It's been five years now, longer than she helped me through school, and money's been kind of tight for me lately. Since she'd been doing well enough to open her own place and make a go of it, I figured maybe she'd understand and let me off the hook early."

His demeanor had gradually changed. Before he'd seemed aloof and slightly bored. Now his foot was tapping rapidly on the asphalt path and he was clenching tightly at the leather leash.

"I'm guessing she didn't agree with your way of thinking."

Stan snorted. "Not hardly. But there was nothing I could do, so I let it go." And then his eyes got wide. "Wait. You can't think that I had anything to do with . . ."

I let him trail off, waiting to see where he'd go with this if I said nothing.

Harry stood and strained on his leash once more, and Stan yanked the dog back to a sitting position. Then, turning his hard gaze on me, he shook his head. "That's just crazy thinking. I was nowhere near Jackie the night she died. Here, I can prove it." He pulled out his phone and clicked and swiped a few times, then held it out for my inspection.

"See?" he said. "I was in Oakland all of last Tuesday and Wednesday, at a continuing ed course. Here's the proof of my registration."

I examined the page, and saw that he had in fact been signed up for the course.

"And I can show you my hotel confirmation, too, if you want," he said, taking the phone back and continuing to swipe at its screen in a manner bordering on the frantic.

"That's okay," I said. "No need." It wouldn't prove anything, I figured, since he could have easily made the one-and-a-half-hour drive down to Santa Cruz from the Bay Area the night Jackie had died, with no one being the wiser.

Stan swallowed, his face softening. "Look, I'm really

sorry about what happened to Jackie. She was a great gal, and a great mom to Evelyn. She didn't deserve that. Would you tell Evelyn for me that if she ever needs anything, all she needs to do is call?"

Not likely that'll ever happen, I thought, but nodded my agreement.

"Now, if you don't mind, I need to finish this walk so I can get home and get ready for work." At the word *walk*, the dog jumped up again, and the two of them made their brisk way down the path.

I let him get a ways ahead of me and then followed behind with Buster. Might as well give him a real walk, since we were out anyway. As we strolled up the coast along with all the joggers, skateboarders, cyclists, and other dog walkers, I wondered how Stan could possibly be hard up for money, given the salary he must make. I'd Googled the pay for nurse anesthetists after Evelyn had told me his job, only to discover they made a whopping $175,000 a year on average.

He likely had a mortgage that, given the price of real estate in Santa Cruz, would be considerable. But that couldn't solely account for his financial straits. A new Ferrari, perhaps? Or a wife with an expensive shopping habit?

Or could he have an expensive drug habit? I thought, remembering how agitated Stan had become during our discussion. I stopped in my tracks, startling both Buster and the jogger coming up behind us. The health care profession was known for its high instances of addiction—especially among doctors and nurses. And although in the past they might have had access to controlled drugs, especially in anesthesia practice, that was becoming much more difficult, what with all the protections that had been implemented in response to the country's opioid crisis.

Which meant that someone like a nurse who'd become addicted back when the drugs were easy to come by would now find himself having to acquire them elsewhere. And on the street, prices could be very high indeed.

If Stan were in that situation, Jackie's death would have provided an enormous financial boon to him. But how could I find out if that was in fact the case? If only I could get inside his house to snoop around. I watched the figure ahead of me as he stopped to let the big black poodle smell a patch of scraggly grass and then lift its leg to add a new mark to the spot. Stan had said he was going home to change for work. Which meant he'd be leaving soon thereafter. *Maybe I could do some snooping around after he leaves.*

But I'd need to follow him home, to find out where he lived.

My car was parked near the corner of the next cross street. I hurried to it, unlocked the door, and got Buster settled onto his cushion. Then, creeping along West Cliff Drive at a dog's pace, I followed Stan and Harry. We were at the lighthouse now, so I figured they had to be near the end of their walk.

They crossed the street at the public restrooms, and I pulled into the far side of the parking area, ducking down so Stan couldn't see my face if he happened to glance over at the bright-yellow convertible that had followed him into the lot. If I ever started tailing people on a regular basis, I'd need to invest in a less conspicuous car.

Stan let the big dog jump up into the back of his SUV, then got in and started his engine. Once he'd turned left onto the road, I pulled out of my spot and followed after, letting two cars get ahead of me. Unlike my T-Bird, Stan's dull-gray SUV looked like just about every other vehicle out on the road, so I had my work cut out for me. Keep far enough back so he didn't notice me following, but not lose him in the process.

The good news, though, is that unless someone has a reason to think they're being tailed, they generally don't pay a whole lot of attention to the cars behind them. I just had to hope Stan wasn't a vintage car aficionado.

I followed him all the way to the freeway and to the off-ramp at Soquel Avenue, at which point it became trickier, as the traffic was light and I had to keep a lot farther back from him to avoid detection. When he turned off 17th Avenue onto a small side street, I waited at the corner to see where he'd go. He pulled into a driveway about a block down the street, opened the tailgate to let the dog out, and walked toward the house.

Ditching my car, I headed down the street on foot, taking Buster along as my cover for skulking around the neighborhood. A pair of gopher mounds in a yard across the street and two doors down from Stan attracted the dog's attention, and while he poked his snout into the holes, I studied the place.

It was ranch-style bungalow with a broad driveway leading to a two-car garage. Several ancient fruit trees—much older than the 1970s-era home—stood in the front yard, suggesting the land had been part of an orchard before being subdivided into a housing tract.

The sound of a powerful engine made me jump, and I looked up to see a shiny red pickup truck pass by. Two bales of hay sat in its bed, and on its bumper was a sticker proclaiming, MY OTHER RIDE IS AN ANDALUSIAN.

The truck slowed, and when I realized it was pulling into Stan's driveway, I ducked behind a tree. After a moment the passenger door opened, and a woman climbed down bearing a bag of groceries. *His wife.*

So much for my idea of snooping around the house after he left for work.

I was trying to decide what to do when the door opened once more and Stan reemerged with a small, gym-style bag slung over his shoulder. As he unlocked his SUV and set the bag in the back seat, it occurred to me that I could follow him to at least find out exactly where he worked.

Walking quickly back toward my car, I kept my face averted till he'd driven by, then watched to see if he appeared to notice the T-Bird parked at the end of the street. No reaction. After he'd turned the corner, I ran the rest of the way down the block, loaded Buster into the car, and took off after him.

I figured he was headed for one of the medical centers just a few minutes away on the other side of the freeway, and I was right. Telling Buster I'd be right back, I followed him into the clinic lobby, where he greeted a man in pale-blue scrubs and long blond hair pulled back into a ponytail, who'd been speaking with the receptionist. I hid behind a large placard encouraging people to get their flu vaccine and watched as Stan and the guy in scrubs laughed about something, then pushed through a pair of swinging doors into an area marked MEDICAL PERSONNEL ONLY.

And so ended my tailing escapade. It hadn't been terribly productive, but it had provided a couple of good reasons for Stan to be in need of ready cash.

Now, how could I find out if he truly had been in Oakland the night of Jackie's death?

Chapter 14

I'd just gotten back home when my cell rang. "Javier. What are you doing up so early? Is everything okay?" It was only a little after nine, far earlier than the chef usually started his day.

"Yeah, everything's fine. Great, actually. I just checked online, and it shows that the purchase money's finally been deposited into your account."

"All right! Here, let me see if it shows up on my end." I switched the phone to speaker mode, then pulled up my online bank account. "Hold on . . . Yes, there it is. Huzzah! Okay, so I'll bring the contract to Gauguin to sign this afternoon after the restaurant association luncheon. We'll need a notary there too, but I've got a friend from my old law firm I bet would be willing to come in exchange for a free drink or two. And then we can celebrate our new partnership!"

Evelyn came into the kitchen while I was talking and flashed a thumbs-up as I told Javier to make sure to bring his driver's license for the notary public.

"Yay!" she said as soon as I finished the call, then gave

me a congratulatory hug. "Can I be there for the official ceremony?"

"Sure," I said with a laugh. "Not that it will be terribly exciting, two people signing a bunch of documents, and then the notary signing and stamping the papers afterwards."

"But it'll be a celebration."

"Yes, it will," I agreed. "And we can talk to Javier about you teaching him how to make pasta as well."

"Great!" Evelyn took a slice of bread from the loaf in the freezer, dropped it into the toaster, and poured herself a cup of coffee, all the while humming a tune sotto voce.

"You seem to be in a better mood today," I said.

"Yeah. Sorry about that, yesterday. It's no fun being around someone as morose as I was being."

"Well, it's no fun losing your mom like that, either. I think you've been amazing, actually."

Evelyn fetched the butter from the refrigerator, then ran her fingers over the various jars crammed into the shelf on the door. "Apricot jam?" she asked, selecting one and holding it up.

"Right," I said.

At the sound of the toast popping up, she set to work slathering the condiments on the bread, then returned them to the fridge. "So did you learn anything last night?" she asked, bringing her coffee and plate to the table. "You know, about the case?"

"I did, in fact. That guy Max was there, and he talked to Eric and me for quite a while."

"What'd you find out?"

I recounted what he'd said about Al and Jackie

collaborating on the recipes, and how Max thought Al had been jealous of his cook, and furious when she left to start her own place. "And check this out," I said, jumping up. I returned with my laptop, pulled up the review I'd discovered the night before, and read her the relevant parts. "And just a month later, the gal gave Tamarind a review that was a full star less than for The Curry Leaf."

"I bet Al didn't like that." Evelyn set down her toast with a frown. "You think there's any chance he's the one who killed my mom?" she asked in a soft voice.

I shrugged, then caught myself giving a nonverbal response. "It's possible, I guess, but it's not really that strong of a motive. Plus, how could he have even been there that night? I don't exactly see him and Jackie hanging out together listening to music and drinking, do you?"

"Not really."

"Oh, and I ran into Sarah from the pop-up downtown yesterday before dinner, and she told me that Rachel *is* planning to reopen the pop-up. According to Sarah, she's using a different name, but it's going to be at the same place and have basically the same menu as The Curry Leaf. And she's doing it right away. It's supposed to open tomorrow."

"Wow," Evelyn said. "That's quick. Almost as if she'd already planned it."

"Maybe. But before you go off on Rachel as a suspect, you need to hear what I did this morning." I told her about tracking down Stan during his dog walk, and about his being at the conference up in Oakland the days before and after Jackie's death.

"Oh," she said, shoulders sagging.

"But it's not an iron-clad alibi," I went on, "because he could easily have driven back down to Santa Cruz that Tuesday night she died. And I found out some other things, too."

"What?" she asked.

I stood up to pour myself a second cup of coffee. "Okay, so I originally suspected Stan might be using drugs, based on how agitated he seemed this morning when we talked, and given how common addiction is among medical workers. I figured that would certainly give him reason to be needing extra money. But then I followed him to his house afterwards, and not only is it a pretty nice-looking place, but it turns out his wife has a big ol' truck that looks brand new. *And*, get this: I think they might own a horse, too."

"Really?"

"Well, the wife's truck has a bumper sticker that says My OTHER RIDE IS AN ANDALUSIAN, and I doubt you'd put that on if it weren't true. Plus, there were a couple bales of hay in the truck."

"Huh," Evelyn said.

"I was one of those horse-crazy girls growing up," I went on, "who read practically every book ever published on the equine species, so I can tell you for certain that owning any horse would cost a bundle, what with boarding and food, not to mention vet bills. And if she has an Andalusian, they're *super* expensive, and it probably means she's into dressage or something. I imagine that even with Stan's high salary, that whole horse show scene could quickly eat up any money he makes—and give him good reason to be in need of a rapid infusion of some big-time cash."

"Which Mom's death certainly provided." Evelyn took

a bite of jam-and-butter toast, her brow creased in thought as she chewed.

"Yep," I agreed.

*   *   *

Four times a year, the Santa Cruz County Restaurant Owners Association hosts a luncheon meeting where we listen to guest speakers, discuss matters such as which state and local initiatives and candidates to support, and gossip with fellow restaurateurs about who's going out of business and who's getting rave reviews on Yelp.

This was my third SCCROA meeting since inheriting Gauguin, so I was prepared for the monotone PowerPoint presentations concerning marketing techniques and the endless recitation of last meeting's minutes and issues pending for discussion. I'd snagged a table near the back of the room with my father, who claimed to detest these events but attended them without fail.

"It's important to be a part of the community," he always said. And that was clearly his primary purpose in coming. Right now he was table-hopping, schmoozing with all the other Italian restaurant owners who, like us, traced their ancestry back to the original "Sixty Families," the fishermen who'd sailed from Liguria to Santa Cruz more than a century ago.

The president called the meeting to order with an official clinking of fork against water glass, and Dad scurried back to our table to take his seat. As she droned on about an upcoming seminar in San Francisco, I scanned the room to see whom I might recognize.

Several of Dad's cronies were at a table near the front, talking among themselves and paying no attention to the announcements being made. The owner of Kalo's was two tables down from them, peering at his phone while the woman next to him took copious notes of everything the president said. Or perhaps she was simply scribbling down a shopping list.

I swiveled in my chair and spotted the sushi chef/owner of Genki Desu, one of Eric's and my favorite dinner spots in town. Catching my eye, Ichirou bowed his head, and I waved back. And then, at the table to his right, I noticed someone who looked familiar. At the sight of the straw hat on the table next to his place—a fancy, Panama-style fedora with a black-and-white-striped hatband—I realized who he was. Al, the owner of Tamarind.

He caught me watching, and I shifted my eyes, pretending to stare at someone behind him. I think he must have bought it, because he immediately turned his attention back to the president, who was finally concluding her opening remarks.

Next up was a talk on newly enacted food sanitation regulations, which thankfully lasted only ten minutes. After the man finished speaking, we moved on to the lunch portion of the meeting. *Finally.* I was starving. Not that I expected much in the way of fine dining from the hotel where we held our meetings.

It seemed more than a little ironic that the quarterly restaurant owners' luncheon would be held at a banquet hall noted more for its ability to be divided into separate meeting rooms than for its creative cuisine. But it was one of the only places in town large enough to accommodate us all.

A server set a tray of composed salads on a folding stand and started distributing the plates among our table. Iceberg lettuce, shredded red cabbage and carrots for a little color, five cherry tomatoes, and a scattering of herb-flecked croutons. "Bleu cheese or oil and vinegar?" Dad said, reaching for the cruets of dressing on the table.

"Bleu cheese. Thanks."

I crunched a crouton. Not bad, actually, given that it likely came from a forty-ounce bag delivered by some restaurant supply warehouse. As I picked at my lackluster salad, I listened to Dad talk about how he and Abby had spent the day on Sunday, when Solari's had been closed due to the blackout. "And then after lunch we took a drive down to Carmel, where the power had already been restored, and spent the afternoon shopping," he said, reaching for more dressing.

"Really? You went *shopping*? You hate shopping."

"Yeah, I know. But it was okay. We stopped for a drink at this fancy wine-and-cheese place, and she ordered these things called fliers of wine—you know, tasting glasses of four different vintages."

"Flights," I corrected.

"Right." He broke his sourdough roll in half and smeared it with butter. "Anyway, it was fun, comparing the different wines."

"Uh-huh." What was happening to all the men in my life? First Eric jogging, and now my dad shopping and wine tasting?

I had the sudden urge to get away. Glancing across the room, I spied a friend who ran a breakfast-and-lunch joint downtown with her husband. "Oh, look," I said to Dad, "it's Jean. I better go say hello."

"That's fine, hon."

Halfway to Jean's table, however, I noticed that someone else I knew was seated next to Al, in deep conversation with the Tamarind owner. The guy was an acquaintance more than a friend, really, but it provided perfect cover for striking up a conversation with Al. Changing direction, I headed their way.

"Ramón," I said, "good to see you!"

He stood and pecked me on the cheek. "Hi, Sally. How've you been? I haven't seen you since the last one of these lunches."

We made small talk about our respective restaurants, and then, as if remembering his manners, Ramón introduced me to Al. "This is Sally Solari, the new—or newish—owner of Gauguin."

"Pleased to meet you," I said. "Which restaurant do you own?"

"Tamarind. But I'm not just the owner, I'm also its head chef," he added, gracing me with a self-important smile. Good. He didn't seem to recognize me from the memorial service.

"Oh really?" I returned his smile with wide eyes, as if being Tamarind's chef made him some sort of local celebrity. "I ate there just the other night and it was fabulous. And *super* busy for a Monday. You're doing a booming business." I punctuated this last with a friendly elbow to his side. "Maybe you can give me some advice on how to increase our customers at Gauguin."

"Yeah, well, it may look that way from the dining room, but from the back room it's not so terrific," Al said with a scowl. "Between you, me, and the wall, our profits have actually been going down recently."

"Really? That's bizarre. How come, do you think?"

"C'mon. You're in the biz—oh wait, you've only been an owner for a few months."

"Eight months now, actually."

He waved a hand dismissively. "Well, my dear, you'll learn soon enough just how difficult it is to keep your restaurant in the black. I run Tamarind on a very tight margin, using only the highest-quality ingredients. So when our sales go down even by only a few covers a night, it's enough to make a difference to the bottom line."

I did my best to soothe my hackles, which had risen in response to his patronizing attitude. What I wanted right now was information, not a squabble. "And to what do you attribute this drop in customers? You have any idea?"

"Yeah, I have an idea, all right," he said, fists clenched. "But I'm pretty sure the reason has now gone away." He started to smile, but it turned into more of a grimace.

Yuck. He was clearly referring to Jackie's death. No way was I going to tell the guy about Rachel and her new pop-up using the same recipes. He'd find out sooner or later on his own.

The waitstaff were now clearing the salad plates and serving the main course—a choice between Chicken Creole and Eggplant Moussaka. I'd opted for the vegetarian dish, as they tend to be the more interesting bet at banquet-style meals.

I was about to head back to my table, but then remembered something else that had been niggling at my brain. "By the way," I said to Al, turning back. "On a totally different subject, I wanted to ask you about the music you had on at Tamarind when I was there. It was really great jazz, and I was thinking maybe I should have something like that at Gauguin."

He poked his fork into a chunk of green bell pepper. "I don't know much about that," he said. "I use one of those monthly service deals, but leave it to my dining room manager to pick which one, since he's really into jazz. I just pay the bills."

"Oh, okay. Thanks."

I headed back to join Dad at our table. So Max was into jazz. Interesting.

Chapter 15

Javier made a great show of reading through the four-page contract, frowning and wrinkling his narrow nose, then nodding sagely and taking up the ballpoint pen with a flourish. Of course, we'd hammered out the provisions of the partnership agreement together weeks before, so he was already intimately acquainted with every section, paragraph, subparagraph, and comma in the document. But it did serve to amuse those of the Gauguin staff who stood by in the office, witnessing the momentous occasion.

The chef initialed the bottom of the first three pages and signed his full name at the end, then handed the papers for me to do the same. I passed it to the notary public—a paralegal from my old law firm stomping grounds—who stamped the agreement and signed her own name to it, then duly entered the information into her journal.

"Okay, that's it," she said after having us sign our names in her notary book. "You are now legal partners in the ownership of Gauguin."

Kris, Tomás, Gloria, Amy, and Evelyn all clapped their

hands, while Brandon popped the cork off a bottle of Champagne and poured us each a small glass.

"To Javier," I said, raising my flute, "the Lennon to my McCartney."

"Ah, so you're the pretty one, are you?" Javier grinned, and I couldn't help thinking that with his silky, dark hair and fine features, he was more the pretty one than I.

We clinked glasses as everyone else raised theirs in salute. "Right," I said after taking a sip. "First order of business now that you're co-owner is I think you need to be the one who goes to the next restaurant owners' luncheon. I thought today's would never end."

"Oh, please, no." Javier threw out a hand as if to protect himself from an incoming projectile. "Anything but that. I detest small talk. And restaurant owners."

"Great. As Bogie so elegantly didn't say, I can tell this is the beginning of a beautiful partnership." I shook my head and took another drink of bubbly. When I looked up, Brian was hovering at the office door.

"Uh, hi, guys," he said. "I wondered where everyone was."

"Well, look what the cat brought in," Javier said, then tempered the remark by waving the cook to come into the room.

Brandon offered a glass of Champagne to Brian, who shook his head. "So what's the occasion?" he asked.

Kris, who'd been off work Saturday night when Brian had stormed out of the kitchen and was thus oblivious to the tension in the room, answered brightly, "Sally and Javier just signed the contract making Javier equal partner in the restaurant. Isn't it great?"

"Yeah, great," Brian agreed, but without his fellow line cook's enthusiasm. He looked my way. "Could I have a word with you, Sally?" he said, nodding toward the hallway.

"Sure." I followed Brian out of the room and to the top of the stairway.

"I want to apologize for the other night," he said. "I was a jerk to act like that, and then leave you hangin' one person short when you were having to deal with the power outage and all." He stared at the floor, shuffling his feet like a high school student called before the principal.

"Yes, it was rather unprofessional," I said. "And I have to say, Javier and I have been wondering what the heck's been going on with you of late. Is there something you need to tell me, Brian?"

He raised his head, his eyes meeting mine. "I am so sorry. I know I've been a pain lately. It's just that, well, me and Roxanne have been having problems. Bad ones, and it's really affected me. I didn't want to talk about it because I know you and she are friends, and I figured I shouldn't be bringing personal problems to work. And then I got sick last week, and that didn't help either." He ran a hand through his buzz-cut brown hair, then dropped his arm with a sigh.

"We had a long talk last night, and I think we've figured a lot of it out. I mean, it's not like you can fix relationship stuff like that all that quickly, but it was good just talking about it. So . . ."

"I take it she advised you to suck it up and come apologize?" I'd met Roxanne the previous summer when we'd sung together in the chorus, and I knew her to be a no-nonsense kind of gal.

He nodded. "Yeah, but I would have done it anyway," he said with a sheepish grin. "I really do like working here. And appreciate how much you—and Javier—do for me."

This was a telling admission, for it had been obvious for several months now how competitive he was with my head chef—no, partner, now.

"And I promise I'll be better from here on out," Brian went on. "No more drama in the kitchen. Scout's honor." He flashed a three-finger Boy Scout salute, with a boyish grin to match.

"Okay, look. I need you to apologize to Javier, also. But I have no doubt he'll agree to let you stay on." I patted Brian on the shoulder. "You're a good cook, and we don't want to lose you any more than you want to lose us."

Tomás came down the hallway, followed by Kris and Amy chatting about the Spiced Persimmon Tarte Tatin Amy had planned for tonight's dessert. After they'd passed, Brian headed downstairs and I went back to the office, where Brandon and Gloria were collecting the empty Champagne flutes on a pair of serving trays.

Javier was sitting on the corner of the desk, leaning over to listen to Evelyn in the pale-green wing chair. "It's all in the rolling out of the dough," she was saying. "If you work it too much, it gets tough, but you have to get it super thin or it won't have that amazing tenderness my *nonna*'s pasta always had."

"Sounds like a combination of bread and pie dough techniques," Javier said. "The kneading part is like with a baguette, where you work it hard and long until it's silky smooth. But then the rolling out has to be quick and dirty, like for a shortcrust pastry."

"Exactly!" Evelyn squealed. She reached out to touch Javier's outstretched hand, causing the chef to grin like an infatuated teenager. *Uh-oh.* What had I set in motion?

"Evie's offered to teach me how to make her grandmother's pasta from scratch," Javier said when I came into the room. *And he's already calling her by her nickname.*

"Sally knows," Evelyn said. "I cooked her my *nonna's* fettuccine the other night, and she thought it could be a best seller for Gauguin." She giggled, reminding me just how young she was. With all that had happened in the past week and the maturity she'd demonstrated in dealing with her mother's death, it was easy to forget that Evelyn was only twenty years old.

And how old was Javier? Thirty? Older? It was hard to tell, since his boyish looks could easily belie his true age. *Funny that I've never asked him.* But no matter what, the chef was certainly a good deal older than Evelyn.

When Javier excused himself to go check on something in the kitchen, I followed him out of the office. "Be back in a sec," I said to Evelyn, then ran and caught Javier by the sleeve of his chef's whites halfway down the stairs. "Do you realize how young Evelyn is?" I hissed.

"Uh . . . twenty-one, twenty-two?" he said. "So what?"

"She's only twenty. Which makes her far too young, I'd say, for you to be hitting on her."

Javier stared at me, mouth agape. Then, taking a step back, he wagged his index finger at me. "No, no, Sally. You've got the wrong idea. I'm not interested in her that way—not at all." His wide eyes, along with the rising pitch of his voice, told me he was telling the truth.

"Oh, sorry. It just seemed like you two were awfully . . . chummy back there in the office."

Javier shook his head with a soft chuckle. "Sure, I like her. She's a sweet girl, and she reminds me a lot of my youngest sister back in Michoacán."

I let out a laugh of relief. "Ah, got it. Sorry for my freak-out."

"No worries." Javier started back down the stairs, then turned and called back over his shoulder, "And I really do want her to show me her pasta-making technique."

* * *

The next morning, Evelyn emerged from her bedroom dressed in tight black pants, black low-heeled boots, and the hot-pink top she'd retrieved from her bedroom closet the previous Friday. She'd braided her hair, applied lipstick, and had on a black-and-white shell necklace.

"My, don't you look spiffy," I said. "Why so dressed up?"

She helped herself to coffee, then joined me at the breakfast table. "I forgot to tell you, but I have to go out to the Vista Center today."

"What's that?"

"It's this center for the blind and visually impaired, out near the hospital. I'm coteaching a technology workshop there with my friend Lucy, and we're having lunch together downtown beforehand."

"Oh, cool. Would you like a ride?"

"That's okay. I can take the bus. You've been doing so much for me that I'm starting to get really spoiled. And I know my way around the neighborhood pretty well now. There's a bus stop just a block down the street from here, so it'll be easy."

We both sipped from our mugs in silence. Buster trotted into the kitchen, nails clicking on the linoleum floor, and went to stand by the back door—his sign that he needed to go out. I got up to open the door and watched through the window as he did his business, then slowly made his way around the perimeter of the yard, sniffing out places the raccoons, skunks, and opossums had visited the night before.

"Oh, I forgot to tell you," I said, letting Buster back in. "I talked to Al, the Tamarind owner yesterday. He was at that restaurant owners' luncheon, and I got the distinct impression he does in fact blame your mom for their recent loss in sales."

Evelyn set down her mug. "So you think it might have been him after all?"

"Not really. It still doesn't seem like enough of a motive. And besides, the killer had to have been someone your mom would have invited into the house, right? But . . ." I paused dramatically to punctuate this next point. "Al did mention that Max was the one who deals with the music at Tamarind, and Al said he was really into jazz. You mentioned before that Max used to come over to the house sometimes. What about him as a suspect?"

"But why would he want to kill Mom? They were friends."

"Who knows. Jealousy, anger, shame, money . . . any of the usual motives for murder could apply. How well do you know the guy?"

"Hardly at all."

"So I don't think we should rule him out just yet."

Evelyn nodded, then pushed back her chair and stood. "Well, I have about an hour before I need to leave, but I better do some studying up before then," she said, and retreated to her bedroom.

And what was on my agenda for the day? Grocery shopping, for one. Grabbing a pad of paper an enterprising realtor had left on my doorstep, I jotted down a list of what I needed to buy: coffee, half-and-half, bread, eggs, lettuce, bananas, bourbon.

Oh, and I should really do some Christmas shopping. There weren't too many people on my list, but my father and Nonna, at least, would be shocked and hurt if I didn't give them a present. And I had to figure out a gift for all the staff at Gauguin—something thoughtful, but not too expensive.

I traditionally bought a present for Eric as well, though right about now I was feeling less than enthusiastic about finding "that perfect something" for the guy. *No doubt Gayle will fill that role this year*, I thought with some chagrin. Because it sure seemed like the two of them were quickly progressing past the "just friends" stage of their relationship, no matter what Eric had said.

And if I saw anything that absolutely screamed Nichole or Mei or Allison or Javier, they'd get a gift too, but I wasn't going to add them to my must-buy list.

After taking the dogs down to Its Beach, where Buster

chased a pair of Huskies through the frigid surf and Coco stole the tennis ball from a Great Dane twice her size, I collected my phone, bag, and keys, then knocked on Evelyn's door.

"I'm off to do shopping and errands downtown. Will I see you before I leave for work this afternoon?"

"Probably not," she called out. "The workshop is supposed to only go till three, but they usually run late."

"Okay, then. See you later. And good luck today!"

Once downtown, I drove around the jam-packed parking garage three times until I found a space, then headed across the street and into Bookshop Santa Cruz. I wanted to look for something for my dad, who was a sucker for big, glossy Italian cookbooks. He didn't tend to make the recipes, but loved to read about the history of the dishes and stare at the photos of cannelloni and tiramisu, painstakingly arranged by food stylists with their tweezers, toothpicks, and glue.

I was in luck, and found the perfect book for Dad with dazzling photos of the cheeses, gnocchi, and roasted meats of Northern Italy. I also found a new thriller for Eric, about an attorney who gets caught up in a smuggling scheme in post-Brexit Ireland. (Okay, so he'd get a present from both Gayle and me this year.)

Shopping bag in hand, I emerged from the bookstore's other door onto the bustling Pacific Garden Mall and made my way down the street in search of inspiration regarding Nonna. My grandmother loved the idea of receiving presents, but never seemed terribly thrilled at the actual gift bestowed. Maybe this year I could surprise her with something she truly loved—perhaps something to eat.

I was musing about chocolate truffles, cheese-stuffed olives, and thinly shaved sheets of *prosciutto crudo* when my stomach let out a rumble worthy of one of the elephant seals up at Año Nuevo State Park. *What time is it, anyway?* Only eleven thirty, I saw from my phone, but I'd had no breakfast.

And then I remembered: Rachel was supposed to open her pop-up restaurant today. If she was doing lunch as well as dinner, perhaps I could get some tasty information as well as food.

Picking up my pace, I continued down the shopping mall, past carol-singing buskers in fuzzy reindeer antlers and hardy souls lunching outdoors under propane heat lamps, till I got to the building that had previously been home to The Curry Leaf. The sign above the door had a schedule listing the days of the week the different pop-ups were in residence. Today's was THE STREETS OF DELHI.

The door was open, and as soon as I stepped inside I was hit by the aroma of cumin and fried bread. *Heaven.* I could see Rachel through the window behind the counter, hefting a baking tray covered with some sort of small pastries into the wall-mounted oven. She banged the oven shut, then turned to speak to Sarah, who was at the stove stirring something in a large pot.

The lunch menu was written in pink chalk on a blackboard standing in the tiny order-and-pickup area. Although the items were available only for takeout, a small table with three chairs had been set up for those who couldn't wait and wanted to chow down immediately on-premises.

I studied today's offerings: Singapore noodles, lamb

curry, spinach dal, Tom Kha Gai soup, pani puri, dosas, samosas, and garlic naan. Peanut sauce and several kinds of chutney were available for two dollars extra. I was tempted to order the noodles to see how they compared to the ones I'd had two nights before at Tamarind, but the samosas and peanut sauce called to me. I mean, really, who can resist deep-fried food once the smell has hijacked your brain?

"Hey, Sally!" a cheery voice called out. I looked up from the blackboard to see Maya at the counter. "We only opened five minutes ago, so I think you may be our very first customer. Unless this guy gets his order in first, that is."

A portly man whose white down jacket gave him the appearance of the Michelin man had come in behind me and looked ready to order. "No, let him go before me. I'm not sure yet what I want."

Once he'd placed his order—lamb curry with a side of potato and onion pani puri—and paid, he stepped aside so I could come up to the window. I told Maya I wanted the samosas with peanut sauce, and she wrote down the order and took both our tickets to Sarah. Returning to the window, she let out a gasp.

"What?" I turned and saw that about eight people had come through the door all at once and were now standing in line, crowding the small room. As Maya hurried to take the next person's order, Rachel stepped up to the window to ask the Michelin man if he wanted his curry hot, medium, or mild.

"Hot," he replied.

Maya put her hand to her mouth. "Oh, sorry. I'll remember to ask that from now on."

The cook nodded, then started toward the stove. "Hey, Rachel," I said, and she turned back with a frown, as if trying to place me. "I'm Sally Solari, Evelyn's cousin."

"Ah." Recognition lit her eyes. And something else as well that I couldn't identify.

"I see you're serving a lot of the same food as Jackie did," I said with a smile. "Did she give you the recipes?" I of course already knew that Rachel and Jackie had done most of the cooking for The Curry Leaf together. But I wanted to know how she'd answer the question.

Rachel stared at me a moment, lips taut, then took the next ticket from Maya. "I don't really have time to chitchat right now," she said. "As you can see, we're kind of busy." She crossed to the stove, placed the ticket on the wheel, and set to work pouring out batter for an order of dosas.

I stood aside to make room for the line of customers, and as I waited for my meal, I caught Rachel glancing my way.

Sure they were busy. But I knew a blowoff when I saw one.

Chapter 16

I had several hours before I needed to be at Gauguin and knew how I wanted to spend at least part of the time. After chowing down my samosas—which were excellent, I have to say—I drove back to the medical center where Stan worked.

Most people tend to park in the same general spot at their place of employment, so when I didn't see his SUV anywhere near where he'd left it yesterday, I figured he likely wasn't there. Which was okay by me. I'd come up with an idea, and it would work far better if Stan wasn't around.

The same receptionist who'd been working the day before was at the front desk and greeted me cheerily when I came in. "Good afternoon," she said with a smile. "Do you have an appointment?"

"Uh, no. I'm actually looking for someone. Stan Kruger, a nurse who works here."

"Oh, I'm afraid he's gone for the day. Is there something I could help you with?"

"Maybe. It has to do with that conference he was at last week, the one up in Oakland."

"Uh-huh."

"I was wondering, do you know anyone else from here who also attended it?"

The smile was replaced by a frown. "I'm not sure I can give out that kind of information. And why would you want to know, in any case?"

"It's just that I was at the conference too—I'm a nurse from up in Alameda—and I met Stan there, and . . ." I did my best to look slightly embarrassed. "Well, he introduced me to this friend of his who was also there, a guy Stan said he worked with. And since I was coming down to Santa Cruz, I'd thought I'd stop by and see if Stan—or his friend," I added with a raised eyebrow, "happened to be here today."

The receptionist leaned over the counter. "Do you know the man's name?" she asked, now very much interested.

"No, I never found out. We didn't talk all that long, actually. But he has a long, blond ponytail. And he's really cute."

She chuckled. "That's gotta be Richard. And he *is* here today. You want me to see if he's available?"

"Would you?" I said, not having to fake the blush that was spreading across my face. *What on earth was I going to say to the guy if he did come out to meet me?*

The woman got on the phone and spoke to someone, then hung up, flashing a thumbs-up my way. "He'll be right out."

Oh, boy.

I paced nervously while the receptionist conferred with a

patient who'd just walked in about his upcoming shoulder surgery. Two minutes later, the guy with the ponytail—Richard—came through the double doors and, glancing around the lobby, walked my way. "Did you want to talk to me?" he asked, confusion on his face. He'd clearly been expecting to see someone he knew, or at least recognized.

"Yeah, thanks for coming out." I led him to the far corner of the lobby so that the woman at the front desk wouldn't know that I'd completely fabricated my story. "So here's the thing," I said. "I met your friend Stan last week at that continuing ed conference up in Oakland, and he was supposed to meet me here today to give back something I left in his car. But he doesn't seem to be here, like he said."

The confused look in Richard's eyes grew even stronger. "Wait, you left something in his car?"

"Yeah, it was . . . a cashmere sweater," I said, pleased to come up with an item that was valuable yet not too intimate. "I left it there when we went to dinner together after the day's classes were over."

"Hold on." Richard made a T with his hands, like a football referee would do to signal a time out. "That's impossible, because Stan didn't have a car with him at the conference. He drove up with me, since his was in the shop. And besides, *I* had dinner with him that night at the hotel, and you were most certainly not with us."

Placing his hands on his hips (another football signal, I believe), he shot me a hard stare. "So what exactly is going on here. Who *are* you?"

"I . . . uh . . . I guess I must have confused him with

someone else," I said, backing away. "So sorry to bother you." With a quick smile, I turned and darted out the door and across the parking lot to my car.

Stan was not going to be pleased when he heard about this. But at least he'd be happy to know I no longer suspected him of Jackie's murder. His alibi had proved to be airtight.

* * *

"We're running low on spot prawns!" I shouted over the banging of sauté pans and roar of ventilation fans in the Gauguin kitchen. It was nine fifteen that night, and the kitchen was finally slowing down after a busy Wednesday dinner.

"On it," Brian called back, then trotted to the prep room to hustle up another quarter-size pan of the delectable crustaceans. Returning to the hot line, he removed the nearly empty pan, dropped the full one into its place, and dumped the few remaining shrimp on top.

"Thanks."

"No worries." Brian tipped an imaginary hat for me. "It's Tomás you should thank. He's the one cleaning the suckers."

I tossed the garlic and sliced onions that I had browning in olive oil, adding several squirts of orange and lemon juice and then a dollop each of butter and spicy harissa. Once these had melded, imparting the onions with a bright, chestnut hue, I dropped in a handful of spot prawns and tossed the pan's contents once again. It didn't take long for the shrimp to cook through, after which I finished the dish with a dozen chunks of fresh orange, keeping the pan over the flame only long enough to heat the orange pieces through.

"Order up!" I called through the pass, spooning the sautéed prawns onto a warm plate next to a mound of rice and garnishing it all with a sprinkling of chopped cilantro.

I wiped my hands on my side towel, then glanced over at Brian at the charbroiler. He'd been true to his word, showing up early tonight and acting the model employee. A real Boy Scout, indeed.

Brian had talked with Javier as I'd requested, and the chef had been satisfied enough to allow Brian to return to work. But I knew Javier was keeping a close eye on him. One more misstep and he'd be out on the seat of his checked chef's pants—a fact Brian no doubt knew, hence his perfect behavior tonight.

I took advantage of a lull between tickets to get myself a glass of ice water from the pitcher in the wait station. Leaning against the sideboard we used for storing flatware, napkins, and tablecloths, I gazed out at the remaining patrons as they finished their main courses and ordered from the dessert menu.

Brandon swept out of the swinging door from the kitchen bearing a slice of Spiced Persimmon Tarte Tatin. It had been such a big hit yesterday that Amy had baked two more for tonight. The pie did look mighty tempting, drizzled as it was with crème fraîche and brandy sauce.

"Yum," I commented as the waiter passed me by. "I think I might have to have a slice of that after work tonight."

"No can do," he replied. "That girl who was here with you yesterday is at table seven and ordered the last slice."

Did he mean Evelyn? I poked my head around the door to get a look at the table, and sure enough, there she was, sipping daintily from a demitasse of espresso. She smiled at Brandon as he set the dessert down before her, then felt for her fork, cut the corner off the slice, and took a bite.

"Ev," I said, crossing the room to her table. "I didn't expect to see you here."

"Oh, hi Sally." She set down the fork and dabbed her mouth, leaving bright red kisses on the white napkin. She hadn't changed out of the black leggings and fuchsia top of this morning, but had added a cream-colored cardigan on top.

"Had a hankering for some dessert, did ya?"

Evelyn smiled. "Yeah, I guess you could say so. I was texting Javier this afternoon about coming in to give him that pasta-making lesson. We're on for this Friday, by the way. Anyway, he remembered me talking with Amy yesterday about the persimmon tart she was planning, and so he invited me to come in tonight to try it out."

"You didn't take the bus here this late at night, did you?" Oh, man, I was starting to sound like my father.

But I guess she was still young enough not to mind my parental attitude. Or at least she managed to ignore it. "No worries, I used a Lyft. And I'm hoping I can catch a ride back with you. I don't mind hanging out till you're finished working."

* * *

We got out of the restaurant at eleven twenty. The last of the gray clouds had finally passed, and it was clear and icy cold outside, the stars gleaming like sequins on a starlet's gown.

Evelyn took my arm as we crossed the parking lot to the T-Bird, and we climbed into the car and fumbled with the old-fashioned seat belts. "So I was wondering, if you didn't mind," Evelyn said, finally managing to click the two pieces together over her lap, "whether we could swing by my house to pick up one of my braille books. I was telling Javier about them tonight, and he's never seen a book in braille before, so I thought I'd bring one for him to look at on Friday."

"Sure, no problem. It's not that far out of the way."

On the way over to her house, I told Evelyn about going to the medical clinic that afternoon and about my conversation with Stan's friend Richard. "So at least that's one person we can cross off our list of suspects," I said.

She nodded. "Good. Even though I never liked the guy, I'm glad he isn't Mom's killer." I pulled up to the curb in front of the house, but as we walked up the path to the front door, something seemed wrong. I couldn't place what it was until we stepped inside the living room.

"The light's not on," I said to Evelyn. "The one on the timer. I know it was on when we left Sunday night." I knelt to examine the devise that was plugged into the wall with the floor lamp cord attached to it. "It's still plugged in," I said. "I wonder if someone could have been here since we left and switched off the lamp."

The sound of a board creaking above us made Evelyn drop to the floor next to me. "I think that someone may be here now," she whispered. "What do we do?"

Before I could answer, however, she stood and started toward the stairway.

"I don't think that's such a good idea," I hissed. "We should just call the cops and wait outside." She either didn't hear or chose to ignore the advice. I pulled out my phone and hit 911. "There's somebody in my house," I said, trying to keep my voice as low as possible. "Upstairs."

The gal asked for the address, told me a unit would be there shortly, then gave the same advice I'd given Evelyn: "Get outside right now and wait for the police to arrive."

But Evelyn had already started to creep up the stairs.

Damn. I couldn't leave her inside alone with whoever was up there. Reluctantly, my pulse quickening in trepidation, I followed after her.

She'd stopped about a quarter of the way up. "Keep to the outside, right next to the railing," she whispered when I came up behind. "The stairs squeak, but not on the very edge."

I briefly pondered why she knew this fact. Had she, like me, discovered the secrets of how to be the most quiet when returning home after your parents' curfew? But any curiosity regarding her rebelliousness as a teenager flew immediately from my head at the sound of yet another creaking board above us.

"Sounds like he's in Mom's bedroom," Evelyn murmured, then continued up the stairs. That room, I knew, looked out into the backyard. So there was a good chance the intruder didn't realize we were in the house.

I took hold of Evelyn's arm. "Really, I think we should wait outside. I called the cops."

But she shook me off. "No. They might get away out the

back door once they realize someone's here. I want to know who it is."

She reached the landing and started down the hallway, me a few paces behind. "Wait. Stop," I whispered. "There's a light on in the room. A flashlight, I think."

The light went out.

"Uh-oh. I think they might have heard us."

"In here," Evelyn hissed back, then turned the corner into her own bedroom. We crouched there silently, listening for any movement in the room across the hall. Nothing. Whoever was in there was likely doing the same thing we were.

"Let's go back down," I whispered, "and wait for the cops."

No longer protesting, Evelyn led the way along the dark hallway, me holding on to her arm this time. I reached the landing and started down the stairs, keeping once more to the edge. Halfway down, a sound came from behind. *Oh, no.*

They were so close I could hear their muffled breathing, yet I was blocked from escape by Evelyn ahead of me. Having no other option, I turned to face the intruder.

But before I could take in more than a vague, dark form, a pair of gloved hands grabbed me around the neck.

I reached up to try to wrest them away, or at least use the advantage of gravity to yank the person down the stairs, but the hands only grew tighter about my throat.

"If you know what's good for you, you'll stay out of this," the person hissed into my ear.

Even if I'd wanted to respond, the firm grip about my

neck would have made it impossible. Strong fingers were pressing into my windpipe, and I gasped for air. As I grabbed futilely at the arms that held me, my head started to swim. *This is it*, I thought, and let myself go limp. Maybe they'd think I'd already passed out and let go.

But no, the grip continued to tighten and the breathing grew louder. Then, with no warning, the hands let go and pushed me down the stairs.

I think I must have lost consciousness at that point, because the next thing I knew, I was sprawled facedown on the living room floor. I rolled over with a groan.

Evelyn touched me on the shoulder. "What happened?" she asked. "I heard the person say something, and then you made a kind of gurgling sound and fell down the stairs. Are you okay?"

I reached up to touch my throat. "I guess so," I said, though it came out more as a rasp. "Are they gone?"

"Yeah. Whoever it was tore past me and out the door. Did you get a look at them? Who was it?"

"No. They were wearing a ski mask. They grabbed me by the throat and told me to 'stay out of this' and then shoved me down the stairs. I guess we must have spooked them with our investigation."

"Ohmygod, how scary! You sure you're okay?"

Slowly, since I was still feeling woozy, I lifted myself to a sitting position and rubbed my shin. I'd been lucky not to break anything, but I could tell my leg was going to host a colorful array of blues and greens by the morning.

"Just a few bruises," I said. "Nothing that won't heal in a few days."

Evelyn exhaled. "Well, that's good. I'm sorry I didn't listen to you and stay downstairs like you wanted." She sank down onto the floor next to me. "And after all that, we didn't even learn anything."

"Yeah, too bad." Taking a few deep breaths, I reached up once again, gently probing the spot on my neck those gloved hands had so tightly gripped. The hissing of the voice came back to me, the face so close to mine.

"Wait," I said. "There *was* something. When they leaned in to warn me off the case, there was a distinct smell." I closed my eyes and tried to recall the elusive aroma. Woody . . . with pepper and citrus . . .

And then, with an intake of breath, realization hit me. "I know what it was," I said. "One of the curry spices."

Chapter 17

A sharp rap at the front door made both of us jump. Through the curtains, I could see the red and blue lights of a police car parked in front of the house.

"I got a call about an intruder?" the uniformed cop said when I opened the door.

"That's right. But they're gone now."

Another cruiser pulled up to the curb. I waited for the second officer, a woman, to join the guy at the door, and then let them both inside.

"You want to sit?" I asked, motioning to the couch.

"That's fine, we're okay," the policeman said. "Why don't you tell me about the incident."

"Sure." I recounted what had happened, but left out what the person had said to me about "staying out of this." No way did I want word getting back to Detective Vargas about how Evelyn and I had been snooping around about Jackie's death. But I did show them my neck and the injured spots on my leg, which had already become discolored.

"You think you should go to the hospital?" the officer

asked. "Your throat's kind of red, and it might be a good idea to get it checked out."

I assured him I was fine, and the woman then went upstairs to check out Jackie's room for evidence while the other guy called in an APB on the suspect. Though a fat lot of good that was going to do, given my account of an average-height, average-build person of indeterminate sex, in dark clothes. That could describe half the population of Santa Cruz.

"You say he had on gloves?" the cop asked, as we waited for his colleague to return.

"Yeah. But like I said, I don't know for certain that it was a man. It was dark, and I was being strangled at the time, so I can't really tell you anything about the person other than that they had strong hands."

"Of course. Sorry." The man glanced toward the dining room and kitchen. "You wanna do a walk-through downstairs to see if anything's missing?"

"Uh, well, I don't live here. It's Evelyn's house—the house she and her mom, Jackie Olivieri, lived in till her mom died last week. Evelyn's been staying with me since then."

Recognition lit up the cop's eyes. "Oh, right. I knew I recognized the address. This is the house where she was found. I'm so sorry about your mother."

"Thanks. But I'm afraid I wouldn't be much help telling if anything of my mom's has been moved or taken," Evelyn said with a wry smile. "You know, because of . . ." She indicated her eyes.

"Right."

The other officer joined us in the living room. "There were several drawers open in the master bedroom," she said, "and it looks like they've been gone through. So I'd say it must have been a burglary in progress that you two interrupted."

"They just told me the house has been unoccupied for a week," the first cop said, "so it makes sense it would be a target."

"I don't think that's what it was," Evelyn interjected, and both officers turned to stare at her. "I think it actually might have been the person who killed my mother, coming back to retrieve something they left here, or maybe cover their tracks in some other way."

"Okay." The man scratched his nose and frowned, as if calculating how to politely respond to this out-of-the-blue theory. "It's my understanding that your mother's death was self-induced."

"But I have—"

I touched Evelyn on the arm. "Let's let it go for the time being," I murmured. "He's not going to do anything more right now."

She exhaled loudly, letting her shoulders fall in defeat. "Fine."

"All right, then." The officer pulled a pen and pad of paper from the pocket of his police jacket. "So why don't you try to figure out if anything's been taken—you know, jewelry, money, other valuables. And in the meantime, I'll file a report and make sure the officers assigned to this neighborhood do periodic drive-bys of the premises. You want to give me your names and how we can contact you?"

The information collected, they took their leave. I watched through the curtains as the two climbed into their respective patrol cars, then sat for a moment making further notes or calling in to dispatch.

"You want to go upstairs and see if anything's missing?" I asked once they'd finally driven off. "I could tell you what's there, and you could tell me if you can think of anything obvious that's gone."

But Evelyn had retreated to the couch and was holding herself protectively about the chest, as she'd done when we'd first met.

"No," she said, then jerked in an involuntary shudder. "I don't think I can." She stood. "What I need to do right now is get out of this house."

*   *   *

Back at my place, Evelyn crawled onto the sofa with Coco and held the dog tightly in her arms as I went to fetch us something to drink—hot chocolate for Evelyn and a stiff bourbon for me.

"You know what's funny?" she said when I returned with our beverages. "After all that, I forgot to get that braille book."

I sat next to her, prompting Buster to jump up beside me. I scooted over to give him more room; the couch was big enough for four, but not all sprawled out lengthwise as my dog insisted on doing.

"We'll just have to go back again," I said. "Whenever you're ready, that is."

Evelyn tested her cocoa and, finding it too hot, set it

back on the coffee table. "I know it's probably irrational, since the person was already gone and there was no more danger, but I just got freaked out once the police came. It made the whole thing about my mom somehow real, if you know what I mean."

"I do." With a shudder, I reached up once more to touch my throat, then slouched down into the sofa. Buster rolled over on his back, asking for a belly scratch, which I provided as I sipped my drink.

"So who do you think it was?" Evelyn asked. "And what do you think they were looking for?"

"Well, even though I couldn't see all that much, I got the feeling it was the same person who stole your mom's laptop from my car. They had the same general build, and it would make sense that whoever took the computer would want her cell phone, too, since it would have a lot of the same stuff on it. So I'm guessing that's what they were after tonight—her phone."

Evelyn picked up the cocoa again. This time she blew on it, then took a small taste. "Yeah, that makes sense."

"And assuming I'm right about that smell," I went on, "that would limit our list of suspects to people who'd be in contact with curry spices."

"And if you're also right about them wanting the computer and phone, it limits the list to people who know the police don't already have them, which includes—"

"Anyone who heard me talk to Detective Vargas at the memorial service," I finished for her.

"Right," Evelyn said with a sigh. "Which doesn't really help. All our suspects were there that day." She pursed her lips. "But what if it wasn't her phone they were after tonight? What else could they have been looking for?"

"Maybe something they left the night she died—something incriminating, like you said to the cops? Or maybe something Jackie had that they wanted."

"Like the recipes," Evelyn said, sitting forward so suddenly that Coco jumped up in alarm. She turned toward me. "What if it was that guy Al? He'd for sure smell like curry, since he works in the kitchen there. Didn't you say Max said he was jealous of Mom as a cook? What if he came to get her Curry Leaf recipes so he could use them at Tamarind?"

I stared across the room at my red-and-white bike. I still didn't think Al was likely our guy, though the curry spice clue did serve to place him back in the running. "What about Rachel?" I asked after a moment.

"Rachel? Really?"

"Well, she is the right height and build, and cooks tend to have pretty strong arms and hands from all the work they do, so it could have been her. What if she went there trying to get more of your mom's recipes, maybe ones she'd kept to herself? It's not all that uncommon, chefs being super secretive about their recipes. Even Javier has been weird about sharing things with me on occasion."

Evelyn mused over this possibility as she drank more hot chocolate. Coco had settled back down, her head in Evelyn's lap. "Maybe. But why wouldn't Rachel just ask me if she could come look for them? It seems pretty extreme to break into someone's house."

"Since she and your mom had had a falling out, maybe

she just assumed you'd say no. Plus, if Rachel was the one who killed her, it's not likely she'd be wanting to call attention to herself right about now by asking about the recipes."

I considered how the ex–Curry Leaf cook had been unwilling to even come talk to Evelyn at the memorial service reception. As if she'd had something to be angry—or guilty— about. And then I flashed on her behavior earlier today, when she'd appeared none too happy to see me at her new pop-up restaurant.

And whoever had grabbed me by the throat tonight and then thrown me down the stairs certainly seemed to hold some kind of personal animus against me.

Chapter 18

Evelyn's door was open when I got home from my bike ride the next morning, so I poked my head into her room to say hi. She was stretched out on the bed listening to something on her phone, but at Coco's sudden movement she pulled out one of the earbuds.

"Hey, girl," I said. "You feeling any better?"

"Yeah, much better." She sat up, removing the other earbud and setting the phone down on her lap. "I don't know what got into me last night. I'm not usually such a wimp about stuff."

I plopped down next to her. "I'd say it's a completely healthy response to want to get the hell out of the place where someone has just broken in and rifled through your mother's possessions, and then committed assault, to boot."

"Yeah, but you're the one who got assaulted. How come you weren't freaked out?"

"I was plenty freaked out, believe me. I guess I'm just a little better at suppressing my feelings is all." As I said this, however, and thought back to what had happened the night before, a wave of heat and nausea swept over my body.

So maybe I wasn't all that great at suppressing my feelings. Maybe I was merely the better liar.

Evelyn traced her fingers over the quilt beneath her, each square of fabric providing a varied texture for her curious hands. "But I am ready to go back there, to look around like the policeman suggested and see if the person took anything."

"We could go now, if you want. And you can pick up that braille book, too."

"Sounds good." Evelyn's eyes took on what I could only describe as a devilish gleam. "And I figure while we're there," she added, "we might as well check to see if the person who was there last night left any clues as to their identify."

*   *   *

Evelyn unlocked the front door, and we stepped into the living room. I yanked opened the curtains, then looked about me. Nothing, of course, had been moved since the night before, but with the addition of the light streaming through the windows, the mood was completely changed. Whereas last night the room had felt eerie and claustrophobic, this afternoon it seemed a warm, inviting place, beckoning me to settle into the reading nook with a fat novel and soothing cup of tea.

"I'm gonna go get that book before I forget again," Evelyn said, and started up the stairs. After a moment, she came back down and deposited the fat tome by the front door. "So," she said, hands on hips, "you want to start in my mom's room?"

"Sounds like the best place, since that's where the person was last night."

Once in the bedroom, Evelyn took a seat on the queen-size bed while I commenced opening dresser drawers and describing what was inside.

"Top drawer, knickknacks and jewelry. The jewelry's mostly in boxes. Let's see . . . a necklace with a piece of turquoise set in a silver backing, a box of various rings, some old-fashioned bracelets—Bakelite by the looks of them. Are there any pieces in particular that you remember your mom wearing?"

"She wasn't that into jewelry, actually. You know, being a cook."

I did know. Jewelry was a no-no in the kitchen. It got in the way and could be a danger if it caught on a pasta maker or Robot Coupe. Even a simple gold band could be a problem if it came off while mixing something with your hands.

"She did wear those plastic bracelets a lot when she went out," Evelyn went on, "but to tell you the truth I don't know what kind of necklaces she wore. It's not like she told me what she was wearing on any given day, unless I asked." Evelyn pursed her lips and thought a moment. "She did have a string of pearls, I remember. Is that still there?"

I pawed around more in the drawer. "Here it is, right in the front," I said, opening a small black velvet box. "They look real, too."

"They are. My dad—my real dad—gave them to her on one of their anniversaries."

I replaced the necklace and shut the drawer. "I'd say

this proves it wasn't a burglar, then. Those pearls must be worth a bundle, so there's no way they would have left them."

"Not unless we scared him off too soon," Evelyn said. "But I'm betting you're right. What's in the next drawer down?"

"That's the one I found the will in, with files and paperwork. I wonder if there's one with recipes," I said, reading through the names of the folders. "Nope, doesn't look like it. Is there an office with a filing cabinet, or somewhere else she might have kept papers and documents?"

"No. I mean, she'd sometimes leave papers and stuff lying around, but we don't have an office. The extra room downstairs is just a guest bedroom. So unless it's down in the kitchen or living room, there wasn't a recipe file."

"Javier stores a lot of his recipes on his laptop," I said. "So Jackie's might all be on hers, wherever it is now."

I sat on the bed and pulled open the drawer of the side table. Nothing but a few magazines and an old copy of the local entertainment newspaper. I was about to close the drawer when I noticed the date on the paper—September 8th. "Hey," I said, "I bet this is the newspaper with that great Curry Leaf review that I read to you the other day."

I leafed through the pages. "Yep, here it is, all right. I'm not surprised she saved it. We had a great review last summer and I kept the hard copy, too. I wonder if . . ." I pulled out the stack of magazines, and sure enough, there was another copy of the same weekly paper, this one dated a month later. "Aha!" I said, flipping to the review section. "She kept the one that had the review of Tamarind, too.

Nothing like a healthy dose of schadenfreude to make a gal feel good."

"Shodden . . . ? Evelyn asked.

"It's a German word for the glorious enjoyment one experiences from another's misery. You know, like how people feel watching golf, when the person they're rooting against misses a gimme putt."

"Oh, right. Or like when the other team misses an easy field goal. Once when Max was over watching a Forty-Niners game with Mom, he started howling like a wolf when the Seahawks missed what would have been a game-winning kick. It was super funny."

I looked up from the article. "So was Max over here a lot?" I asked.

"It depends on what you mean by 'a lot.' I mean, I guess he was one of Mom's better friends. Like, he'd come over every week or two, and they'd hang out watching a game or a movie or something." She turned to me on the bed. "Why? You thinking he might be the one?"

"Well, given what Al told me the other day about Max being really into jazz, it sure seems like he should at least be on the list. And even though he's not a cook, he does work at a restaurant that serves curry, so it's not that far-fetched to think he might carry the smell with him."

"Yeah, I guess so."

"So the next question is whether you remember Max ever playing your albums when he was over here."

"No, never. But Mom wouldn't have let him. She knew I didn't want people messing with my records. When she wanted to listen to music, she'd use her phone."

"Well, do you remember anything unusual ever happening when he was over? Any argument or conversation they had?"

Evelyn lay back on the bed and drew up her knees toward her chest as she contemplated my question. "There was one time," she said. "It was pretty late at night, and I came down to get a glass of cranberry juice. When they heard me on the stairs, they got quiet all of a sudden, like they didn't want me to hear what they'd been talking about."

"*Did* you hear?"

"Only a little. It was about the recipes, how Al was telling people that Mom stole them, I'm pretty sure."

"Do you remember anything specific that they said? The exact words?"

"Well, I definitely heard the word *recipes* while I was still upstairs in the hall, but as for anything else . . ." Evelyn closed her eyes, brows wrinkled in concentration. "Wait, I do remember something." She sat up and turned to face me. "Right before they stopped talking, I heard Max say 'Rub my back' or something like that. Because I remember worrying—from the way he said it—that maybe I was interrupting them in the middle of, you know . . ."

"You think they were romantic?"

"Mom never told me they were involved, but I'm not positive she would have, if they were."

"Huh." This put a whole new spin on things. "You know whether he likes cranberry juice, by any chance?"

"I have no idea." Evelyn slid off the bed and started for the door. "I'm going to use the bathroom. Back in a sec."

I perused the closet while she was gone but found

nothing other than clothes, shoes, and a collection of handbags. I'd just opened a leather messenger bag to see if it might contain Jackie's cell phone when I heard a shout from the bathroom.

"Sally, you have to come in here! I think I found something!"

Dropping the bag, I tore down the hallway. Evelyn was standing at the sink, holding out her index finger as if pointing at the wall. "What is it? Where am I supposed to be looking?"

"Here on my finger, and on the counter, too—between the soap dish and the wall. Some kind of powder."

I examined her finger and saw several tiny grains of something white. Next I looked where she'd indicated on the white tile surface. "I don't see anything on the counter," I said.

"Look closer. That's where this stuff came from."

Leaning over, I squinted at the white tile and finally saw it—a scattering of minuscule white granules. But it would have been easy to miss if I hadn't known exactly where to look, lying as it was on the white tile.

"Yeah, you're right," I said. "I wonder if it could be some kind of drug."

"Drugs? Are you sure?"

"Well, it's not like I'm an expert or anything, but it sure looks like it could be a drug to me."

Evelyn reached out for the white powder, but I grabbed her arm. "No, don't touch it again. We need to call the cops. Here." I took hold of her hand and brushed the granules from her finger onto the counter at a spot away from the others.

Next I pulled out my phone and called 911. After telling the guy who answered what we'd found and where, and how it was the same location as where Jackie Olivieri's body had been found the week before, he said he'd send out a unit right away.

"Well," I said to Evelyn once I'd hung up, "we might as well go down and see if anything else is amiss while we're waiting for the cops. And we can look for your mom's cell phone, too."

After a thorough search of the entire downstairs, however, there was no sign of either the phone or anything else out of place in the house—other than a bent screen and open window in the laundry room, which told us how the intruder had gained entry to the house.

"I'm impressed you discovered that powder on the counter," I said as we waited for the police on the living room couch. "I could barely see it, even after you pointed it out to me."

"I was just looking for the soap dish and my hand touched the stuff. I could tell right away it was something weird."

At a knock on the front door, I jumped up and was surprised to see Detective Vargas standing on the front porch.

"Ms. Solari," he said with a half smile. "We meet again."

"Yeah. Sorry about that." The smile spread to the rest of his mouth. "But really, I think we've known each other long enough now that you can call me Sally."

"All right. And in that case, I suppose you should call me Martin."

Ah, so that's what the M *on his name tag stands for.* "Will do. So I'm surprised to see you here. I figured they'd just send the cop on the beat."

"I heard the call come through while I was in my car, and since I wasn't too far away, I thought I might as well stop by and see what you found."

"Well, that's actually a good thing," I said, "because there's something I wanted to tell you about what happened last night."

"Yeah, I read the report this morning. You okay?" The concern in his eyes was evident as he studied me for signs of the attack.

I resisted the urge to reach up and touch my neck. "I'm fine," I said. "Though it was pretty scary. Anyway, neither Evelyn nor I believe the break-in was a simple burglary. We think it's related to Jackie's death, that it might have been her killer coming back to look for something they left here that could incriminate them."

"Do you have anything concrete to support this theory?"

"I do. I was still kind of out of it when the cops came last night, so I forgot to mention it to them at the time, but whoever attacked me had a distinct aroma about them. They smelled strongly of one of the curry spices used in Southeast Asian cooking."

Vargas frowned. "So who do you suspect . . . ?"

"Well, both Al, Jackie's old boss at Tamarind, and Rachel, the woman who worked at The Curry Leaf with her, are cooks at Southeast Asian restaurants. So they would for sure smell like curry spices. But between the two, for my money, I'd go with Rachel."

Evelyn was nodding. "I agree. I don't see my mom inviting Al in for drinks, which must be what happened that night. But Rachel? Sure. Especially if she'd wanted to come over to try to make things right with Mom."

"Okay." Vargas was jotting down some notes on the pad he kept in his pocket. "I'll check out this Rachel woman. In the meantime, you wanna show me what you just found?"

Evelyn and I led the detective upstairs and into the bathroom, and I pointed out the white power on the counter. Vargas peered at the granules, then shook his head with what sounded almost like a growl. He turned toward me, his face severe. "Has anyone been in this room since the night of Ms. Olivieri's death?"

"No," I said, suddenly defensive. "Unless the person who broke in last night came in here. But the officers who responded to our call didn't do much of a search of the house, since they were so convinced it was just a burglary that we'd interrupted."

Okay, Sal, I chastised myself. *Don't lose your cool.*

I took a slow breath before going on. "In any case, though, I doubt whoever was at the house last night took the time to come in here and snort drugs. I'm thinking this must have been here ever since Jackie died."

The detective's expression softened. "I'm sorry. I guess I'm just taking out my frustration with my officers—who should have been the ones to discover this, not you. I should be thanking you, Sally, instead of being so snippy."

"It was actually Evelyn who discovered it," I said.

"Indeed?" He turned to Evelyn, new respect in his eyes. "Well, thank *you*, then."

Reaching into his jacket pocket, he removed a point-and-shoot camera and took several photos of the counter and the white powder. Next, he pulled out a pair of disposable exam gloves and a packet of small plastic evidence bags, then extracted a business card from his wallet.

"These over here were touched by Evelyn," I said, indicating the granules that had been on her finger. "And she may have touched some of the other powder, too."

Vargas nodded as he snapped on the gloves, then used the card to scoop up the grains and place them in two separate bags. Removing a felt-tip pen from his shirt pocket, he wrote several lines of information on each bag and slipped them into his jacket.

"We'll get this tested right away," he said, heading out to the hallway. "But I'm sorry to say, I suspect it will only end up supporting our initial finding of intentional overdose."

Once downstairs, he shook Evelyn's hand, then mine, and opened the front door. "Thanks for your good work," he said. "And do let me know if you happen to run across any *more* evidence my officers missed." I couldn't tell for certain, but I was pretty sure he was chuckling to himself as he headed out to his car.

Evelyn plopped down onto the sofa. "So you think there's any way he's right? That Mom was doing drugs the night she died? I know that's what he was implying."

"I don't know." I leaned against the arm of the couch, thinking it certainly now appeared that might at least be possible.

She sank down lower, shoving her hands into the cushions behind her, as if she could maybe hide herself away within the guts of the couch. Kind of like what Buster did during a thunderstorm. "Maybe I'm being naïve," she said, "but I just don't believe it. I would have known if she'd been taking drugs."

Digging her hands even deeper, she let out a moan that reminded me of a wounded animal. It was obvious that, despite her protestations, part of her believed it to be true about her mom. Why else would she be so despondent?

But when she let out a yelp, I jumped up and grabbed her by the shoulders. "Evelyn, snap out of it. Really, it's gonna be okay."

She rooted farther into the depths of the couch, and I held on to her even tighter, worried she might be having some sort of fit. "C'mon, you gotta get it together, girl."

Her right hand popped out of the cushions. "Ohmygod!" she shrieked.

"What?" I shrieked back.

Thrusting her hand toward me, she opened it to display the prize she'd extracted from deep within the sofa.

It was a smartphone.

"Oh, wow." I stared at it a moment before asking, "Is it your mom's?"

"Is it a Droid?"

Taking the black phone from her, I examined it. "Yep."

"Then I bet it's hers."

I clicked the button to activate it, but nothing happened. No surprise there, since the device had been hidden away in the couch for over a week now. "The battery's dead," I said. "You know where the charger is?"

"I have no idea."

Chapter 19

Concentrating on work that night was difficult.

Evelyn had come up with the bright idea of trying her mom's car for a phone charger, and—after locating the keys on a hook in the kitchen—we'd been elated to find one inside the Subaru parked in the driveway. I'd plugged the phone and charger into my T-Bird's outlet (which had been originally designed as a cigarette lighter), but when I turned on the ignition, the screen remained black. After the fifteen minutes it took to drive home, when the device still hadn't lit up, I decided something had to be wrong.

Googling the issue quickly informed me that when a phone battery is allowed to go completely dead, it's not uncommon for it to no longer take a charge at all. We'd likely need a new battery to get the thing working again. And since I needed to be at Gauguin for work in a half hour, we'd have to wait till tomorrow to do anything.

So there I was, deglazing a pan with brandy and butter, monitoring a saucepot of beurre blanc, keeping an eye on a tray of duck confit in the oven, and sautéing an order of broccoli rabe with anchovy butter, all the while trying to take my mind off that stupid phone that wouldn't charge. *Could it hold the secret of who killed Jackie?*

I was plating the broccoli rabe up next to a medallion of pork tenderloin that Brian had just sent over from the grill station when Tomás came darting out of the *garde manger*, a pair of small metal trays in his hands. He swapped out the full containers—sliced red onions and spot prawns—with the nearly empty ones in the *mise en place* area next to the hot line, then started back to the cold food room.

"Hold on a sec, Tomás," I said, and he came to stand by my side. "I was wondering if you'd heard any news about your friend who got taken into custody."

"Yeah. His wife brought in his papers, and it took a while, but they finally let him go yesterday."

"Oh, good. Glad to hear it."

Javier, who'd been listening in as he sautéed a pan of our Spot Prawns with Citrus and Harissa, leaned over once Tomás had gone and asked, "What was that about?"

I started to tell him about the immigration raid down the street the previous week, but before I could finish, the sound of a pan crashing to the floor across the room made me jump.

"Sorry," Tomás said, then crouched down to retrieve the metal insert that he'd dropped.

While Javier turned to give the prep cook some good-natured ribbing, I wiped my brow with a side towel and tried to calm my shaking body.

"Wow, you look like you just saw a ghost," Javier said, returning to his shrimp. "You okay?"

"I'm fine," I answered with a forced smile. "It just

startled me is all." Javier scattered a handful of orange chunks in his pan, tossed everything together a few times, then spooned it over a bed of basmati rice. "So, Evelyn's still coming over tomorrow to show me how to make her grandmother's pasta, right?"

"Yeah, that's the plan. How 'bout if I drop her off around two? That'll give you a couple hours."

"Sounds good." Wiping clean his sauté pan, he grabbed the next two tickets off the rail, handed me one, and set to work on an order of Duck á la Lilikoi.

I heated my pan for another side of broccoli rabe. But as I swirled clarified butter about its stainless-steel surface, I couldn't help but keep glancing behind me. For the image of those gloved hands reaching out to grip me by the throat was now seared into my brain.

* * *

Two hours later, the tickets had slowed to a trickle and Javier and Brian were discussing the specials for the coming weekend. As a concession to Brian for having to switch nights with him this coming Saturday, Javier had asked the cook if he wanted to come up with some dishes of his own.

"I had this idea for a turmeric chicken," Brian was saying. "I found a bunch of fresh turmeric and galangal today at this Asian market over the hill, and I was thinking we could serve it with lemongrass-scented rice and a papaya chutney."

Javier nodded. "Sounds great. Go for it."

"Awesome," Brian said, and headed back to his grill station. I followed him over to the charbroiler.

"So, do you know a lot about curry spices?" I asked.

"A fair amount. We had a few Indian and Thai dishes on the menu at Le Radis Ravi, that place in Los Gatos I worked at years ago." And then he spun to face me, his eyes flashing anger. "What, are you worried my turmeric chicken will suck?"

"No, no," I said. "Not at all. I have utter confidence in you as a cook." Though my confidence in his ability to handle stress had just fallen back a notch again. "It's just that I'm wondering if you'd be able to describe the smell to me of some of the curry spices."

He tilted his head. "Huh? How come? You thinking of trying some out in a recipe?"

"No, it's just that, well . . . I met this person who had this smell on them that I thought might be a curry spice, and I've been wondering what it was."

"Okay . . ." Brian still seemed puzzled by my request, but with a shrug, he grabbed a chicken quarter from the cooler and threw it on the grill, then motioned for me to follow him. "Here," he said, leading me into the walk-in fridge. "You can check out these spices I bought today for the turmeric chicken. Can you describe the smell you're looking for?"

"Sort of woody, I guess."

"This?" Brian plucked a stalk of lemongrass from the bunch on the shelf and thrust it at me.

"No, I know the smell of lemongrass. This was more, I don't know, spicy. Like black pepper, and maybe citrus?"

Brian frowned, then handed me a knob of something

that looked like ginger but was much more orange. "How about this? It's fresh turmeric."

I lifted it to my nose. "No. This is woody, but not in the way that smell was. It was almost like pine needles."

"Aha!" With a smile, the cook pawed through the cardboard box of produce and came up with another knob of something that was much paler in color. "I bet it was this."

"Ginger?" I said, taking the root from him. "I don't think so." But when I inhaled its pungent fragrance, a wave of nausea swept over me as the memory of the masked face leaning in to hiss in my ear came flooding back.

"That's it," I managed to say. "What is it?"

"Galangal," said Brian. "It's a common Southeast Asian spice, but it's probably most known in this country for being used in Tom Kha Gai. You know, that chicken-coconut soup?"

I did know. It was one of my favorite Thai dishes.

And it had been one of the offerings chalked onto the board at The Streets of Delhi, Rachel's new pop-up, the day I'd been attacked.

* * *

Evelyn and I didn't get to the cell phone store the next morning until almost eleven, since both of us had slept in. The salesman examined the device with the same mixture of distain and boredom I'd come to expect whenever being assisted by a twenty-something tech geek.

"Well, it looks like it's probably the battery," he finally said after trying in vain to get it powered up via his charger.

I snorted and gave Evelyn a "which is exactly what we said when we came in" nudge to the shoulder.

The man took the phone into the back room to search for the correct battery and emerged several minutes later. "There ya go," he said, plugging the device into the charger once again and setting it on the counter with a self-satisfied smile.

The screen was lit up and the icon at the top right informed us that the charge was at one percent. "Yes!" I said. "How much do I owe you?"

As soon as I sat down in the T-Bird, I plugged the phone into Jackie's charger, and this time when I started the car up, the phone sprang to life. I let the engine idle as I swiped the black screen.

Oh, no. ENTER PIN, it read.

"I don't suppose you know your mom's phone password, do you?"

Evelyn frowned. "No. I wonder if it's different from her computer. Try *Coco*. Or maybe my name?"

"Nope," I said, when neither this nor any variation on *Evelyn* worked. "And I don't suppose you even know how many characters she used."

She shook her head. "Sorry."

Great. No way would we be able to unlock the thing. Jamming the car into gear, I headed out of the parking lot. "We should take it to the police," I said. "They for sure have some techie cop who can get it unlocked. We could drop it off now, on the way back to my place."

"No," Evelyn answered with a vigorous shake of the head. "I bet I can come up with the password. I really want to see what's on the phone before we turn it in. Just give me a day or two, and if we can't figure it out in that time, we can take it to the police then."

"Okay," I said. "But it better not get stolen like that computer was. And you have to promise you won't tell Vargas when we found it when we do give it up."

"I promise."

Once home, Evelyn brainstormed password ideas, which I tried, only to have all fail. Birth date? No. Previous pets' names? No. Wedding date? Nope. Divorce date? Well, Evelyn didn't know that one for sure, so who knew.

After about ten minutes of this, I got bored. "Just jot your ideas down, and I can try them all at once," I said, heading to the kitchen for a second cup of coffee. "I'm going to go work on my staff scheduling until it's time to leave for Gauguin."

"Will do." Evelyn tapped a forefinger on her phone a few times, then began murmuring words into its voice recognition app.

I retired to the study, and after an hour and a half of work, had come up with a tentative schedule that seemed like it would make everyone in the front of the house fairly happy. Everyone, that is, except the hostess, Gloria, who'd asked for both Christmas and New Year's Eve off. No way was that going to work, nor would it be fair to the other staff.

I'd just finished penciling in all the names on my scheduling pad when the Indigo Girls' "Closer to Fine" rang out from my phone. "Hey, Nichole," I said. "How's it?"

"Good. Great, actually. Mei just found out she has tomorrow off at the gym, so we thought we'd come down to Santa Cruz to stay the night tonight, if it's not too late notice."

"No way. It's great timing. I'd normally be working, but Javier's off tomorrow to go to a wedding, so he's taking my place tonight. We can have a night on the town together."

"Nice! I'll text you later to let you know when we'll be there."

After hanging up, I stood up from the desk and stretched, then went in search of Evelyn. "Time to go make pasta," I said, poking my head into her bedroom.

Fifteen minutes later, we pulled into the Gauguin parking lot. "You need help getting inside?" I asked as Evelyn started to climb out of the car.

"Nope." She popped open her cane and stepped onto the uneven concrete surface. "I've done it enough times now that I know where all the potholes are. I'll be fine. As long as the door's unlocked, that is."

Javier's car was already parked in the driveway, and I could see his silhouette through the window of the *garde manger*. "Yeah, I'm sure it is. But I'll wait just to make sure."

Once she was safely inside the building, I locked my car and headed on foot for the Pacific Garden Mall a block away. I was hungry and knew exactly where I wanted to have a bite to eat: The Streets of Delhi.

Chapter 20

The pop-up was far less busy than when I'd been there on Wednesday, as it was now that slow period after lunch yet well before dinner. Two customers were sitting at the small table in the waiting area, but they got their food and left before I finished studying the offerings on the chalkboard. I'd been hoping to try out the Singapore noodles this time, but they weren't listed today. The Tom Kha Gai soup, however, was still on the menu, and the sight of the name sent a little shiver down my back.

Stepping up to the counter to place my order, I poked my head through the window to check out who was in the kitchen. I could see Sarah at the far counter dumping the contents of a saucepot into a large plastic container, but she appeared to be alone. No sign of Rachel. Which came as a bit of a relief, but was disappointing at the same time. I would have liked to get another good look at her, to see if she could in fact have been my attacker the other night. And to observe how she reacted to seeing me again.

Oh, well. Maybe Sarah would spill something important about Rachel if I could get her talking. Which—based on our previous conversations, when she'd been quite the chatterbox—wouldn't be too hard, I figured.

Looking up, Sarah smiled and flashed a "just a sec" gesture, finished scraping the pot clean, and then came over to the window.

"Hey, Sally," she said. "We actually just closed for the day at two, but I could get you something real quick if you want."

"Oh, you're not open tonight?"

"No. The other pop-up that shares the space has Friday nights. We have to be out of here by three-thirty so they can come in for their prep work."

"Ah. Got it. Well, I'd love some of the Butter Chicken if you still have any."

"No worries," Sarah said. "That's what I was putting away, but I can heat up an order for ya. Rice?"

"Sure. Jasmine, if you have it."

"You got it."

Remembering what she'd said about playing bass in a band, I asked if she had a gig tonight, to get her talking.

She ladled a portion of the creamy orange-colored chicken back into the pot and set it on the stove, then returned to the window. "Yeah, I do, as a matter of fact," she said. "So I'm actually glad we're closed Friday nights. Tonight's our first night at this really cool jazz bar."

"Oh, yeah? Which one?"

"Nick's, that retro place out in Aptos Village. Why? You thinking of coming?" Hope spilled from her eyes at the possibility of a few additional patrons. The more drinks the bar sold tonight, the better the group's chances were of being asked back.

"Maybe. I have some friends coming down from the City, and it might be a fun thing to do tonight. Are you expecting a lot of people?"

She shrugged. "Rachel and Maya both said they'll be there, and I've asked a few other people too, but you never know if they'll actually come or not."

She left to stir my chicken and, deeming it sufficiently heated, heaped a mound of rice into a to-go box, then spooned the curry on top. "Here ya go," she said, sliding the cardboard container into a paper bag and passing it to me.

"Thanks." I handed her a twenty and she made change. "So, speaking of Rachel," I said, "last time I was in here she seemed kind of . . . I dunno, gruff, like she really didn't want to talk to me. I can't imagine any reason she'd be mad at me, can you?"

Sarah closed the register and leaned on the counter. "I'm not sure why she'd be upset with you. Unless maybe it's because of your relationship to Evelyn—and by extension, to Jackie."

"Oh, because of whatever caused Rachel to quit, you mean?"

"It turns out she didn't quit. Jackie fired her."

"Really?"

Sarah nodded. "Yeah, I just found out the other day. Rachel told me that when she and Jackie had started up The Curry Leaf, she'd thought of it as belonging to them both, but after a while it became clear that Jackie felt like it was *her* place. That she was the creative person behind it all and Rachel was just an employee. Even though Rachel had helped tweak the recipes and the curry spice mixtures and everything." Sarah frowned and chewed her lip. "Maybe I shouldn't be telling you this. But then again, you own a restaurant, so I guess you'd understand."

"No, it's okay," I said. "And I totally understand how Rachel would feel. That would really suck, doing so much to make a place so successful and then have the owner not even appreciate how much of it was because of you." *Exactly how Javier must have felt before I asked him to be co-owner*, was what I was thinking. "And it's not as if I was friends with Jackie," I added. "The last time I saw her was like twenty years ago."

This seemed to satisfy her. "Well, anyway, I guess they had a big fight about it one night when Maya and I were gone, and Jackie ended up firing Rachel."

"Whoa. I wonder why Rachel had told you she quit?"

"I guess she didn't want me to be uncomfortable still working for Jackie. Or maybe she was just embarrassed, I dunno. But now that she's running this place, she probably figured she might as well tell me what really happened. You know, since it looks like it might actually work out between us. It's not good for couples to have secrets." Sarah smiled and stood back up from the counter. "Anyway, I really should get back to cleaning up."

"Right. No problem." I picked up my to-go container, grabbed a fork and napkin from the box on the counter, and started for the door. "So see you tonight, maybe."

"I hope so. That would be awesome!"

It'll be even more awesome, I mused as I headed down the street, *if I can get Rachel to talk to me.*

I had almost an hour to kill before picking up Evelyn after her pasta-making session, so I took my chicken curry up to Abbott Square to pass the time. This close to the winter solstice, the light cast by the low sun was not all that warming, but nevertheless, the tables at the public piazza were nearly full. Folks out for their holiday shopping, or merely taking a late lunch, sat with panini and glasses of beer, their faces turned toward the weak sun. Everyone was simply happy to enjoy some time outdoors after the previous weekend's gusty rainstorm.

Taking a table near a group of women chatting and knitting with brightly colored skeins of yarn, I opened the box of curry and dug in with my bamboo fork. The seasoning was perfect—hints of cardamom, black pepper, and cumin with none overwhelming another, the chunks of tender chicken blanketed in a creamy sauce spiked with tomato and ginger.

Wow. This was far better than any butter chicken I'd had before. Was it one of the recipes Jackie had created at Tamarind, or had she and Rachel developed it on their own afterward? I didn't remember it ever having been on the menu at The Curry Leaf. Had it been, I would have surely noticed, since it's one of my favorite Indian foods.

Curious, I took out my phone and pulled up the Tamarind website to check their menu for the dish. Yes, there it was: "*Makkhani Murghi*, Chicken in Butter Sauce."

My thoughts returned to the intruder at Jackie and Evelyn's house on Wednesday night. Ev and I had discussed the possibility of it being someone out to steal any recipes Jackie might have kept at home, which theory jibed with their smelling like freshly grated galangal. My attacker obviously hadn't been holding anything in their hands (*Don't think about those gloved hands, Sal*), but they could have had a small notebook or stack of recipe cards in their pocket.

As I savored the luscious butter sauce enveloping my chicken curry, I became even more convinced that was indeed what the intruder had been after. A recipe like this—along with all the others Jackie had no doubt compiled—would be a colossal boon to any purveyor of Indian or Southeast Asian food.

Especially someone like Rachel, who was just starting out and needed to make a quick splash in order to establish her own clientele. And then I realized something that made my breath catch: the Butter Chicken had first appeared on Rachel's menu two days after the break-in at Jackie's house. *Coincidence?* I wasn't so sure.

I finished my curry, tossed the box into the trash can in the corner of the piazza, and headed back to Gauguin.

No one was in the *garde manger* when I got there, but white dish towels covered most of the counter space, upon which strands of flour-dusted pasta lay like golden tresses cut from the head of a fairy-tale princess.

I found Javier and Evelyn upstairs in the office. "They make drying racks," Evelyn was saying. "These things with dowels sticking out at all angles, that you can hang the pasta on."

"Well, we'll have to get some of those," Javier said with a laugh. "Because right now it's taking up all the counter space of my cold food prep area."

"Hey, guys," I said, coming into the room. Javier, I noted with amusement, started at my sudden entrance but Evelyn did not. Was her sense of hearing so much better than his that she'd heard me walking down the hall? "You finished up early, I see."

"Yes, Javier was quite the quick learner. I don't think he'll ever be as good as my *nonna*, but for a non-Italian, he's not bad." Evelyn stood. "You ready to head back home?"

"Yeah, it'd be nice to have a little time before Nichole and Mei arrive." At a buzzing in my pants pocket, I pulled out my phone and examined the screen. "Aha. Speak of the devil."

It was a text from Nichole: MEET AT YOUR PLACE AT 5?

PERFECT, I sent back. AND I HAVE A PLAN FOR TONIGHT.

Now, even more than before, I hoped I could talk Nichole and Mei into going to hear some jazz tonight. I had a few questions to ask Rachel.

*   *   *

I hadn't been to Nick's in years. Eric and I had gone there a few times when we'd still lived together. We'd sit at the bar sipping Manhattans and pretending we were someplace like the Blue Note in New York City. Although, from what I've heard about those famous big-city jazz clubs with their squished-together tables and how-many-drinks-can-we-sell-you ambience, I'm guessing Nick's is probably a far more pleasant venue for simply relaxing and listening to music.

On weeknights, it's an old-fashioned piano bar with this guy who looks close to ninety tinkling out the Great American Songbook, occasionally singing along with himself in a raspy yet soothing voice. On Friday and Saturday nights, however, they have combos perform, sometimes local groups like Sarah's and occasionally better-known jazz musicians. So it was a bit of a coup for her trio to have scored this gig.

Tonight, by the time Nichole, Mei, and I finally arrived after our leisurely dinner at the Szechwan place down the street, the joint was jumpin'. At least a dozen couples were packed onto the tiny dance floor, swing-dancing to a blistering version of Ellington's "Take the 'A' Train." We found a table at the far back of the room, ordered a round of drinks from the cocktail waitress, and—since it was far too loud to do any talking—sat back to enjoy the band.

They were good. Really good. Especially the pianist, a gal with coal-black hair and eye shadow to match, whose hands flew over the keys with a finesse recalling the Duke himself. I turned my attention to Sarah, her fingers a blur as they attacked her upright bass. She and a young guy on the trap drum kit were focused solely on each other, their playing locked together in a tight rhythm.

The tune came to an end, and we all clapped. A lithe woman with a Joni Mitchell *Court and Spark* look now stepped up onto the small stage. Sarah moved a mic stand that had been sitting behind her to the front of the stage and introduced the woman as their special guest, Liz Lacey.

Liz uncoiled the microphone and slid it from its clip, then nodded to Sarah, who commenced a languid bass melody accompanied by brushes on the snare drum. After eight bars the pianist joined in, at which point I thought I recognized the song. I was proved right when the woman began to sing.

"Oh, I love this one!" I said to Nichole and Mei. It was

"Cry Me a River," and the singer was doing her best breathy Julie London imitation. I started to sing along, then noticed I wasn't the only one doing so. There was a woman standing at the bar who obviously knew every single word to the song.

It was Rachel. She must have either just arrived or come from the ladies' room, because I'd scanned the place for her when we'd first gotten there. As I watched, she not only mouthed the lyrics along with the singer but punctuated the accents of the bass and kick drum with a burlesque shake of the hips.

The next song was an up-tempo rendition of "Little Did I Dream," which got the crowd back out on the dance floor. I kept an eye on Rachel, curious to see if she'd respond to this lesser-known song with as much familiarity.

She did indeed. If anything, she seemed even more into this one, snapping her fingers and bobbing her head, then applauding enthusiastically at the end of the piano solo. Like a true jazz aficionado.

"Thanks, everyone," Sarah spoke into the mic after the song was over. "And thanks, Liz, for that sweet singing. We're going to take a short break now, but we'll be back up here in just a few minutes."

Sarah laid down her bass, then jumped off the stage and headed for the bar. Rachel gave her a hug and a kiss on the lips, causing Nichole to jab me in the ribs. "Cute couple," she said.

"Yeah, real cute. Although one of them may well be a burglar or a murderer—or both."

"Very funny," Nichole said, then frowned. "Wait. You're serious."

"Maybe. I don't know." I sipped from my Maker's Mark.

"Okay, what gives." Nichole leaned across the small table, prompting Mei to do the same.

I gave them the *Reader's Digest* condensed version of Evelyn's and my theory regarding her mother's death, and why Rachel was currently one of my favorite suspects.

"And now I find out that she's totally into jazz," I finished. "So it could easily have been her who was playing that Artie Shaw and Mel Tormé album the night Jackie died. I just wish I could get her to talk to me, but she acts like I have the plague every time we meet."

The three of us stared at the couple, who had their backs to us, oblivious to our fascination. After a bit, Sarah set down the pint glass of water she'd been drinking, patted Rachel on the shoulder, then pushed off from the bar. Walking over to where the drummer and pianist sat, she pulled out a chair and joined them.

Nichole stood. "I'm gonna go chat her up." She jabbed a thumb toward the bar. "That Rachel chick. Maybe I can get her to come join us. You know, 'cause of my winning personality an' all." With a grin that was pretty darn charming, I had to admit, she headed for the bar.

Mei and I watched as she went to stand next to Rachel and tried to catch the bartender's eye. It took a while, since everyone in the place had apparently been holding off until the break to order another round of drinks. While she waited, Nichole casually glanced Rachel's way, flashed a flirtatious grin, and said something to the other.

Rachel took the bait and leaned over to reply, causing Nichole to let out a boisterous laugh. *Overacting*, I thought.

But then again, Rachel couldn't know that Nichole's natural state tended more toward sarcastic understatement than exuberance.

Her beer finally ordered and delivered, Nichole lingered at the bar, chatting with Rachel. After a few minutes, I could see Nichole motion our direction, to which Rachel responded with a smile and a nod. The two of them picked up their drinks and headed our way.

Swiveling around in my seat so as to not appear over-anxious, I waited for the two to arrive. *Yes.* I'd finally get to have that talk with her. *Way to go, Nichole!*

Mei extended her hand to shake as Nichole made the introduction, and Rachel pulled out a chair to take a seat, turning her attention to the other person at the table. But as soon as she saw who it was, her face froze.

Our eyes met for the briefest of moments, and there was a hardness there that was a little scary.

"Uh, I just remembered something," she mumbled to Nichole, then hightailed it to the other side of the room. But not before I got a good look at her hands—the large, muscular hands of someone who does a lot of cooking.

And then I noticed the drink she held. It was one of those bright-pink cocktails—a Cosmo or Cape Cod, I wasn't sure which.

But it was most definitely a drink made with cranberry juice.

Chapter 21

"How was the music last night?" Evelyn asked, pulling out her earbuds as I came into the kitchen the next morning. Buster and Coco sat at their usual place under the table, hoping that her slice of buttered toast would miraculously spring off the plate and onto the floor.

"It was great! I'm so sorry you couldn't come with us."

"No worries. Me and my friend Molly ended up going out for Mexican food, so it's all good. And hey, I turn twenty-one next week, so you and me will just have to go to the jazz club together sometime after that." She raised her coffee mug as if it were a glass of Champagne, then took a sip. "Was Rachel there like you'd hoped?"

"She was." I helped myself to coffee and half-and-half and sat down. "And it turns out she's totally into jazz."

"No kidding? Huh." Evelyn drummed her fingers on the Formica table, causing both dogs to sit up in anticipation. Tearing the top crust off her toast, she held a piece out in each hand. Coco accepted hers delicately, but I was afraid Buster might bite off part of Evelyn's finger, he was so excited by the sudden appearance of the treat.

"And that's not all," I said. "She was drinking a Cosmopolitan or a Cape Cod."

Evelyn frowned. "I'm not sure I get what that has to do with anything."

"They're both made with cranberry juice."

"Ah." The confusion in her eyes turned to profound interest.

"And get this," I went on. "I found out that Rachel didn't quit working at The Curry Leaf; she was fired by your mom."

"No way."

"Way," I said, and recounted what Sarah had told me yesterday about Rachel and Jackie's falling out.

"Wow." Evelyn took a deep breath. "So Rachel really could be the one who was there that night. And the one—"

A sharp bark from Coco caused both of us to start. Nichole and Mei stopped at the doorway, then came the rest of the way into the kitchen once Evelyn had grabbed the dog by the collar.

"They were here just last night," she chastised Coco, making her sit. "Have you no memory?" Then, to the humans who'd just entered the room: "Sorry about that. She'll be fine once she remembers who you are."

"How was the hide-a-bed?" I asked. Since Evelyn was occupying the guest bedroom, Nichole and Mei had been relegated to the saggy sofa bed in the study.

"Let's just say that had I been given prior notice of its age and condition, I might have opted for an Airbnb for the night."

Nichole drained the last of the coffee from the carafe into a mug and handed it to Mei, then set about brewing a second pot. "So, I heard you talking just now about that

Rachel gal from last night. Did you tell Evelyn how she ske-daddled as soon as she saw it was you at the table? Like you have big-time cooties or something," she added with a chuckle.

"I hadn't gotten to that part yet. But it's not really all that funny," I said, shooting a glare at Nichole. "If she is the person who . . ."

"Sorry." She finished pouring water into the coffee machine, then took a seat at the table with the rest of us. "So you really think someone killed your mom on purpose?" Nichole asked, serious now. "Sally told us about it last night at the bar."

"Yeah, I do," Evelyn said. "And it's starting to look more and more like Rachel's our prime suspect."

"Who are the others?" asked Mei.

I glanced at Evelyn to see if she was going to field this question. "There's a couple," she said. "First, there's Mom's ex-boss, Al, who was super mad at her for quitting and then using some of the recipes from his place at her new pop-up restaurant."

"Al thinks he started losing profits because she stole away his customers," I put in.

"But Rachel makes more sense to me now," Evelyn said. "Since she has a motive, *and* she's into jazz and therefore could have been the one who played my records. And also because now we know she drinks cranberry juice. That would explain both the red stain on the carpet and the bottle being moved in the fridge."

"But couldn't it have been your mom who spilled juice on the carpet?" Mei asked.

"It's possible, but that wasn't her usual drink. She liked vodka and tonic."

"I'm assuming the cops didn't find more than one glass at the scene?" Nichole said.

I shook my head. "No, but it's easy to wash and dry a glass and put it back in the cupboard."

Nichole slapped the Formica table. "Sounds to me like it's most likely that Rachel chick, then."

"I don't know. The problem with Rachel—and with Al," I said, "is that it's not that likely Jackie would have been socializing with either of them. And given the record albums and juice that had been moved, whoever killed her must have been someone she invited in to hang out with."

"There is Max," Evelyn said.

"Who's Max?" Nichole and Mei asked in unison.

"A friend of Mom's. Who it turns out also really likes jazz and could easily have been with her that night. But I have no idea why he'd want to do anything to hurt her, much less kill her."

"Except . . ." I stopped, not sure if Evelyn would want me to repeat what I'd been about to say.

"Oh, right," she finished for me. "Except it's possible they were involved."

"Aha!" Nichole said. "That's your guy, then. It's *always* the lover."

"If only we could get Mom's phone unlocked," Evelyn said, oblivious to the collective eye roll Mei and I had given to Nichole's last remark.

"You have your mom's phone?" Nichole stood up in

response to the coffee machine's beep, announcing it had finished brewing.

"Yeah, but we don't know the password."

"Have you tried her pets?"

"Uh-huh. And her address, phone number, birthday, my name, my dad's name—the real one—and Stan. And the name of her pop-up, all the other restaurants she worked at, the name of her schools."

"I still think we should turn the phone over to the police," I said. "They'll be able to unlock it, for sure."

Evelyn shook her head. "No, I know I'll be able to come up with the password. Detective Vargas said at Mom's memorial that their tech guy doesn't even work on weekends. So just give me till Monday."

"Okay, fine," I said. "Monday *morning*."

* * *

Brian was not a happy camper that night at Gauguin. This was the evening he was supposed to have had free—a big deal, since staff in any professional kitchen only rarely get Saturdays off. But because of Javier's friend's wedding up in San Francisco, the head chef had pressed Brian into service tonight. And Brian wasn't letting anyone in the kitchen forget it.

"What's taking so long with those apps for table seven?" he hollered, wiping clean a sauté pan as he peered at the tickets lined up on the rail. "I've been waiting at least ten minutes to fire their entrées, and we've got a second service at that table tonight, people!"

Slamming the pan onto the Wolf range, Brian stomped over to the door of the *garde manger*, nearly colliding with Tomás. The prep cook, who'd been moved up to the appetizer station for the night, held an order of our Tahitian sea bass starter in each hand.

"Got 'em right here," he said, then rushed with the plates to the pickup counter, tapped the bell, and shouted, "Order up!"

"About time," Brian muttered, then returned to the hot line and grabbed the next ticket in line.

"You don't have to be so hard on Tomás," I said, reaching for the bottle of sriracha-mayonnaise to squirt atop an order of spicy fried chicken. "For someone who's not used to working that station, I'd say he's really stepped up to the plate tonight."

Brian ladled clarified butter into his sauté pan and swirled it about, then set the pan down over the blue-white flame. "I know," he said with an impatient shake of the head. "I'm sorry. It's just that I have all these chemicals flowing through my body right now. Angry chemicals. And I can *feel* them—like they're shooting up and down my veins or nerves or something."

"Sounds like a case of menopause. I know the feeling well. I don't suppose you're getting hot flashes, too?"

"I doubt I'd be able to tell if I were," Brian said with a snort, "given the heat blasting from the oven and stove right about now." He laid a plump pork chop into the butter, then wiped his hands on his side towel.

I studied the cook. His jaw was clenched as he squinted

angrily at the meat sizzling in his pan. "Look, Brian, I need you to be honest with me. Are you okay? Because it seems like something's been going on with you lately. Something besides just your problems with Roxanne."

He continued to stare at the slice of pork, then lifted the pan from the heat and deftly flipped the chop. It was perfectly browned, the ribbon of fat along the top edge delectably crisp. With a slow nod, the cook glanced my way, then returned his attention to the pan. "I did cut back on my drinking recently," he said softly.

"Ah."

"But it's not like what you're thinking. I never drank before work. Or during. But afterwards, and on my days off I was probably drinking more than I should have." He shrugged. "I'd been having problems getting to sleep when I got home at night and the beer helped. But I guess I just kind of let it get out of hand."

"Well, that could certainly affect your mood, especially if you go cold turkey or cut way back all of a sudden."

"I guess." Brian added brandy and dried apricots to his pork dish and then tossed the onions he had going in another pan. "Anyway, Roxanne was the one who first got on my case about it. That's one of the reasons we'd been having problems. So I've been limiting myself to only one beer after work, and two on days I'm not working."

"And how's your relationship with Roxanne been going since then?" I asked.

"Much better. She was totally right." He shook out his arms, then clenched and unclenched his hands a couple of times. "Don't worry. I'll apologize to Tomás later, I promise."

"That'd be great. And I'll try to do what I can to make things less stressful around here tonight."

"Good luck with that," Brian said with a nod toward the line of tickets awaiting us.

* * *

An hour later the kitchen was in full swing. Brian and I were on the line, tending sauté pans at six of the eight burners, when Brandon darted up to the pass and stuck his head through the window. "Cancel the orders at table seven!" he shouted.

I examined the tickets on the rail to check their table numbers, then shook my head. "Too late. They're already fired." It was one order of Coq au Vin au Gauguin, which I'd just plated up, and another of the spot prawn special, now sizzling in the sauté pan before me.

"Damn. One of the people just got a text saying there's some sort of emergency, and the other guy left along with her, so I had to void the ticket. Sorry I didn't catch you in time."

"It's okay. These things happen. Here, lemme see if any of the next few orders are for either of these dishes. Nope, no dice." I shook my head, and the server started back for the dining room. "Wait, hold on a sec," I said, dumping the order of shrimp onto a plate and setting both entrées onto the pass. "Go ahead and take these out to the wait station for you all to share."

Brandon grinned as he took the plates. "Thanks, Sally."

"Yeah, well, no reason they should to go waste."

But of course it *was* a waste to the restaurant—not only of the food itself and the labor that had gone into preparing

225

it, but also of the potential profit on what would otherwise have been two additional covers that night for Gauguin.

Good thing this doesn't happen very often, I thought as I wiped off my pan with a paper towel. Because it wouldn't take many voided tickets to have a serious effect on our bottom line.

I set the sauté pan down on the stove with a frown as I remembered Al lecturing me about Food Service Economics 101 at the restaurant owners' luncheon earlier in the week. Tamarind had been down only a few covers a night recently, but it was enough to make a difference to their profits.

I stared out through the pass window at the diners, some finishing up their meals, others digging into orders of pot stickers, duck confit, and crème brûlée. Brandon was at the point-of-sale terminal, entering information onto the computer screen and printing out the check for one of the tables.

How easy it would be, I realized, for someone with access to the POS codes to steal from a restaurant. All they'd have to do would be to void tickets after the customer paid, then pocket the money themselves. And in the case of a cash payment, no one would ever be the wiser unless they happened to check the "voided ticket" category in the system, something I only rarely did.

I bit my lip as I watched Brandon place the bill on a tray, drop two wrapped chocolate mints on top, and take it out to table four. If I hardly ever checked to see about our voided tickets, it was unlikely Al did either.

Could that be the reason Tamarind had been losing money of late? Here at Gauguin we didn't get a lot of cash sales, but there were often one or two a night. And as Al had said, it only takes a few lost covers a day to make a difference between profit and loss for a restaurant running on a very tight margin.

But if someone were voiding tickets and pocketing the cash at Tamarind, they'd have to have been given access to the POS codes. So it would have to be someone like the dining room manager.

Someone like Max.

"Sally, you okay?" Brian startled me out of my reverie, and I realized I'd been standing there at the stove, staring blankly out at the dining room, for almost a full minute.

"Yeah, fine," I said with a quick smile. "Just thinking about something is all." Grabbing the next ticket in line, I set to work on two orders of the pan-fried Petrale sole special.

But why would Max be embezzling from Tamarind? That aspect of my hypothesis didn't seem to make any sense. His job as dining room manager surely paid well, and he'd be risking everything by such an action. Since only a limited number of employees would know the POS codes, it wouldn't be at all difficult to figure out who the culprit was, once it was discovered someone had been voiding tickets.

And then I wondered if my embezzlement theory could have anything to do with Jackie. According to Al, the lost sales had started right around the time she opened The Curry Leaf. Could Max—or whoever it might be—have decided that her new pop-up would provide perfect cover for the sudden drop in sales at Tamarind? If so, they'd been right, as Al certainly believed that was the cause.

Okay, then, I mused as I ladled a pool of *sauce normande* onto two plates, then set the golden-brown sole fillets on top. *Assuming my new pet theory to be true, how could the thefts be related to Jackie's murder?*

Maybe she had known about the embezzlement.

And maybe the thief had killed her to shut her up.

Chapter 22

It was after midnight when I got home that night, exhausted and achy. Having two complete dinner services with each table filled is terrific for the pocketbook but miserable on the body. Brian, however, had been a trooper. Unburdening himself like that must have released some of his pent-up anger, because after our conversation he'd reverted back to the Brian of old, joking around with the staff and whipping out the hot-line orders like a master chef.

Evelyn was in the living room watching another old movie when I let myself into the house. Fetching a nightcap, I joined her on the couch.

On the screen, Katherine Hepburn spoke on the telephone in a rapid patter, listing the names of all of Santa's reindeer. Several bottles of Champagne sat atop the gray metal desk before her.

"Ah, another classic," I said. "*Desk Set*. Perfect for the Christmas season."

"This was one of Mom's favorite movies," Evelyn replied. "She thought it was funny how even way back then they were having the exact same argument about whether computers can ever replace humans. Hey, I wonder if Siri can name all the reindeer."

She grabbed her phone and held it up to her mouth: "Siri, what are the names of Santa's reindeer?"

"All right, here's what I got," the perky voice spoke up. "Dasher, Dancer, Prancer, Vixen, Comet, Cupid, Donner, and Blitzen."

"Yeah, well big whoop," I said. "She's nowhere near as charming as Katherine Hepburn."

"Totally." Evelyn set the phone on the coffee table next to her mom's Android.

"So any luck with that password while I was gone tonight?" I asked.

She shook her head. "Nada. Nothing I could come up with worked."

"Well, don't feel bad. Hackers spend hours using all sorts of complicated algorithms to break into people's devices. But I do have some good news about the case. Well, not really news, but I think I might have figured something out tonight at work."

"Oh, yeah?"

I told her my theory about Max embezzling from Tamarind by voiding tickets, which would explain the loss of sales at the restaurant over the recent months.

"Yeah, I like it," Evelyn said. "It would prove once and for all that Mom didn't do anything wrong."

"But the thing is," I continued, "it doesn't make a lot of sense *why* Max would risk his job by embezzling, given how risky it would be to do so. But if we can prove I'm right, *and* that your mom knew what he was doing, it would certainly provide a strong motive for her murder, especially if he was afraid she'd bust him."

Evelyn sat forward eagerly. "Okay, so how do we prove you're right?"

"Well, first off, I think I need to pay a visit to Tamarind tomorrow to talk to Al."

*   *   *

Another storm front had been predicted to roll in on Monday, so the next morning—Sunday—Evelyn and I took advantage of the sunny weather to cruise home from grocery shopping via the beach with the top down. "So, how would you like to celebrate your big twenty-first birthday this week?" I asked her. Though I had to shout in order to be heard over the rush of wind and roar of the T-Bird's engine. "What day is it again?"

"Tuesday."

"Oh, dang. That's too bad. I'd thought it was tomorrow. I have to work Tuesday night."

"Yeah, I know." Evelyn pulled back her hair, which had been whipping about in her eyes, and fastened it into a ponytail with a rubber band. "But I was thinking maybe we could do something at Gauguin. I could come in for dinner with some friends, and then once it slows down, you and Javier could maybe join me for dessert—and my first legal cocktail."

"Good idea. Tuesday's usually pretty slow, so it should be no problem for us to join you by around eight or eight thirty." Coming to a stop at Woodrow Avenue, I waited for a woman with a stroller and two gray-muzzled black Labs to make their way across the street. "You're coming to Nonna's this afternoon, aren't you?" I asked once we'd turned the corner toward my house.

"Absolutely. I can't wait to taste her Sunday gravy."

"And I promise you won't be disappointed." I pulled into my driveway, and we carried our shopping bags from the T-Bird up to the house. Once inside, Evelyn set about wrapping rubber bands around the canned food we'd bought (one for corn, two for black beans, three for sliced beets), while I stowed the produce and dairy goods in the fridge.

"Okay, what time is it?" I said, consulting my phone after all the food had been put away. "Eleven fifteen. Which means if Al's working the lunch shift today, he should be there by now. Guess I'll go down and see what I can find out."

"Good luck sleuthing!" Evelyn shouted after me as I grabbed my keys and headed back out to the car.

Since Tamarind didn't open till noon, the front door was locked when I got there. I walked around the side to the kitchen entrance and poked my head inside. I was hoping Max wouldn't be working lunch today, but figured that even if he was, he'd be out in the front of the house prepping the dining room for the midday service.

A busboy carrying a rack of glasses passed by and asked, "You looking for someone?"

"I am, actually. Is Al around?"

"He's in his office," he said, and nodded toward a closed door next to the walk-in refrigerator.

"Thanks." Ignoring the questioning stares from the two twenty-something cooks setting up the *mise en place* for the hot line—the same tattooed guys I'd seen at Jackie's memorial service—I strode across the kitchen and knocked on the door.

"What is it?" came a sharp voice.

I took this as an invitation to enter and stepped into the room. Al was seated at the desk, but swiveled around on his wheeled office chair at my entry. The scowl he wore faded and his eyes took on a look of confusion. "Who . . . ? Oh right, you're that girl who owns Gauguin. What the hell do you want?" He spun back around to face the desk and picked up a piece of paper. "I'm kinda busy here."

I was pretty darn sure Al wasn't the one who'd murdered Jackie. The motive seemed far too weak, plus—now that I saw that paunch sagging over the waistline of his hot-chili-decorated chef's pants—I realized he was far heavier than whoever had stolen the laptop from my car and attacked me Wednesday night.

But that didn't mean the guy wasn't still a total slimeball.

Keep your cool, Sal. Remember you're here to get information, not engage in a spitting match. "I wanted to talk to you about those sales you said you've been losing over the past few months."

This got his attention. Setting down the paper, he turned back around. "Yeah?"

"I think I may know why it's been happening."

He flashed a patronizing smile. "I *know* why I was losing sales," he said. "And the fact that they're now back up to normal proves I was right all along."

"I wouldn't be so sure about that," I said. "The person

cheating you may have stopped for now, but once they get the taste for it, it's hard to give it up for good."

"Cheating me?" He shook his head. "No, it wasn't that."

I took a seat on a barstool in front of several cases of Jim Beam. "Look, I know you're convinced it was Jackie's pop-up that was siphoning business from you, but I think you need to consider another possibility—that one of your employees has been embezzling money from the restaurant."

"That's preposterous," Al said. "I'd be the first to know if that were happening."

"No, actually, you probably wouldn't. Not if someone were voiding tickets that had been paid in cash and then pocketing the money. How often do you check the voided ticket page of your POS?"

"I . . ." From his frown, I could tell it must have been something he did about as often as I, which was pretty much never. But Al was clearly not one to admit he could possibly be wrong. "No, I know I'm right," he said. "Now if you don't mind, I have a lunch service starting in a few minutes." And with a wave of the hand, he dismissed me from his presence.

*　*　*

Evelyn and I arrived for Sunday dinner fifteen minutes early, but my grandmother was thrilled to see us—or Evelyn, anyway. "Ah, my dear!" Nonna exclaimed, taking her into her arms before Evelyn could even get all the way through the front door. "I am so sorry I did not make it to your poor *mamma*'s service, but I was feeling so poorly that day."

"It's okay, Nonna," she said. "But wait, that's not what I should call you. You're my, what, some kind of aunt?"

"Huh, good question," I said as Nonna continued to clasp Evelyn in a tight hug. "Let's see. My dad would be your grand-uncle, so Nonna would be your great-grand-aunt. I think. Don't hold me to it."

Nonna released Evelyn with a laugh. "I like that, being both grand and great! But you can just call me Aunt Giovanna, if you like. Here." She took hold of Evelyn's hand and started dragging her down the hallway. "You come into the kitchen while I finish the cooking."

Nonna sat Evelyn down on the tall stool next to the stove, and while she strained the meat from the gravy in her hefty enameled Dutch oven, she recounted stories about our extended family. The relationships were all very confusing, but the stories—which bordered on the risqué—soon had all three of us laughing like schoolgirls.

"And then," Nonna said, her lips forming a wicked smile, "Nonno Salvatore told his sister, 'You no marry that man. I seen him in the locker room and he never gon' give you no children, that is sure.' And she turned red as the tomatoes in my *papà*'s garden and went running off to her room."

"And is that who she ended up marrying?" Evelyn asked with a giggle.

"No, no. She only dated him for about four months. She met your great-grandfather later, when she and I worked together at the cannery. And dat man, he had no problem like the other one," Nonna added with a wink in my direction.

"What's so funny?" my dad asked, coming into the kitchen as the three of us exploded in laughter at Nonna's last story. His new flame, Abby, stood behind him.

"Never you mind." My grandmother swatted him lightly on the hand. "It's just girl talk."

"Well, I'm a girl," said Abby brightly. "So how about we send Mario out of the room, and then you can tell me?"

I expected Nonna to scowl at this familiarity from someone she'd never even met before, but instead she merely clucked a couple of times, waiting for Dad to make the introductions.

"Ma, this is Abby. She recently moved up here from Southern California."

"So pleased to meet you," Abby said, leaning over to give Nonna a quick half hug.

"Nice to meet you, too," my grandmother said, accepting but not reciprocating the embrace. "You like the pasta?"

"Oh, yes! I love it—all kinds. Lasagne, spaghetti, fettuccine . . ."

"Good." Nonna turned back to the stove and gave the pot of gravy a few swift stirs as my dad introduced Abby to me and to Evelyn. She then clapped her hands. "Ready to eat. Here, you take this." Nonna thrust the bowl of green salad into Abby's hands and directed her to the dining room table. "Where's Eric?" she asked, turning to me with a frown. "You say he was coming, no?"

"He is, but you know Eric. He's never on time."

"Yes I am!" Eric strode into the kitchen and kissed my grandmother on the cheek, causing her to break into a broad smile. Nonna adores Eric, even though he's not Italian, and her most fervent wish is for us to marry and bear her multitudes of grandchildren. *So much for that dream,* I mused. *Maybe in a few years he can bring all the babies he's made with Gayle over to visit her once in a while.*

These sour thoughts were interrupted by Nonna poking me in the shoulder. "Sally, go tell your *papà* to come back out here an' open the wine. And take this with you." She handed me the platter of antipasti—prosciutto and salami, marinated cauliflower, carrots, and peperoncini, and provolone and mozzarella cheese.

I'd just set the food on the table when my cell rang. The number was unfamiliar, but since we still had a couple minutes before dinner, I walked down the hallway to take the call.

"Hello?"

"Sally, is that you?"

"Al?" I wasn't positive it was the Tamarind owner, but the rudeness of his tone made me think of him. "How'd you get my number?"

"From Ramón."

Ah. Our mutual acquaintance who'd been sitting with Al at the restaurant owners' luncheon.

"Anyway, I wanted to let you know you were right," Al said with a growl. "I checked the point-of-sale records for voided tickets, and there's been a rash of them over the past few months. A couple most nights, all cash transactions, just like you said." He cleared his throat. "So, well, I just wanted to thank you is all."

Huh. Maybe I'd been wrong about the guy. Maybe he wasn't such a slimeball after all.

"You know who did it?" I asked. "Can you tell if it was the same person for all the voided tickets?"

Al didn't answer right away. It wasn't any of my business, of course, so why would he tell me? But then his anger got the better of him. "It was my dining room manager, Max," he spat out. "Except for a couple isolated instances—which were probably valid cash-outs—every single voided ticket was approved by him. And boy, is he going to regret it."

"When exactly did the activity start?" I pushed on, since he seemed eager to vent.

"About five months ago, it looks like, and there were a few more instances over the next couple weeks after that. But then they really started to increase four months back, as if he'd gotten confident that his little scheme was working."

So he started while Jackie still worked at Tamarind, but then ramped up the activity significantly once she'd left.

"Are you gonna go to the police with the information?" I asked.

"I think it'd be more fun to tell him when he comes into work tonight that I know, and then let him stew over it a few days, wondering if I'm going to turn him in or not. Let him suffer some of the same anxiety I did the past few months." With a harsh laugh, Al disconnected the call.

Wow. So I'd been right about Max—at least about his embezzling from the restaurant. I couldn't wait to tell Evelyn.

I headed back to the dining room, where Nonna was herding everyone to get seated at the large, oak table. *Oh, well.* I'd have to wait till after the meal to give her the news.

"Pass the bread, please," Eric said, and I handed him the basket of thickly sliced ciabatta.

"No eating till we make our toast," Nonna said, raising her glass of Barbera d'Alba. "*Salut, cent'anni!*" she said, and Dad, Eric, and I all joined in. My great-grandfather, Ciro, who had arrived here from Liguria as a teenager in the 1890s, and his young bride, Lucrezia, stared down at us with somber expressions from a hand-painted photograph mounted in an oval frame.

"What's it mean?" asked Abby. "Chen-tanni?"

"Health for a hundred years," Dad said, clinking glasses with his date and holding her eyes as he sipped his wine.

I glanced at my grandmother to see how she was taking this show of affection by her son for a new woman. But although Nonna eyed Abby with a hint of distaste, she said nothing. It was sad, actually, how much vinegar the old gal seemed to have lost over the past few years.

Evelyn lifted her glass of water. "I know this isn't wine, but I can still offer a toast as well. It's one Javier taught me the other day. Too bad I don't remember how to say it in Spanish: May you truly *live* for all the days of your life."

"Well, since we're sharing toasts," Eric said, "I have one: May misfortune follow you the rest of your life . . ." He paused, allowing everyone at the table time to take this in and then frown. "And never catch up!" he finished with a flourish.

Nonna patted him on the shoulder with a wide smile. "Ha-ha, I get it. Very nice."

"Let me guess," I said before I could catch myself. "Gayle taught you that."

"No." Eric shot me a why-the-hell-would-you-think-that look. "It's an old Irish toast that my granddad used to say."

"Sorry," I mumbled. "It's only because . . . Oh, never mind." Shaking my head and hoping Eric didn't notice the blush I felt spreading across my cheeks, I took a long drink of wine.

"Who's Gayle?" Nonna asked, her mouth now tight. I chuckled to myself. She was more concerned with Eric's love life than that of her own son.

"Just this woman I've been working with on a case," Eric said. "Or rather, we've been working against each other, since she's on the opposite side."

This seemed to appease my grandmother, who turned her attention to Evelyn, touching her on the arm and asking if she'd like more antipasto. I reached for the wine and refilled Eric's glass as a sort of olive-branch gesture, then topped my own off as well.

"Thanks," he said with a quick smile, popping a rolled-up slice of salami into his mouth and washing it down with some of the wine.

Good. I was afraid my previous remark had annoyed him, but he appeared to have already forgotten it. "So, what do you say about hanging out tomorrow night?" I asked. "There's this French movie at the Del Mar that's getting great reviews, and we could have an early dinner beforehand."

He shook his head. "Sorry, Sal, no can do. I'm already busy." He kept his eyes on his plate as he spoke, and I detected a slight tightening of the muscles around his mouth.

"Oh." I glanced at the others at the table, but Nonna and Evelyn were still talking, and my dad was leaning over speaking into Abby's ear. "You're doing something with Gayle." It was a statement, not a question. Because of course that's what it had to be.

Eric shrugged, then gave a slight nod. Turning to face me, he smiled faintly. "Yeah. We're actually going to see that movie you mentioned. But hey, you could join us if you wanted."

I waved him off. No way was I interested in being the third wheel on their "not date." "That's okay. I could use a night off, anyway."

Which was probably true. But it still stung. Back when I'd worked at Solari's, Tuesday had been our traditional night to hang out together, since that was the day the restaurant was closed. It had never been an "every Tuesday" thing, but Eric and I had both thought of that as "our night," even after we broke up. Then, once I'd inherited Gauguin, which has the more traditional Monday closing, we'd switched to that night.

Biting into a slice of creamy buffalo mozzarella, I glanced from Dad to Eric—both pairing up right before my eyes. *I should be happy for them, right?* But it was hard to be supportive of the speeding love lives of others when my own was stalled in neutral, if not reverse. And whose fault was that? Mine, of course, all mine.

Just two months ago, Eric had made clear he wanted to rekindle our relationship as a couple, but I'd been so afraid of it blowing up again—and this time maybe destroying our friendship entirely along with the romance—that I'd put a damper on his smoldering emotions before they'd even had time to reignite.

What I'd failed to consider, though, was that I was likely to lose him anyway. There'd been no way the bright, boyishly blond Eric would remain single for long. And once he did get involved with someone else, it was a sure thing our friendship would slip into the background as his new relationship grew. Like spending Monday nights with his new gal instead of me.

Maybe I should sign up for one of those online dating services, like Dad, I thought, helping myself to more wine.

But the thought of that only made me more lonely.

Chapter 23

I waited till we were back home to tell Evelyn about Al's phone call. With the convertible's top down, it would have been hard to carry on any kind of real conversation, and there were a few questions I wanted to ask her about Max.

She sucked in her breath when I told her the news, causing Coco to trot over to the kitchen table and paw at her leg. Evelyn reached out to stroke the dog's chocolate-brown forehead. "I can't believe Max would do that to Mom," she said. "Make it look like she was the reason the restaurant was losing money when he was the one stealing. Why would he do that? They were friends."

"Who knows why people do stuff." I found a place in the fridge for the leftover Sunday gravy Nonna had sent home with us, then joined her at the table. "But now that we know he was in fact embezzling from Al, the next question is, did that have anything to do with your mom's murder?"

"I don't know how we can ever find that out," Evelyn said, shoulders sagging.

"Well, do you remember anything else from that night

you heard your mom and Max talking? Anything to suggest she might have known he was stealing from the restaurant?"

"Not really. Just the stuff about the recipes is all. And that . . . romantic talk I heard."

"Hang on," I said, "You heard Max say something about her rubbing his back, but you couldn't remember exactly what he said, right?"

Evelyn nodded.

"So, what if he said 'scratch my back,' not 'rub' it? Is that possible?"

"Sure, I guess he might have."

"Don't you see?" I stood up from the table, startling Coco from the near coma she'd descended into as a result of the face massage by Evelyn. "If he said 'you *scratch* my back,' then he could have been talking about an agreement between the two of them—that she'd scratch his, too."

"By not telling Al about his stealing from the restaurant," Evelyn filled in.

"Right. But if she then reneged on that agreement and threatened to tell, that would be a hell of a motive to get her out of the picture."

Evelyn clenched her hands. "And Al said that Max was really into jazz music, too."

"I wonder if Max is the one who stole your mom's laptop," I said, thinking out loud as I began to pace back and forth across the kitchen. "As the manager, he could've left Tamarind whenever he wanted that night and come to Gauguin."

I came to a stop by the back door and gazed out at the row of fruit trees lining the fence at the far end of the yard.

Their gnarled branches glowed like burnished copper in the late-afternoon sun. "I have to find out if he's the one who took it. Because if he did, that would *prove* a serious connection to your mom—and prove he was scared enough by something on the computer to risk breaking into my car. And breaking into your house, too, I bet."

"So how are you going to do that?" Evelyn asked.

"Well, Al mentioned that Max is working tonight. So if I can find out where he lives, maybe I can do a little snooping to see if there's a MacBook Air lying around his house."

I grabbed my computer from the kitchen counter and pulled up the white pages website, only to realize I didn't know Max's last name. But then I remembered the business card he'd given me that night I'd been at Tamarind with Eric. Had I kept it?

Yes. It was stuck in the book I'd been reading the same night, a dog-eared copy of *Kitchen Confidential* that had belonged to my Aunt Letta. Sitting back down at my laptop, I typed MAXWELL LACROIX into the search box. An address came up near downtown Santa Cruz.

"Got it," I said to Evelyn, and jotted down the number. "And he doesn't live too far from Gauguin. Looks like maybe I'll be the one taking a little time off from work tonight."

As I returned my computer to the kitchen counter, I noticed Jackie's phone charging in the wall socket. I unplugged it and brought it to the table. "You want to brainstorm more ideas for your mom's password? I've got a little time before I have to be at the restaurant, and today's the last chance before you promised we'd give it to the police tomorrow morning."

"Okay." Evelyn sat up and placed her palms flat on the kitchen table. "I can't imagine her picking anything all that hard or original. It must have been something easy for her to remember. Like . . . maybe her favorite food or something?"

"What was her favorite food?"

Evelyn thought a moment. "Probably *aloo gosht*—it's a kind of lamb-and-potato curry. Here, lemme try that." I handed her the phone, and she punched in the name of the dish. "Nope, didn't work."

"Good thought, though. How about other foods she liked?"

Evelyn entered several other Indian food names: *tandoori*, *basmati*, *chapati*, *vindaloo*. "Oh, and she loved French fries, too." But none unlocked the phone.

"It's no good," she said with a sigh. "We'll never figure it out."

I stared past her into the living room, and my eyes came to rest on the television. "I know something else she really liked," I said. "Classic films. What was her favorite old movie?"

Evelyn thought a minute. "That's hard to say. Maybe *You Can't Take It With You*? But she also really liked *Mr. Deeds Goes to Town*."

"Those are kind of long for a password. But wait, aren't they both Capra films?" I grabbed my computer again and did a search for the director Frank Capra. "Yep, they are. Try his name. It's spelled C-A-P-R-A."

"Nope." Evelyn set the phone back down.

"Oh, well." I drummed my fingers on the red Formica as I stared at my computer screen. "Hey, here's something. It says both those movies starred Jean Arthur." Grabbing the phone, I entered her name. And, voilà, a green screen opened with the word MESSAGING.

"I'm in!"

"Oh, man, she was totally Mom's favorite actress. I shoulda thought of that. So is there anything there?"

I scrolled through the recent messages: a long string from Evelyn and then one that made me catch my breath. "Ohmygod," I said, "there's a text from Rachel on the date your mom died. It's from seven forty-two that night."

"What's it say?"

I tapped the entry to open the message and read it aloud: I HAVE TO SEE YOU."

* * *

Javier was in high spirits that night at Gauguin. He'd come straight to work after his trip back from San Francisco and proceeded to recount in great detail the fabulous wedding he'd attended the night before. The reception had been held at some hoity-toity private club on Nob Hill, and they'd been served designer cocktails and canapés to start, followed by a four-course meal with waiters in white jackets and black ties.

"They had herb-and-panko-crusted rack of lamb as the main," Javier told us as he checked on a baking sheet of balsamic-glazed butternut squash roasting in the oven. "It was served with individual watercress and cauliflower timbales and perfectly cooked Hasselback potatoes. Usually when I've had them, they've been half raw inside, but these were crispy on the outside and soft and creamy in the center. And they were drizzled with some kind of amazing cheese sauce." He closed the oven door and tucked his side towel into the strap of his white apron. "Maybe we should try them here sometime."

"Sure," I said. "Why not?"

"But it wasn't only the food that was great," he went on. "The whole room was decorated in this classy nineteen thirties style, with an old-style jazz band to match. It was super cool—just like one of those old black-and-white movies." Javier smiled as he reached for a spoon to stir the pot of *sauce normande* for tonight's pan-fried Petrale sole special, then went on to describe the massive tier of pink and white cupcakes they'd served in lieu of a traditional wedding cake.

But I was only half listening. At the mention of old black-and-white movies, my thoughts had flown back to the message we'd discovered on Jackie's phone.

I'd been so caught up with the idea of Max as the murderer that I'd nearly forgotten about Rachel—someone who had an actual, proven motive to want Jackie gone, and who not only loved jazz music but also had a known taste for cocktails made with cranberry juice.

And not only that, but the Streets of Delhi cook was sure to carry the aroma of curry spices about her person if she'd just come from work. *As she would have at eleven thirty last Wednesday, the first night the new pop-up was open . . .*

"Hey, Earth to Sally. You gonna cook something in that butter, or what?"

I refocused on Javier, who was pointing at the clarified butter simmering away in the sauté pan I held. "Oh, sorry," I said. With a chuckle, he pulled the now-browned butternut squash from the oven and set the hot baking sheet on the far side of the range top.

Tipping my pan away from me, I laid a thick pork chop into the hot butter. *Oh, well,* I mused. *Even if Rachel has now jumped back up as a prime suspect, there's nothing I can do about that right now.*

But there was something I *could* do tonight. "Hey, Javier," I said. "I was hoping you wouldn't mind if I took off for a half hour or so once the rush dies down. I have an errand I need to run."

*   *   *

At nine fifteen, I parked my car around the corner from Max's house and walked as nonchalantly as I could down the sidewalk. A single light shone from the front room, but there was no sign that anyone was home: no car in the driveway or out front, no sound coming from inside.

Smiling at a woman with a rotund pug pulling at its leash, I waited for her to turn the corner, then crept down the driveway. I'd worn dark clothing for my clandestine adventure but was still worried about a nosy neighbor spotting me, so I kept to the edge of the large hedge that bordered the property.

A low gate with a simple latch provided entry to a concrete patio. I pulled on the vinyl gloves I'd grabbed from the box in the *garde manger* at Gauguin, opened the gate, and stepped into the backyard. *Okay, Sal, you've now crossed both the literal and figurative thresholds of criminal trespassing.*

With a deep breath, I made my way to the nearest window and peered in. Dark. *Should I risk using my flashlight app?* Glancing around, I saw that a tall fence prevented any neighboring property from having a view of Max's back-yard, so I decided to take the chance.

I shined the light through the window and found myself looking into a bathroom with 1960s-style tile and white ceramic fixtures. A stack of magazines sat on the floor between the toilet and sink, and several towels were draped over the side of the tub.

I moved on to the other window facing the backyard. It was the kitchen, which boasted tile from the same era as the bathroom. Shining my phone around the room, I saw a stack of dirty dishes in the sink and several pots with drips of food running down their sides atop an old gas stove. Not much of a housekeeper, was Max. Which struck me as slightly odd, given his job as dining room manager at Tamarind.

A small table was on the far side of the kitchen, with only one chair. So he probably lived alone. Several more dishes sat on the table, as well as something flat that reflected back the light from my phone. *A laptop?* Yes, it was definitely the right size and shape. But from my angle, I had no way of knowing whether it was a MacBook Air or not.

Heart now thumping, I switched off my light. What to do?

Tons of people owned silver laptops, so what were the chances it was Jackie's? Certainly not worth the risk I faced if I tried to break into the house.

And yet . . .

I crept up the steps to the back door. What if he had a key hidden somewhere? Then it wouldn't really be "breaking" in, right? But the ex-lawyer in me knew damn well this was a distinction without a difference. Whether I gained access by way of a key, an unlocked door, or a battering ram, it would constitute an illegal entry into a private property.

Nevertheless, I lifted up one of the flowerpots to the right of the door. Nothing. Emboldened, I looked under the others. No key.

Ah, well, probably for the best, I thought as I turned to go. But then I spotted the ceramic elephant on the far side of the patio. I walked over and turned on my light once again. The sculpture was about a foot tall, cobalt blue with white stars sprinkled about its fat body, and had its trunk and right front leg raised as if trumpeting a call.

Switching off the phone, I stashed it in my pocket and used both hands to lift the elephant off the ground. And there it was, the glint of metal. Before I could talk myself out of it, I grabbed the key, dashed to the back door, and inserted it into the lock.

It worked; I was inside the kitchen.

Before I got halfway across the room, I saw the Apple logo and white sticker on the laptop, causing a prickling sensation to spread across my shoulders and down my arms. *So he* was *the one who took it.* Although I'd suspected as much, having the actual proof right here in front of me was chilling.

Next to the computer lay a sheet of paper with a list of words written down and then crossed out. By the dim light coming from the living room, I saw they were the same sort of password ideas that Evelyn and I had originally brainstormed, to no avail: *Evelyn, Coco, Curry Leaf,* Jackie's birth date, her street address. But Max had obviously not gotten in, based on the lines drawn through all the words—not to mention the fact that he hadn't yet ditched the computer.

Now that I knew he was the one who'd stolen the laptop from my car, I should have skedaddled out of there. I'd already checked Jackie's email remotely, via her phone, so what would be the point of logging on to her computer?

Still, I couldn't resist.

Okay, I thought, sitting down at the chair. *Let's hope she used the same password for both her devices.* I opened the lid and was greeted with the familiar login screen that had stymied me over a week ago. I typed J-E-A-N-A-R-T-H-U-R into the password box (though I fumbled the keys some, what with wearing gloves) and was rewarded by the screen immediately switching to Jackie's desktop graphics—a photo of Evelyn standing in a field of wild mustard, the yellow flowers set off by a vibrant blue sky behind.

Several dozen icons crowded the screen, and I scanned their titles to see if anything struck me as relevant to the case. Most looked to be related to the pop-up, with names such as "CL Invoices" and "Scheduling." But then my eyes landed on an icon entitled "ML."

Max Lacroix's initials.

Holding my breath, I clicked on the file. Four jpg files bearing dates from the previous July were inside. I opened the earliest of the photos and found myself looking at a screenshot of a point-of-sale terminal. It showed a partial list of the night's tickets, one of which was a voided cash payment of eighty-six dollars and thirty cents that had been approved by manager number two.

Which had to be Max. I was about to click open the second photo when a noise made me flinch.

What was that? I closed the laptop to extinguish its light and ducked down. Had a car door slammed out front? Heart thumping, I grabbed the computer off the table and squatted on the floor.

A man's voice could now be heard outside the house. From the volume, I guessed he was talking on his cell phone.

A key turned in the front door lock. *Uh-oh.* My hands now trembling, I closed the files, logged off the computer and slid it back on the table, then dashed across the kitchen and out into the backyard, closing the door silently behind me. I'd just replaced the key under the elephant's foot when the light went on in the kitchen. Through the window, I could see Max pull off his jacket and throw it onto the chair.

Why was he home now? Had Al confronted him about the voided tickets and he'd left Tamarind in a huff? Or perhaps it had simply been a slow Sunday and the place had cleared out early.

Crouching down, I watched Max take a beer from the fridge and lean on the counter as he drank deeply from the bottle. He would no doubt discover soon enough that his back door was unlocked, but hopefully he'd simply assume he'd left it that way by accident.

As I crept back down the driveway and out to the street, I took a series of deep breaths, trying to calm the shaking that had spread to the rest of my body. But nothing was going to calm the agitation that had overtaken me when I'd seen the screenshot of that voided ticket.

Not only had Jackie been aware of Max's embezzlement, but she'd kept proof of it on her computer.

Chapter 24

At eight the next morning the buzzing of my cell phone jarred me from a deep slumber. I'd stayed up only a half hour after getting home from work the night before, hoping to catch up on some of the shut-eye I'd lost of late. But it was not to be. Once in bed, visions of Max and Rachel, crouched over Jackie's dead body, had kept me tossing and turning for hours before I finally was able to nod off.

And then—after way too little sleep—my stupid phone woke me. I'd purposely switched off the ringer the night before, but the walnut dresser upon which it sat unfortunately acted as an amplifier for the vibrate mode I'd switched it to. As a result, the percussive throbbing that jarred me awake was at least as loud as my normal ringtone.

"What do you want?" I said groggily into the device, not even bothering to see who was calling.

"*Mado*, do you sound cranky this morning," a perky voice sang out.

"Marta. I should have known it was you. No one else ever calls this early. What, you looking for a riding partner this morning? Isn't it supposed to rain today?"

Marta was the director of the chorus Eric sang with, which I had joined the previous summer as an alto. She and I had bonded over our love of cycling, and even though I no longer sang with the chorus, we still rode together several times a month. It was always a good workout, as Marta—a dynamo of a gal from Naples—was fiercely competitive, which tended to bring out the same quality in me.

"Look out the window, *cara mia*. It is a glorious day for the *ciclismo*!"

I wasn't eager to leave the confines of my warm bed, but curiosity won out, so I crossed to the window and peeked through the curtains. She was right, as I'd known she would be. Marta was always right. Although the forecast had been for a big storm to roll in today, I was greeted by an electric-blue sky dotted with cotton ball clouds, and had to shade my still-dilated pupils from the bright sunlight streaming into the room.

I dropped the curtains back into place. Maybe an invigorating ride would help chase away thoughts of Rachel and Max, whose faces continued to haunt my thoughts even this morning. "Okay," I said. "I'm game. What's the plan?"

"Eight thirty, at the clock tower on Mission. We can head up to the university."

"Sounds good, but make it nine. I need some caffeine first."

*   *   *

Bombing back down High Street after our ride up to the UCSC campus, Marta and I took the middle of the pavement to prevent any cars from attempting a dangerous pass on the narrow road, then slowed for the right onto Storey. Three minutes later we were back where we'd started, under the Town Clock that stands as guardian at the top of the Pacific Garden Mall.

"Good workout," Marta said, pulling her phone from the pocket of her cycling jersey to check our time on Strava. "Over two minutes faster than last time." She enlarged the map with her fingers, nodding. "I thought so. We improved along the road at the top, coming up to Science Hill. But I am sure next time we can cut even more time off the climb, yes?"

"Right." I was still catching my breath from the hair-raising descent, where I'd done my best to keep up with the fearless Napolitana careening full-throttle down the hill, fingers not even touching her brake levers. "Maybe if I have about six more cups of coffee before we go, that could happen."

She slipped the phone back into her pocket and clipped into her right pedal. "I should go. I have to get home and call my mother before it's too late in Italy. Perhaps later this week we can go riding again?"

"Sure, weather permitting."

Marta sniffed. She considered my refusal to ride in the rain a serious character flaw. "You buy a bicycle that is named for the Paris-Roubaix," she'd once chided me, referring to the famous one-day bike race nicknamed the "Hell of the North" due to the rough cobblestone roads and brutal weather that often accompany it. "Yet you will not ride your *preciosa* Roubaix if there is even the slight wetness outdoors," she'd finished with a derisive shake of the head.

Whatever. I went on bike rides not simply to stay in shape, but also for enjoyment. And slogging through puddles, dodging detritus in the gutter, and worrying about being hit by cars to due poor visibility was definitely not my kind of fun.

After Marta took off for home, I pedaled leisurely down Pacific Avenue, taking advantage of the green "contraflow" bike lane that had been added a few years back. The shop- and restaurant-lined street was just coming to life, with vendors sweeping the sidewalk and setting out tables of sale merchandise to entice customers inside. Cruising by the alcove in front of an empty storefront, I waved at the Great Morgani, a local icon who—dressed in an outrageous black-and-white-striped costume from which at least fifty pointed cones protruded—was regaling the early-morning shoppers with his lively accordion music.

My plan was to head home to finish up work on the Gauguin scheduling, but first I had to drop Jackie's cell phone off at the police department. Carrying my bike up the cement stairs leading to the station, I wheeled it into the lobby and leaned it against the wall.

"Uh, no bicycles allowed inside," the woman at the reception window called out.

No one else was in the lobby, so I was able to come straight up to speak with her without waiting in line. "I don't have a lock, so I can't leave it outside. But I'll just be here a sec."

She frowned, but didn't order me and my bike outside, so that was a small victory.

"I just have something I need to drop off for Detective

Vargas," I said. I pulled Jackie's cell phone from the back pocket of my cycling jersey and set it on the counter. "It's the phone that belonged to Jackie Olivieri, the woman who was found dead in her home a couple weeks ago. He asked me and Jackie's daughter to look for it, and we found it on, uh . . . the other day. But you were closed over the weekend, so I had to wait till today to bring it in. I don't suppose he's in right now."

"No, he's not." She eyed the phone for a moment, then picked up a pen to maneuver it into a plastic evidence bag.

"It was buried under the cushions of Jackie's sofa," I said in an attempt to justify not having protected the device from contamination. "I'm sure she just lost it there, so I doubt it had any useful fingerprints or anything on it."

The woman ignored my remark as she wrote something on a sticker and affixed it to the bag.

"Oh, and you should write down the phone's password for Detective Vargas. It's Jean Arthur, no caps or spaces." At her blank look, I wrote it down for her. "She was a movie star from the thirties and forties. And make sure he reads the last text, the one from Rachel, because I think it might be important."

She stopped writing to stare at me. *Tampering with the evidence by using the phone,* her expression said, *as well as contaminating it?* With a soft exhalation, she finished writing what I'd said, jotted down my name and phone number, and slipped the paper into the bag with the phone. "Anything else?" she asked.

"No, that's all. Thanks."

"No, thank *you*," she said, finally cracking the hint of a smile. "But next time bring a bike lock."

*   *   *

Evelyn was at the stove when I got home, stirring a pan of scrambled eggs with a wooden spoon. "Late night last night?" I asked, setting my helmet on the Formica kitchen table.

"Yeah. I didn't fall asleep till about three, I think. But I only just woke up, so it's all good. I got plenty of sleep."

She touched the eggs to gauge their doneness, then turned off the burner and scraped them onto the plate she'd set out on the counter. At the sound of her toast popping up, she buttered the two slices and brought her breakfast to the table. "How was your ride?" she asked.

"Good." I pulled off my cycling shoes, which must have been making quite the racket. "But that Marta is a demon. She says she prefers riding with women because they're less competitive, but I sometimes think it's really because she has a better chance of beating me up the hills than she would with a guy."

I padded across the linoleum floor, poured myself coffee from the pot Evelyn had brewed, and took the cup to the fridge. "I was wondering if you might want to hang out tonight," I said. "Since Gauguin's closed, I thought maybe we could get a pizza delivered and watch a movie, as a sort of pre-birthday celebration."

"Oh, that's super sweet," Evelyn said with a smile. "But I actually already have plans for tonight with Molly and

Anne, since they can't come tomorrow. It'll just be me and Lucy for my real birthday dinner at Gauguin."

"That's okay. It's good you'll get to hang out with them tonight, then. And I could probably use an evening off, anyway. I've been going gangbusters the past few nights and I'm pretty beat." I poured a glug of half-and-half into my cup, then pulled out a chair to join Evelyn at the table, taking care not to bonk Buster on the nose. "I think I'll just stay in and watch something on Netflix. And maybe go ahead and order that pizza all for myself. One with linguica sausage. And extra cheese."

"Now you're making me wish I could stay home with you," Evelyn said with a laugh. I took a sip of coffee and then, noticing I still had on my cycling gloves, peeled them off and tossed them into my helmet. "So I need to tell you what I found out last night."

"You got into Max's house?" Evelyn set down the egg-laden fork she'd just raised to her lips.

"I did. And your Mom's laptop was in fact there."

"Ohmygod." She blinked a few times, then shook her head.

"And not only that," I went on, "but there was a file on the computer desktop with photos proving Max had been voiding tickets at Tamarind. So we now know that not only did your mom have the dirt on him, but she was keeping proof of it. He must have known about the photos, which was why he was so desperate to get her laptop."

"So that's it, then," Evelyn said softly. "He's the one who did it. To keep her from blabbing."

"Maybe. But there's also that text Rachel sent to your

mom that night, asking to see her. Which potentially places Rachel at the house the night she died."

"You're right. It could be either of them." Evelyn slumped over her half-eaten eggs. "So we're back to square one."

"Well, I'd say we've gotten to at least square two, having narrowed it down to Max and Rachel. Oh, and I dropped your mom's phone off at the police station just now, so maybe after Detective Vargas sees that text from Rachel he'll finally believe us about the murder and do some real investigating of his own."

"Did you give them her computer, too?" Evelyn asked.

"No. I left it at Max's house."

"Really? But—"

"I don't see that I had much of a choice," I interrupted, perhaps a bit too impatiently. "It was totally illegal what I did, breaking into his house like that. So first of all, no way do I want to get arrested for criminal trespass, and second, the evidence would probably be inadmissible in any case if they confiscated it based on my actions."

"Right." Evelyn frowned and pushed her plate to the center of the table. "But we can't just sit around and do nothing. One of those two murdered Mom, I'm sure of it."

"Agreed," I said. "And I sure don't relish the idea of waiting to see which one acts again first, since whoever did it likely knows we're on to them."

Chapter 25

Maria Callas was feigning a lightheartedness and nonchalance she did not feel. Or rather her character, Violetta, was. The Violetta for whom my Aunt Letta had been named and who, like my aunt, ended up in her grave far too young.

I was stretched out on the sofa listening to *La Traviata*, and Callas's fluid coloratura, as she sang of the pleasures of being free from love, struck me as simultaneously exultant and sad:

> *Sempre libera degg'io*
> *Folleggiare di gioia in gioia . . .*

"Ever free and aimless, I frolic from joy to joy," Verdi's famed courtesan insisted to the world. But it was a facade. What Violetta truly craved was the simplicity and consistency of one steadfast love—that of the provincial, bourgeois Alfredo.

And I could relate. Not to the bit about wanting a provincial lover, but to the part about lying to yourself. Or at least not knowing your desires as well as you'd thought you did. And now I had only myself to blame for spending the evening alone, ordering out for lukewarm pizza and listening to tragic heroines sing of passion and despair.

I'd put on the opera CD and poured myself a bourbon-rocks in the hopes of dispelling both my melancholy at the thought of Eric and Gayle spending "our" night together and my frustration at having finally narrowed the list of Jackie's possible killers down to two, only to hit a dead end.

But it wasn't working on either count.

The storm had finally arrived late this afternoon, and each time a tree branch knocked against the living room windows, I jumped, my thoughts returning to Max and Rachel. One of those two had killed Jackie and later attacked me, I was now sure. And whichever one it was would no doubt be eager to finish the job once they suspected I was truly on to them.

The CD came to an end, and I abandoned the comfort of the couch to slip in disk two and refresh my glass. Maybe having another drink would allow me to wallow in a pool of good, old-fashioned self-pity about Eric and at least temporarily forget my fears of being the killer's victim number two. I would then eat my pizza, watch a few episodes of *Chef's Table*, and collapse into bed by nine o'clock.

As I was dropping a trio of ice cubes into the glass, my cell buzzed from the kitchen table. I was in no mood for conversation but walked over to see who it might be. M VARGAS, the screen read.

Grabbing the phone, I swiped right to pick up the call. "Detective Vargas."

"Hi, Sally," he replied. "And yes, it's Martin."

"Right. Martin. Sorry. It may take a while to get used to that. But isn't it a little late for you to be working? It's after six."

"No rest for those of us fighting the never-ending battle for truth, justice, and the American way," he said with a chuckle.

"Uh-huh, that's how I always think of you. As the Man of Steel—minus the steel, that is." I poured a large splash of bourbon over my rocks and took a drink. "I gather you got the cell phone I dropped off?"

"I did. So where'd you find it?"

"Evelyn found it. Under the cushions of the living room sofa."

I heard him sigh, no doubt in part at the thought of us having contaminated the evidence by handling it. But he was also likely frustrated that his people hadn't found the phone when it had been in such an obvious spot.

"It was hidden down there pretty deep," I said in their defense, and by way of distracting him from the other issue. "The only reason Evelyn found it was because of her own superpowers. You know, of heightened touch."

"Right."

"Anyway, we figured it must have fallen out of her mom's back pocket or something and slipped down there the night she died." I cleared my throat. "So, uh, what did you think of that text from Rachel? You gonna talk to her?"

"I already did, and she has an alibi for the night Jackie died. She was at the rehearsal of her girlfriend's band until eleven, and then the four of them went out for drinks till well after midnight. I spoke with the members of the band, and her story checks out."

"Ah, that's good," I said. Though in truth, I was a little disappointed, as I'd wanted it to be Rachel. Which was unfair, since this was based largely on the cook's surly behavior toward me—not the best reason to suspect her of murder.

"When I asked why she'd sent that text," Vargas was going on, "she told me that even though she was still angry at Jackie—who apparently had fired her from The Curry Leaf—she wanted to give her a heads-up that she was going to be opening her own place, using some of the recipes the two of them had developed together."

"Yeah," I said, "that makes sense. Thanks for letting me know."

"No problem," he replied. "But there's actually another reason I'm calling. The lab report came in this afternoon for that substance you found on the bathroom counter."

"That Evelyn found, you mean."

"Noted. Anyway, the results are pretty interesting. It came back positive for Ambien and Percocet—"

"Like the bottles found next to her body," I cut in. "But why would there have been powder of those on the counter? They were in pill form."

"Good question," Vargas said. "But an even better one is, why would there also be cocaine mixed in with the other two? Because the lab results came back positive for that as well, which is what I suspected all the powder would be."

"Whoa. That's weird."

"Maybe not. I'm thinking it actually supports our finding

of suicide, that Jackie Olivieri simply took all the drugs she had available to her to, you know, do it."

"I don't know . . ." I thought a moment. "But what about that note using Evelyn's full name, when her mom never called her that?"

"Who can say? Maybe being as out of it as she was, she just wrote the full name without thinking."

But knowing what I did, I wasn't convinced. *Should I tell him about Jackie's computer being at Max's house?* It was absolutely the right thing to do, even if it would get me in a load of hot water. But maybe there was another way to get him interested in Max.

"I found out something else that might be important to the case," I said. "Al, the owner of Tamarind, told me he just learned his dining room manager, Max, has been embezzling from the restaurant by voiding checks and pocketing the money."

"I'm not sure exactly how that would relate to Jackie's death," Vargas said.

"It's relevant because if Jackie knew about it and threatened to tell Al, it would provide a strong motive for Max to want her dead."

"*If* she knew," he repeated. "But we don't know that, do we?"

I chose not to answer this rhetorical question, on the grounds that it could incriminate me. "Well, couldn't you get a warrant to search his house based on his theft?" I asked instead.

The detective snorted. "Doubtful," he said. "But I will talk to the Tamarind owner and see what evidence he has that this Max character has been stealing from the restaurant. In the meantime, I want a promise from you not to try and do something stupid like going over to Max's house yourself."

"How could you possibly think that of me?" I asked with a laugh.

"I'm serious," he said. "No snooping around there on your own. I don't want you fouling up our investigation, and I don't want to see you end up in the ER again, either, like last time."

"That so was not my fault!"

"Uh-huh." He made no attempt to hide his sarcasm. "So you promise?"

"Yessir. I promise."

"Good."

He ended the call, and I returned to the living room with my cocktail. Boisterous male voices were now booming from the speakers—the pack of matadors hired to entertain the party guests in act two—so I skipped the CD forward several tracks to something more sedate.

Stretching out once more on the couch, I listened as the two lovers sowed the seeds of their tragic demise and thought about what Vargas had told me. *Could it have been Jackie's cocaine?* If so, that would likely mean she'd been using it before that night as well. She had, after all, been under extreme stress in the weeks leading up to her death, according to Evelyn. And she surely could have gotten the drug if she'd wanted, working in the restaurant business where it was such a common menace.

But I'd known a couple of cokeheads in my day, and it was hard for me to believe her daughter wouldn't have noticed if Jackie had been one. In my limited experience, they tended to experience wide swings of emotion, all lovey-dovey when high, then depressed and snarky-mean after the come-down. And the one I'd known who'd used the stuff in large quantities had ended up a complete jerk—selfish and manipulative, able to turn on the charm in a flash if he thought he could get something out of you.

The results of Jackie's toxicology report wouldn't be available for weeks or even months to come, but I knew in my heart that she hadn't used cocaine the night she died—at least not willingly.

And then it hit me—who it was that oozed a combination of charm and smarm. Max, who'd laid on that have-I-got-something-for-you familiarity the night Eric and I had been at Tamarind, just like a druggie. He'd been smarmy, all right—unctuous and eager to please, even though he barely knew me. And although some of it could be chalked up to his being maître d' of the restaurant, he hadn't even been working that night.

Visions of Max flashed through my mind: wiping his nose at the memorial service, scratching and pinching it that night he'd talked to us. By itself, this behavior would likely mean nothing. But one of the most common tics of drug users is to fuss with their nose, as if worried that tell-tale signs of the powder are still there.

I sat up, startling the two dogs asleep at the foot of the sofa. And the other thing I knew about cocaine was that it could be a very expensive habit. Which would explain why someone like Max, even though he had a well-paying job, could succumb to the temptation to steal from his place of employment.

Buster jumped onto the couch next to me, and as I stroked his rough, brown coat, I considered what this could all mean. If Max was indeed a drug addict, that would be something else he'd want to keep from his boss—and yet another reason to want to shut Jackie up if she'd threatened to tell.

I got up and started pacing across the living room, my brain churning. This was the first time all the pieces of the puzzle had seemed to come together in a way that made sense. Max must have gone upstairs to the bathroom, where he'd discovered the Ambien and Percocet in the medicine cabinet. And then he'd gotten an idea of how to be rid of Jackie forever. But he'd needed some extra courage to do the deed, so while crushing the drugs to slip into Jackie's drink, he'd ingested some of his own.

But did the other pieces fit? Jazz lover? Check. Fan of cranberry juice? Who knew. But Max did likely drink, given his hanging out at the Tamarind bar that night Eric and I had been there. And besides, whoever had slipped the crushed Ambien and Percocet into Jackie's drink would have wanted a cocktail that hid the taste of the drugs, so maybe it was Jackie who'd had the drink with cranberry juice, not the killer.

And finally, the scent of curry spice on the person. Max wasn't a cook at Tamarind, but I knew from my experience running the front of the house at Solari's that he'd be in and out of the kitchen all evening for various reasons. So he could certainly carry the aroma with him.

I ceased my pacing and strode back to the kitchen to check the time on my phone: a quarter to seven. And it was Monday, the same night Max had been hanging out at the Tamarind bar last week on his day off.

Would he be there again tonight? Maybe not, depending on what had happened between him and Al last night. But I also knew that Monday was Al's night off. So it was worth a shot.

Forgetting my plans to spend the evening with a linguica pizza and Netflix, I headed upstairs to change clothes. Yes, Detective Vargas had made me promise not to go to Max's house, but he hadn't said a thing about going to Tamarind.

Chapter 26

I parked the T-Bird on a side street around the corner from Tamarind and hurried to the entrance through the steady rain. The steam blanketing the inside of the windows made it difficult to see inside the restaurant, but I could tell the place was once again popping.

As soon as I opened the door, I was hit by a rush of warm air and the seductive smell of sesame oil and garlic. Raised voices echoed off the black-and-white tile floor, and the same host who'd been on duty last Monday had to call out over the din to inquire whether I wanted a table.

Shaking my head no, I paused a moment, peering over at the bar area. About a dozen people were there, most standing around waiting for tables, but a few seated with their backs to me. I quickly spotted Max. He was near the end of the bar, chatting with the bartender as she placed dirty glasses in the washer rack. Laughing at something she'd just said, Max took a sip from what looked like a Martini.

Okay, now or never. I made my way to the bar and took an empty stool three down from his. The bartender shoved the now-full rack into the under-counter washer, closed the door, and switched it on. Glancing up, she caught my eye and came over to where I sat. "Evening. What can I get for you?"

"A Martini up would be great. You have any of that local gin?"

"The Venus?" She turned to examine the bottles behind the bar. "Yeah, looks like we've got their oh-one."

"Perfect. And go easy on the vermouth."

While she shook my cocktail in a stainless-steel shaker and strained it into a chilled, olive-garnished glass, I pretended not to notice Max, who I could see from the corner of my eye *had* noticed me. I'd opted for a Martini, rather than my usual bourbon-rocks, with the idea that he'd be pleased to see me ordering "his" drink, making it more likely he'd come chat me up.

My ploy worked. As soon as the bartender had served me my iced delight, there came a voice from behind. "Nice choice of cocktail."

I swiveled around on my stool. "Oh, hi," I said with a smile. "It's . . . wait, I'll remember . . ."

"Max," he supplied. "Do you mind?" He indicated the stool next to mine.

"Be my guest."

"What brings you back to our lovely restaurant so soon?"

I sipped my Martini. My, that gin was delicious. In addition to the customary juniper, I got hints of lemon and ginger as well. "Two things," I said, setting down the stemmed glass. "One, I enjoyed those spring rolls with peanut sauce so much last week that I couldn't resist coming back for more."

"And the second?"

I swiveled back around and put on a glum face, staring at the shelves of liquor, made double by the massive mirror behind them. "The guy I asked out tonight turned me down for another woman, so I decided to drown my sorrows with a Martini."

I'd made a snap decision to act the jilted lover, figuring Max wouldn't be able to resist turning on the charm in response. And maybe if I was lucky, he'd drop his guard and simultaneously drop some revealing information.

But it wasn't going to take much acting to put on a persuasive show, since I was in fact feeling pretty darn glum right about now.

"That guy who was here with you last week?" The flicker of Max's eyes told me his interest had jumped up a notch. "Well, his loss."

"Uh, thanks."

I flagged down the bartender, hoping to order some food. I'd started to feel the effects of that bourbon I'd had at home and, with a fresh cocktail before me, thought it best to take in some sustenance. But it also seemed wise not to give Max the impression I'd come there that night in the hopes of seeing him. Hard-to-get seemed the better tactic.

The gal behind the bar poured a pair of frothy yellow drinks into glasses, set them on a cocktail tray at the server station, then came back over to where I was sitting.

"Could I get an order of spring rolls with peanut sauce?"

"Sure thing." She entered the order into the POS system and returned with a glass of water and a set of flatware wrapped in a green cloth napkin.

"Thanks." I sipped from the water, staring at the computer

screen behind the bar—very likely the terminal from which Max had been voiding all those tickets. But how on earth was I going to get him to show his hand and give me something to prove his connection to Jackie's death?

I swiveled back around on my stool and flashed what I hoped came across as an encouraging smile. If I played *too* hard to get, I might lose my fish entirely. "You're still doing a booming business here, I see."

"Yep. Kind of exhausting, but it's better than the alternative."

"I hear ya." I tipped my glass to him, then took another taste of my aromatic gin.

Max grinned, revealing the crooked teeth in his lower jaw. "So what do you do when you're not running a restaurant?" he asked.

"Oh, I keep pretty busy," I said. "It's not like I have a whole lot of free time, but when I do, I ride my bike, walk my dog, hang out with friends, listen to music."

"What kind of music do you like?"

"Lots of kinds. Rock, new wave, opera . . ."

He wrinkled his nose at the mention of this last category. "I dunno, I could never get into that opera stuff. All those screeching women and people jabbering in German and Italian."

I've heard this reaction enough times by now that it no longer raises my hackles to the extent it used to. But I still have to fight back the urge to respond with a lecture on the aesthetics of grand opera.

"Yeah," I said instead with a shrug, "it's not for everybody. Oh, and I like jazz, too."

Max perked up at this, as I'd hoped he would. "Jazz, now that's my thing." He nodded his head enthusiastically, then drained the rest of his Martini. "What sort do you listen to?"

"Well, I like whatever's on right now." I knew damn well that what was playing over the bar speakers was what's known as "cool jazz," a style marked by its more subdued playing and relaxed tempos as compared to the often-frenetic improv employed in bebop. But I wanted to give Max the chance to show off and try to impress me, an invitation he eagerly accepted.

"That's Chet Baker," he said. "He's pretty unusual, in that he was both a singer and a horn player. An amazing dude."

We listened to the whisper-voiced singer, who, after coming to the end of the chorus of "My Funny Valentine," launched into a pensive trumpet solo. Cranked up as the music was in order to be heard over the chatter of the restaurant patrons, Baker's playing still came across as intimate and vulnerable.

"This style is sometimes called West Coast jazz," Max said in a lecturing voice when the song had come to an end. "Because so many of the guys who played it back in the fifties lived in LA and San Francisco." A more up-tempo tune had followed the Chet Baker song, and Max was bobbing his head and drumming his fingers on the bar in time to the syncopated beat. "If you like this kind of jazz," he said, reaching up to scratch his nose, "you should really check out guys like Miles Davis and Paul Desmond and Stan Getz."

"Thanks, I will." I had several CDs by those well-known artists at home, but wasn't going to tell him that. "But I'm actually more into jazz vocals," I said. "So who's your favorite jazz singer, if you had to pick only one?"

"Oh man, that's hard. There are so many." Max put his elbows on the bar top and frowned. Tapping a finger against his front tooth, he considered my question. "I'm tempted to say Ella Fitzgerald, but I think if I could only pick one, I'd have to go with Sarah Vaughan. She was more free, more uninhibited, I guess."

"Sounds kind of like what my mom always said about Frank Sinatra and Mel Tormé. That Sinatra was more suave and controlled with his phrasing, but that Tormé could sing circles around Frank, especially when he was young. What do you think?"

I'd been watching Max closely as I brought up the subject of Mel Tormé, whose record we'd found misplaced in Jackie's house. I was hoping to catch him flinch or suck in his breath, but all he did was chew his lip and stare at the Kingfisher beer poster behind the bar.

"I'd have to go for Frank," he said after a bit.

So maybe it hadn't been Max who'd played that album that night. But I wasn't ready to give up yet. "But you must like Mel, too. Talk about a smooth voice. I mean c'mon, who doesn't like 'The Velvet Fog'?"

He turned to face me, his eyes searching mine. Then, with a quick shake of the head, he said, "No, not really. I'm more of a bebop kind of guy. You know, Charlie Parker, Dizzy Gillespie, Coltrane."

Climbing off his barstool, he smoothed out the front

of his gray silk shirt. *Oh, no. I've blown it and scared him off.*

But I was wrong. "Just gotta hit the men's room," he said, pointing a thumb toward the back of the restaurant. "Be right back."

"Oh, okay. I'll be here."

A waiter appeared with my spring rolls. *Good.* I was famished. I picked one up but immediately dropped it again. Way too hot. Making do with dipping my fork into the ramekin of peanut sauce, I waited for the rolls to cool.

Max plopped back down onto his stool and wiped his nose once again. I couldn't be sure, but I thought I detected a tiny streak of white on its aquiline tip. Had he gone to the restroom to snort a few lines of coke? Or was my imagination simply concocting evidence to support my suspicions regarding the guy?

He held up his empty glass to the bartender, then glanced over at me. "Can I buy you another?"

I drained my Martini and smiled. "Sure, that would be great."

While Max ordered, I took a tentative bite of my spring rolls. Max was eyeing the plate, so I shoved it his way. "Help yourself, if you'd like."

"Okay. Thanks." He picked one up, dunked it into the peanut sauce, and ate half the crispy roll in one bite.

The bartender set down our Martinis, and Max and I clinked glasses. He finished off his spring roll as I nibbled mine. It was still pretty hot, and I was impressed he could take such big bites without burning his mouth. But then again, he was chasing them with gulps of icy gin.

Dipping the unchewed end of my roll into the peanut sauce (since we were sharing, I thought it rude to double dip), I raised it to my mouth, only to have a dribble of sauce fall onto the front of my yellow blouse.

"Dagnabbit," I said, staring at the oily brown splatter. It had managed to fall onto not only my shirt but also my green tweed blazer. "I better wash this off right away so it doesn't stain."

I set the roll back on the plate, slid off my stool, and headed for the restroom. But as I reached the far end of the room, something made me turn back. A niggling at the back of my brain—something I'd read about never leaving a drink unattended at the bar, which seemed especially apt if you were with a guy you suspected might be a murderer.

Peeking out from behind a large potted palm like someone out of an old Marx Brothers movie, I stared at Max. He was fishing for something in the pocket of his pressed blue jeans, then glanced quickly to either side.

No way. Could I be right?

Waiting till the bartender was occupied with ringing up a sale on the POS screen, he pulled my drink toward him. My glass—as well as Max's hands—were now blocked from view by his body, but a few seconds later he shoved the Martini back to its place in front of my barstool, then picked up his own drink and took a sip.

No one appeared to have noticed his actions, but then again, the only one who likely could have was the bartender, and she had her back to Max. *Whoa.* This was unreal.

In a bit of a daze, I pushed open the door to the women's room and set about rinsing the peanut sauce off my blouse.

I must have gone too far, after all, with my questions about Mel Tormé. Which meant Max *was* the one who'd been at Jackie's house that night playing Evelyn's jazz records. And now, fearing I was on to him, he was trying to drug me— just as he'd done to Jackie.

Thank goodness I'd seen what he'd done. But now I had to figure out how to play this. If I confronted him about dosing my drink, I'd simply end up making a scene, and any chance of getting information out of him would be forever lost. So how best to act, to make him think I suspected nothing?

I crossed back to the bar and bought a little time by eating more of my spring roll and washing it down with a drink of water. And then it hit me: if I could replace the gin in my glass with water without his seeing, he'd be none the wiser that I was on to his despicable plan.

But the "without his seeing" part would be difficult, given how closely he was monitoring my every move. *Go on, drink your Martini*, I could tell he was thinking. I had to distract him, somehow. Did I have anything on me I could use? I reached into my blazer pocket and felt a handkerchief and several loose coins. *Aha.*

Feigning a sneeze, I pulled out the hankie, making sure I had the coins in my hand as well. As I opened up the cloth to use it to wipe my nose, I let the money fall to the floor. It got the desired reaction. Max immediately jumped off his stool and crouched down to collect the jingling coins from the tile floor.

"Oh, thanks," I said as I dipped the hankie into my drink, then dumped the contents of the stemmed glass into the drip tray along the bar top and quickly refilled it with water from my tumbler. I'd just retrieved the olive and dropped it back into my glass when Max stood up and handed me my quarters.

Accepting them with a broad smile, I took a long drink from my faux Martini, which prompted an equally broad smile from Max. I shoved the coins and the handkerchief—which now contained evidence of the adulterated drink, or so I hoped—into my jacket pocket.

And along with them, I pocketed my fork. Just in case.

Now all I had to do was play-act that the drug was working. *How long would it be before whatever he put in my drink would take effect?* Best to finish the drink quickly, not only to hasten whatever time frame that would be, but also so he didn't look too closely and notice that it was water in my glass rather than gin.

With a flirtatious laugh, I drank down the rest of the drink. "That Venus really is good," I said. "I'm going to have to buy a bottle to have at home." I picked up my partially eaten spring roll, and Max reached for the last one on the plate. I wondered if he was afraid that if I ate too much, the drug wouldn't work as well. Or maybe he was simply one of those uncouth boors who took more than their share of the appetizers at restaurants.

"So, I told you what I did with my time off work," I said, licking peanut sauce off my fingers. "How about you?"

Max launched into a detailed description of his hobbies: mountain biking up at Wilder Ranch, tasting and collecting wine, going to jazz clubs, traveling. "I have a trip planned this summer for Italy, actually," he said. "Have you ever been?"

"Not yet. But someday I hope to make it there. I'm told I have a ton of relatives back in Liguria."

We actually had a lot in common, I realized. Too bad he was such a scumbag, or we could perhaps have been pals. But no way would I ever want to be alone with this creep, much less be a friend of his.

"Where ya gonna go 'n It'ly?" I asked, purposely starting to slur my words.

"Let's see. Rome, Florence, Pisa, Venice. I really want to see Venice before it's covered in water. What with the rising tides from climate change, it won't be long before it's completely—"

"Innn . . . dated," I interrupted, then giggled. "Man, thas hard to say. I think that last drink kinda went to my head. Maybe I should order something else to eat."

Max was staring at me intently, the hint of a smile forming on his lips. "Or I could give you a ride home, if you wanted. I'm thinking you probably shouldn't drive, even if you do have something more to eat."

I thought a moment. *What do I want to do?* It didn't look like I'd be getting any more information out of him tonight, and since he'd clearly moved into full-on aggressor mode, it seemed time to bail. I did have that handkerchief that I could give to Vargas to have analyzed, so the evening wasn't a total loss.

"No, I'm okay to drive," I said. "But I do think you're right that I should probably get home." I slid off the stool and took my purse from the hook under the bar. Pulling a twenty and a couple singles from my wallet, I laid them on the bar to pay for my drink and spring rolls. "Thanks for the Martini, and maybe I'll see you here again some-time soon."

I walked to the front entrance, doing my best to act slightly wobbly, but not so out of it that he wouldn't believe I could drive home. On opening the door, however, I was nearly knocked off my feet, which certainly heightened the realism of my act. In the short time I'd been at the Tama-rind bar, a virtual tempest had apparently descended upon Santa Cruz, and gusts of wind and pelting rain came flying into the restaurant as I tried to regain my balance and make my way outdoors.

"Close the damn door!" someone shouted from a nearby table.

"Sorry . . ."

A steadying hand grasped me on the shoulder, and I turned to see who it was.

"Here. I have an umbrella. At least let me walk you to your car."

It was Max.

Chapter 27

"No," I said. "I'm okay. But thanks." I tried to get past him and out the door, but he still had hold of me by the shoulder.

"Really? In this downpour? You'll get drenched. C'mon." Max steered me outside under the Tamarind awning, then opened his large black umbrella. "So where are you parked?"

I stood there buttoning up my blazer, trying to decide what to do. The last thing I wanted right now was to have Max accompany me to my car. But short of going back into the restaurant, I didn't see as I had much choice. And even if I did dash inside and accuse Max of accosting me, the dining room staff all worked under the guy, so realistically, what were they going to do?

"Okay, fine," I said, stepping out from under the awning. "It's this way."

Max held the umbrella over the two of us as we made our way down the sidewalk, continuing to chat about the trip he had planned to Italy this summer. I did my best to act slightly out of it, wobbling a bit as I walked, but he didn't appear to notice. He was too busy telling me how excited he was to finally get to see the Roman Pantheon, which, despite being almost two thousand years old, he told me enthusiastically, still boasted the largest unreinforced concrete dome in the world.

Maybe I'd been wrong. Maybe he hadn't doped my drink after all and only wanted to walk me to my car out of chivalry—or at least in the hope of continuing our relationship, such as it was. The way he was going on and on about that ancient Roman building sure didn't suggest anything other than a purely innocent objective.

I turned the corner at the side street where my car was parked a block down. Now that we were off the main drag, the road was darker due to the lack of streetlamps and the cars few and far between. I quickened my gait, and Max had to trot a few steps to catch up. He'd now moved on to the subject of the superiority of Italian pizza over the American variety and wanted to know my opinion.

"Well, now that a lot of places here have those wood-burning ovens, I think you can get just as good pizza in the States as there." I stopped at the T-Bird. "This is me," I said.

He whistled. "Nice car." I watched to see if he had any reaction to the patch job I'd done on the car's ragtop, but he showed no sign of noticing it.

"Thanks," I said. "And thanks for keeping me dry getting here." Walking around the car to the driver's side, I waved goodbye, then unlocked the door.

Max tipped an imaginary hat from where he stood on the sidewalk.

I dropped into the bucket seat, started the ignition, and switched on the wipers and fan. With a sigh of relief that the ancient car had started right up, I let out the clutch, jammed the stick into first, and started forward—only to realize the windshield was so fogged up I couldn't see a thing in front of me.

Cursing the car's Precambrian-era defogger, I hit the brake and grabbed the towel I keep in the driver's-side map compartment. But before I could take even one swipe at the condensation dripping down the windshield, the passenger side door opened and Max slid into the seat.

What the—? How could he have gotten in? I always kept the car locked.

But then I remembered: I'd driven Evelyn to Sunday dinner the day before, and she must have neglected to lock the door. It's a common occurrence with people who ride with me, since these days everyone is in the habit of letting the driver lock all the doors at once with the push of a button. But the sixty-plus-year-old T-Bird, of course, came with no such automatic locking system; it has those old-school button locks you have to push down manually.

"What are you doing?" I asked.

He set the dripping umbrella at his feet. "Just thought I'd come in out of the rain. It's nice and cozy in here."

"Okay," I said, "you need to get out of the car and let me drive home."

But he made no move to leave, instead turning to me with an unfriendly smile. I leaned as far back against the door as I could. "Get out. *Now!*" I shouted. When he still didn't move, I reached for my door handle. If he wasn't going to get out of the car, then I would.

Max reached out to grasp my right hand in a tight grip.

"Not so fast," he hissed in my ear. A whiff of galangal spice lit up my senses like an electric shock. *Ohmygod, it* was *him that night.* The smile had now become a grimace. "We have some unfinished business to complete, concerning a certain party who's no longer with us."

Struggling to pull free, I started to scream. "Help! He's attacking me!" The street was empty of people and cars, however, and even if there had been anyone nearby, they likely wouldn't have heard over the sound of the hard rain.

"Shut up," Max said hoarsely, leaning in close once more. I screamed again in response, even louder this time. "Help! *Help* me!" I was taking a deep breath to redouble my efforts when something soft was shoved against my face, forcing me back, against the car door. The intense smell of wet dog hit me briefly, only to be quickly shut off as I realized I could no longer breath.

Buster's pillow. He was trying to suffocate me with the dog cushion that had been at his feet.

As I struggled to free myself, the conversation with Detective Vargas about Jackie's death flashed through my brain—how the opiates she'd consumed had caused her to essentially die of suffocation. So if Max had finished her off with a pillow, no one would be the wiser.

"*No!*" I managed to utter into the dense mass of cushion. I was not going to go out like Jackie.

I had one thing in my favor. Max believed I'd drunk that drug-laced Martini, so he'd assume I was weaker and more out of it than I actually was. I had to use that to my advantage.

Letting my body relax, I slumped down as if losing

consciousness and, at the same time, let my hand fall into the pocket of my blazer. It was scary, because Max's first reaction to this was to press the cushion even harder against my face. But another thing he didn't know was that I had strong lungs from all that cycling, and could go without oxygen for longer than he likely suspected.

After a moment he stopped pushing. I could hear his loud breathing, as if he were the one who'd been under attack. I figured he was wondering what to do now. Was I unconscious? Dead?

Time to act, before he realized he needed to keep the pillow tight against my face in order to finish me off. With my right hand, I shoved with all my might against the cushion. Caught unawares as he was, he fell back slightly, letting the pillow slip from his grasp. In that brief moment, his face was exposed, and I looked into a pair of surprised brown eyes with enormous, dilated pupils.

Closing my own eyes, I stabbed the fork into Max's face. I wasn't sure exactly where it landed, but the jab was followed immediately by a howl of pain. He brought both hands to his face, and I turned and fumbled with the door latch, finally managed to get it open, and jumped out.

Without turning to see whether or not he was following, I tore down the middle of the dark, wet street as fast as I could.

* * *

The next afternoon I sat once more on the small couch in the SCPD interview room, Detective Vargas—no, Martin—on the chair opposite me.

"He of course denies everything," the detective was saying. "He claims you invited him into the car and then all of a sudden just freaked out and attacked him with a fork. He wants me to press charges against you and claims he's going to sue you for damages."

"Do you believe him?"

Vargas shook his head. "Not one bit. He was high as a kite when we picked him up last night, with pupils the size of golf balls. And," he said with a smile, "we found about a gram of coke on him, as well as an empty vial with traces of ketamine—the same substance the tests showed to be on that handkerchief you gave the cop last night."

"Ketamine?"

"Uh-huh. Special K, they call it. It's a party drug, and folks sometime like to mix it with uppers—such as that cocaine our guy had on him. It's fast acting and causes, among other things, impaired motor function, distorted perceptions, and, get this: problems breathing."

"Whoa."

He nodded, and I imagined we were thinking the same thing: if I'd actually drunk that ketamine-laced Martini, my chances of surviving the encounter with Buster's cushion the night before would have been slim indeed. "Are you thinking that's what happened with Jackie?" I asked.

"I think there's a good chance it is, especially given what happened to you last night. And that would explain the crushed Percocet and Ambien in the upstairs bathroom. He must have found them in the medicine cabinet, come up with his plan, and then crushed and dissolved them in Jackie's drink."

"Exactly my thought," I said. "And he used the cranberry juice to disguise the flavor. That would explain how the bottle got moved and also the red stain on the carpet."

"Great minds think alike," Vargas said. "I'd come to the same conclusion."

"And Max was obviously the one using the cocaine upstairs in the bathroom."

The detective tapped a finger on the file in his lap. "We'll have to wait to see what the tox report on Jackie says when it comes back, to be sure. But I'm guessing you're right and it'll be negative for cocaine."

Shifting on the saggy couch, I studied the colorful photo on the wall of the Giant Dipper roller coaster, trying to organize my thoughts. "And I'm pretty sure I know *why* he did it, too," I said. I told Vargas what Evelyn had overheard Max say to Jackie and explained my "scratch your back" theory. "Max promises to get Al off her case about the recipes, and in exchange, Jackie agrees to keep quiet about Max stealing from the restaurant—and maybe his drug use, too. But then Al keeps on bad-mouthing her around town, so Jackie threatens to tell Al about Max. Max freaks out and decides to kill her."

"Yeah, makes sense to me," he said.

"So what do you think?" I asked. "You have enough evidence to charge Max with murder?"

He grinned. "If that was all we had, I'd say maybe not. But we actually have something to place him at the house the night Jackie Olivieri died."

I leaned forward. "What?"

"Well, it was what you told the responding officer last

night about that record album that had been moved—Mel somebody?" he said, opening the file in his lap.

"Tormé."

"Right. That guy. We had it dusted for prints this morning, and guess whose were on it?"

"Max's."

He nodded. "You got it. So with Evelyn's statement that the record had been moved sometime after she left that afternoon to go to her friend's house, along with those prints, we've got him there the night Jackie died. I also had that upstairs bathroom checked for prints, and they found a partial on the counter that looks like it belongs to Max, too."

"Yes!" I pumped my fist.

"And there's even more," the detective said, a glint in his eyes. "We got a warrant to search Max's house and found Jackie Olivieri's laptop there."

I tried to hide my smile, but it didn't matter, since Vargas had looked down and was studying the case file.

"And there was a file on the computer," he went on, "with photos showing instances where Max had voided out sales, which goes a long way toward supporting your theory about his motive for killing her. So, with all that, along with what happened last evening, it's not looking too good for the guy."

Vargas closed the folder and stood. "Okay, well, I'm going to need an official statement from you sometime in the next day or so, but I think we're done here for now." He shifted from one foot to the next, fidgeting with something in his slacks pocket. "I know you need to get going to work, so . . ."

"You look like there's something more," I said.

"Uh, yeah, actually there is. I was just wondering if, well, maybe you wanted to go grab a bite to eat sometime." He smiled uncomfortably, then cleared his throat. "It just kind of seems like the gods have been throwing us together an awful lot lately. Maybe we should just go ahead and get to know each other a little better. You know, when there's no dead body involved."

"Sure," I said, returning his smile. "That sounds fun. But maybe not Southeast Asian food. I think I need a break from that for a while."

Chapter 28

"You *what*?" Lucy came close to spitting out her mouthful of Kahlúa, vodka, and cream, only managing to clap a palm over her lips just in time. I'd been telling the story of my encounter with Max the night before, and she'd had the unfortunate timing to take a large drink of her White Russian right as I got to the bit about the fork. "Oh, man, that is *so* gross! But pretty awesome, too."

Evelyn patted her on the forearm. "I told you my cousin was super cool."

Lucy laughed and reached out with one hand to locate the top of the table, then set the drink she held in the other on the white tablecloth. "Do you know where you got him with the fork? I mean, did you *see* it?"

"Ewwww!" Evelyn shrieked, and the two friends erupted in giggles.

"No," I answered. "I took off as fast as I could once I heard him scream, so I didn't get the chance to see the results of my handiwork. But the detective told me this afternoon that I got him pretty bad on the cheek and that the fork missed his eye by only about an inch."

"Lucky guy," said Javier. "Not that he didn't earn it, but no one really deserves to lose an eye. Though I have heard that women sometimes go for guys with an eye patch." He started to laugh, then stopped, as if suddenly realizing that jokes about the loss of eyesight might not be all that appropriate in the present company.

But Evelyn and Lucy had no such qualms. Both burst out laughing once again, and Evelyn slapped Javier lightly on the arm.

I watched the two women with a smile. Evelyn was enjoying her first-ever cocktail—a Pink Squirrel, just like we'd joked about her ordering to celebrate her twenty-first birthday. The Gauguin bartender had needed to look up the recipe on his phone, he'd said, because it was the first time he'd made the drink in about twenty years. And since Gauguin didn't stock crème de noyaux, he'd had to substitute amaretto and a splash of grenadine for the almond flavor and pink color.

But Evelyn didn't care. She'd proclaimed it "amazingly yummy," especially the dollop of whipped cream that topped the already intensely sweet concoction. I was monitoring her closely, because the ice cream in the cocktail hid the potency of all the liqueur that also went into the drink. I didn't mind if she got slightly tipsy, but I sure as hell didn't want to be the cause of her first hangover.

For the time being, however, it was clear the two friends were simply being silly. As well they should. Although they'd seen each other at the memorial service and taught that workshop together at the Vista Center the previous week, this was the first time they'd gotten to just hang out and have fun since Jackie's death.

I looked up to see Brandon striding across the dining room bearing a pair of large plates. "Incoming!" I called out.

"Who has the Divine Decadence?" the server asked.

"I do." Lucy's hand shot up, and she leaned back to allow him to set the chocolate monstrosity before her.

"And the bread pudding?"

"That's me," I said. I don't order dessert all that often, but I figured I merited one tonight. And the thought of the moist challah bread soaked in cream, sugar, and egg—really more of a baked French toast than an actual pudding—drizzled with a rich crème anglaise, had been too much to resist.

"Be back with the others in a jiff," Brandon said, then scooted across the dining room.

I leaned over to tell Lucy where things were on her plate. "Okay, so there's a scoop of chocolate mousse at twelve o'clock, two chocolate-and-coconut macarons at three, a slice of bittersweet chocolate hazelnut tart at six, and two pieces of chocolate bark with ginger, fennel, and sea salt at nine o'clock."

"Ohmygod. I'll never be able to eat all that."

"I warned you," Javier said with a chuckle.

"No worries," Evelyn chimed in. "I'll help you with—" But she was interrupted by a chorus of voices coming our way.

"Happy birthday to you," the waitstaff sang, and the few diners besides us still left in the restaurant all joined in. "Happy birthday, dear Evelyyyyyyn . . . Happy birthday to you!" Brandon set a puffy lemon soufflé down in front of the birthday girl as we all clapped.

"There's a candle," Javier said, leaning over to touch her on the shoulder. "Make a wish and blow out the flame."

She thought a moment, then grinned and blew, missing the pink-and-white-striped candle by about four inches.

"A little more to your right," he prompted.

Evelyn did as Javier said, but the fact that she was laughing at the same time made the blowing difficult. Nevertheless, the flame sputtered and went out.

We all clapped once again, and Brandon set down Javier's dessert—a slice of apple pie with a scoop of French vanilla ice cream nestled at its side.

"There's a certain way to eat soufflés," Javier said to Evelyn as she picked up her spoon. "Want me to show you how?"

"Absolutely." She offered him the spoon, which he accepted.

"First, you make a hole in the top." He punched out the dome of the puffed marvel, releasing a burst of steam. The walls held momentarily, then sagged. "Next, you pour in some of the crème anglaise. How much would you like?"

"Lots! I love cream. Just like Sally," she said, turning my way with a grin.

Javier picked up the small pitcher Brandon had left and poured a stream of the creamy custard into the center of the soufflé, then handed Evelyn the spoon. "Okay, all ready," he said. "But be careful, because it's still very hot."

The table became quiet as we savored our desserts in silence, save for the occasional "uhhh" and "yuuum."

Lucy was the first to speak. "Maybe we should try making some of these desserts when we live together," she said, coming up for air from her quartet of chocolate delights.

"You think we could make a soufflé?" Evelyn asked.

"Well, maybe not that. But I bet we could handle the chocolate tart, and maybe even the mousse."

I turned to look at Evelyn. "You're going to live together?"

"Oh, I forgot to tell you." She set down her spoon. "I figured out a way to keep the house. Lucy and Sharon are going to rent rooms from me. Lucy will move into Mom's old room, and Sharon will take the guest room. They've both been wanting to move out from their parents, so it's perfect. And with the rent money I get, I should have enough to make the mortgage and pay the other bills."

"That's a great idea!" I said.

"We're going to make quite the trio, living all together." Evelyn took a sip of her Pink Squirrel, leaving a frothy mustache on her upper lip. "But this way," she added with a laugh, "we can arrange the house exactly as we need, with none of those annoying sighted people messing things up."

Lucy and Evelyn went on to discuss their future household: what kinds of food they'd prepare together, how they'd set up the living room as a place for them all to study, what music they'd listen to. ("No Justin Bieber," they both agreed.) I was only half paying attention when I looked up to see a familiar form come through the restaurant door.

Eric. What was he doing here?

I waited to see if he had anyone with him, but no. He was alone. No Gayle.

He stood a moment looking around till he spotted us, then crossed the dining room to our table.

"Hi, Sal. Hey, Javier. Evelyn."

I introduced him to Lucy and asked if he wanted to pull up a chair, which he did.

296

"So what brings you here?" I asked.

"Well, I ran into your dad downtown this morning, and he told me what happened last night."

"Oh, shoot, Eric. I'm so sorry. I should have called to tell you . . ."

And why hadn't I? At any other time in the last seven years, Eric would have been the first person I called.

He held my eyes a moment, then frowned and looked away. He knew why, as did I. Gayle was the reason. But what he didn't know was that talking to Martin Vargas had also driven the need to call and tell him what had happened straight out of me.

"Anyhow, Mario told me you were having a celebration here tonight for Evelyn's birthday after it slowed down some, so I thought I'd come by. Happy birthday, by the way." He stood and walked over to give her a hug and kiss on the cheek, then sat back down.

Brandon appeared at our table. "Hey, Eric. Can I get you anything?"

"Don't order any dessert," Lucy said. "There's more than enough here to share."

"A Calvados would be great. Thanks."

The arrival of Eric caused the rest of us to become more subdued. Brandon brought him his snifter of apple brandy, and he raised it in a toast. "Here's to the next twenty-one years, Evelyn. May they be filled with health, prosperity, and good cheer."

"Is that another Irish saying?" she asked.

"Nah, I just made that one up right here on the spot." He turned to me, raising his glass once more. "And may your next years, Sally, be filled with less stress and hopefully not quite as many murder investigations."

I shook my head, in no mood for a scolding at this moment. But when I looked back up, I saw that Eric's expression wasn't one of reproach but rather concern.

"And I want you to know that no matter what happens between us," he went on, "no matter where we end up—or with whom—I'll always be around for you, Sally. You know that, right?"

I smiled, not attempting to hide the tears springing to my eyes. "Yeah, Eric. I do. And the same goes for me. I'll always have your back, kiddo."

We clinked glasses, then Eric stole my spoon. "Okay," he said, "so who's going to tell me about all these amazing desserts?"

Recipes

Roasted Leeks With Walnut Oil, Lemon, and Thyme

(serves 6)

Most folks cut off and discard the dark-green ends of leeks, but because of the added flavor and color they impart, I like to use them for this dish (do, however, discard any yellow or brown parts of the plant). Cut off the roots, then slice the leeks down the middle and rinse off any dirt or grit you find between the layers. Then cut them into 3-inch pieces.

If you don't have a citrus zester, you can use a fine cheese grater instead (as long as it's good and sharp). Wash and zest the lemon first, then cut it in two and squeeze out the juice for the recipe.

Ingredients

6 medium leeks (about 2 pounds), split down the middle and cut into 3-inch lengths

4 tablespoons roasted walnut oil

3 tablespoons lemon juice (from 1 large or 2 small lemons)

½ teaspoon salt

½ teaspoon black pepper

1 tablespoon lemon zest (from 1 large or 2 small lemons)

1 tablespoon fresh thyme, finely chopped (stripped from the woody part)

⅓ cup grated Parmesan or pecorino cheese

Directions

Place the leeks in a large roasting pan, drizzle on the walnut oil and lemon juice, sprinkle on the salt and pepper, then toss and spread out evenly over the pan.

Roast at 375° F until the leeks start to soften (about 15 minutes). Sprinkle the lemon zest and thyme over the leeks, toss, and return to oven until lightly browned and tender (about 15 minutes more).

Serve topped with the cheese.

Singapore Noodles With Roast Pork and Broccolini

(serves 4–6)

These are the luscious noodles that were served by the pop-up restaurant The Curry Leaf. It's a perfect way to use up leftover barbecued or roast pork, but you can also buy *char siu*–style Chinese pork, or make your own roast pork especially for this dish (*recipe follows this one). Both black bean and oyster sauce can be found in jars in the Asian food section of the supermarket.

The steps set forth in the "Prep" section of the directions can be completed several hours beforehand, but then the "Stir-Fry" portion should be done right before service.

Ingredients for the Stir Fry

1 pound broccolini, uncut (may substitute broccoli florets)
1 pound dried Chinese egg noodles or spaghetti
2 tablespoons sesame oil
2 tablespoons peanut or canola oil
1 medium onion, halved, then thinly sliced (about ½ pound)
2-inch chunk of ginger, minced (2 tablespoons)
4 cloves garlic, minced (1 heaping tablespoon)
1 pound roast pork, sliced into 1 × ¼–inch strips

3 green onions, chopped
2 tablespoons cilantro, roughly chopped

Ingredients for the Sauce

1 cup chicken stock
1 tablespoon brown sugar
2 tablespoons black bean sauce
2 tablespoons oyster sauce
2 tablespoons white vinegar
1 tablespoon soy sauce
½ teaspoon black pepper

Directions

Prep

Bring a large (at least 4-quart) pot to a boil. Add the broccolini and cook 2 to 3 minutes, till bright green but still firm. Remove with tongs to ice bath and cool, then drain. Cut into 2-inch-long pieces and set aside.

Bring water back to a boil and add noodles. Cook according to instructions till al dente (still slightly firm in the center), stirring occasionally to prevent sticking. Drain, then toss with 1 tablespoon sesame oil. Set aside.

Combine all sauce ingredients in a medium-size saucepot, bring to a simmer, and cook until reduced by half, stirring occasionally. Set pan aside, keeping sauce warm (or you can reheat it while the noodles are frying).

Stir-Fry

In a very large wok or heavy skillet, heat 1 tablespoon peanut or canola oil over medium to high heat till shimmering, then add broccolini and fry, tossing often, till it softens slightly and starts to brown. Remove to bowl and set aside.

In the same wok, heat 1 tablespoon peanut or canola oil and 1 tablespoon sesame oil over medium to high heat till shimmering, then add the cooked noodles and fry, tossing often, till they start to brown. Add the onions, ginger, and garlic, and continue to fry, stirring or tossing often, till onions soften and start to brown. Add the sliced pork and browned broccolini, and continue cooking till they are heated through. Pour in warm sauce, and toss to coat noodles and vegetables.

Served garnished with chopped green onions and cilantro.

*To make roast pork for this dish, cut 1 pound pork (any cut will work, but I like to use shoulder) into four chunks and season with salt, pepper, garlic powder, ginger powder, and five-spice or garam masala powder. Wrap in aluminum foil and place in roasting pan. Roast at 250° F for 2 hours. Unwrap pork and continue to roast (still sitting in juices on foil) 15 more minutes to allow top to brown. Let cool enough to handle, then slice into strips and pour liquid from pan over sliced meat.

Spot Prawns With Citrus
and Harissa

(serves 4)

Gauguin prepares this recipe with spot prawns (a kind of large shrimp) because of their sweet, almost lobsterlike flavor and because the seasonal harvest is limited and sustainable, thus allowing for the continued health of the species. But if you can't find spot prawns, feel free to substitute a different variety of shrimp (just be sure to check with your seafood supplier to learn which varieties are deemed the "Best Choice" by the Monterey Bay Aquarium Seafood Watch program). We peel the shrimp before cooking but leave the tails intact for eye appeal and added flavor.

Harissa is a spicy North African condiment made from roasted hot chili peppers, garlic, olive oil, cumin, coriander, caraway, and other spices. Tubes or jars of this paste can be found in most supermarkets in the United States, but if you can't locate it, feel free to substitute another hot chili sauce such as sriracha (to which you could add cumin, coriander, and caraway to make for an even better substitute). If you are sensitive to spicy food, use only half the amount of harissa specified, then taste and add more if needed.

This dish is best served with steamed basmati or jasmine rice, and would pair nicely with a crisp green salad.

Ingredients

2 tablespoons olive oil

2 medium onions, halved, then thinly sliced (about 1 pound)

3 cloves garlic, minced (1 tablespoon)

¼ cup lemon juice

⅓ cup orange juice

3 tablespoons butter

1 tablespoon harissa

1 pound raw spot prawns or other shrimp, peeled (with tails intact)

2 seedless oranges, pceled and white pith removed, then cut into chunks

salt and pepper to taste

2 tablespoons cilantro, coarsely chopped

Directions

Heat the olive oil in a large skillet over medium heat till shimmering, then add onions and sauté till they soften. Add the garlic and continue to cook till the onions start to brown.

Pour in the lemon and orange juices and continue to cook until the liquid is reduced by half. Then add the butter and harissa and toss to incorporate.

Once the butter has melted, add the prawns/shrimp and sauté until they turn from white to pink. Add the orange chunks and toss just long enough for them to heat through.

Season with salt and pepper, and serve garnished with the chopped cilantro.

Nonna Sophia's Pasta With Peas, Onion, Porcini, and Garlic

(serves 4–6)

This is the dish Evelyn learned as a young girl from her grandmother. It's best with homemade egg pasta (the recipe follows this one), but you could use a store-bought variety instead. If so, try to find dried fettuccine or pappardelle made with eggs. (Avoid the "fresh" pasta sold in the supermarket, as it tends to be too thick and overworked, and can turn gooey when cooked.)

It's important to sauté the peas and onions separately from the mushrooms and garlic so that the flavors remain distinct. Once they're cooked, however, they can be combined into one pan to await mixing with the pasta.

If you can't find dried porcini mushrooms (also called *boletes* or *cèpes*), you can substitute fresh creminis—small brown, button mushrooms—or portobellos.

Ingredients
2 ounces dried porcini mushrooms (or ½ pound fresh)
6 tablespoons olive oil
1 large onion, diced (about ¾ pound)
¾ pound peas (fresh or frozen, thawed)
½ teaspoon salt

½ teaspoon black pepper

6 cloves garlic, minced (2 tablespoons)

2 tablespoons flat-leaf parsley, coarsely chopped

¼ pound Parmesan or pecorino cheese, finely grated
    (about 1½ cups)

1 pound dried egg fettuccine or pappardelle (or use pasta
    recipe below)

1 tablespoon salt (for pasta water)

Directions

Pour enough boiling water over the dried porcini to cover them and let soak for an hour. Slice the mushrooms into thin strips, reserving the liquid in a separate bowl.

Heat 2 tablespoons oil in a large skillet over moderate heat till shimmering, then add the onions. Sauté till they soften, then add the peas and continue to cook until the onions start to brown and the peas are cooked through. Season with ¼ teaspoon each salt and pepper. Set aside.

In a separate pan, heat 2 more tablespoons of oil till shimmering, then add the mushrooms (squeeze out most of the liquid first so they don't spatter). Sauté till they cook through, then add the garlic. Continue to cook till the mushrooms start to brown. Season with ¼ teaspoon each salt and pepper. Add the chopped parsley and ½ cup of the mushroom liquid, stir to incorporate, and set aside.

Bring a large (at least 4-quart) pot of water to a boil. While the water is heating, reheat the peas/onions and porcini/garlic over medium heat.

Add the salt and pasta to the water and cook, uncovered, over medium heat until al dente (still slightly firm in the center), stirring occasionally to prevent sticking. If using homemade pasta, it will cook very fast—in about 3 minutes. If using dried pasta, it will take about 10–12 minutes to cook.

Reserving ½ cup of the cooking water, drain the pasta and dump it back into the cooking pot (without rinsing). Add 2 tablespoons of olive oil to pasta and toss to coat all the noodles. Pour in the ½ cup of cooking water, then add the reheated vegetables and toss. Finally, add 1 cup of the cheese and toss once again.

Serve garnished with the rest of the cheese.

Nonna Sophia's Homemade Egg Pasta

(serves 4–6)

Like her Nonna Sophia before her, Evelyn always rolls out her pasta by hand with her *mattarello*—an Italian rolling pin. But as this is a fine art requiring years of practice, the recipe here calls for a pasta rolling machine instead—which is far easier and makes for perfectly fine pasta.

Ingredients

3 cups unbleached, all-purpose flour (called "00" in Italy)

4 large eggs, at room temperature

Directions for Dough

Pour the flour into a mound on a large smooth work surface such as wood (don't use marble, as you want to keep the dough warm). Make a large well in the center of the flour with your fingers and crack the eggs into the center. With a fork, beat the eggs until the whites and yolks are evenly mixed together. Then start drawing in some flour from the sides of the well as you beat. This mixing needs to happen slowly, to avoid having clumps of flour. (Be careful not to break the wall, lest the eggs escape!) Continue incorporating the flour into the eggs until they are no longer runny—a bit like a thick pancake batter.

Using both hands, quickly bring the rest of the flour over the egg mixture so that it's completely covered. Then work the mixture with your hands until all the flour is combined with the eggs. The dough should feel moist but not too sticky (if so, add a little more flour; if it's too dry, add a tiny bit of water). Form it into a ragged ball and wrap tightly in plastic wrap.

Scrape clean your work surface and wash and dry your hands. Then unwrap the dough and begin kneading. Use the palm of your hand to push the dough down and away from you, then fold it back over itself. Rotate the dough a quarter turn and repeat this process. Continue kneading until the texture of the dough is uniform and smooth, with no specks of unincorporated flour—about 10 minutes. (It should be "smooth and silky as a baby's butt," Nonna Sophia would say.)

Wrap the ball of dough in a clean sheet of plastic wrap and let it rest on the counter for at least 20 minutes.

Rolling and Cutting the Pasta

Cut the ball of dough into six pieces and wrap five back up in plastic so they don't dry out. Flatten the first piece of dough with your hands and feed it through the roller at its widest setting (usually 0). Fold the dough in thirds (like an envelope) and feed it again through the same setting, with the folds at the sides. Do this three more times.

Reduce the roller width one notch and run the piece through one time. Reduce the width another notch and run the piece through one time. Continue reducing the width and running the piece through once until you get to notch number 7. (If the sheet becomes too long to handle easily, cut it in half.)

Lay the rolled sheet of pasta on a clean dish towel or wax paper, and repeat this process for the other five balls of dough, starting each time with the widest setting.

Let the sheets of pasta dry until they feel leathery (so the cut noodles don't stick to each other), but not so dry as to be brittle and crack. Once leathery, run the sheets through the widest setting of the pasta machine's cutting mechanism (for fettuccine), and lay the strips out flat to dry.

If you want pasta wider than fettuccine (such as pappardelle), you'll have to cut it by hand. Dust the sheets of pasta with flour to keep them from sticking, then roll each sheet loosely so it's about 3 inches wide, cut it into wide ribbons with a large knife, then unroll the ribbons and lay them out flat.

If you're not going to cook the pasta the same day, you can roll the cut strands into loose nests. (Make sure they're dried enough not to stick together; dusting them with flour helps.) Let them dry completely, then wrap in plastic and freeze. To cook, simply drop the pasta into salted boiling water (it will take slightly longer to cook if frozen).

Acknowledgments

I owe an enormous debt of gratitude to the people who took the time to share with me their experiences of being blind: Erin Byrne, Stacie Grijalva, Beverly Heninger, Patrice Maginns, and Herman Rubin. This book would not exist but for your generosity and candor.

In addition, my heartfelt thanks go out to those who provided advice and information regarding their various areas of expertise: Craig Gillespie and Nancy Lundblad (medical and eye issues), Cathy Kriege (restaurants and POS systems), Bill Ong Hing (immigration law), Detective Wes Grant of the Santa Cruz County Coroner's Office, Christie Tall of the Vista Center for the Blind and Visually Impaired, and Daria Siciliano (who cooked for me her Nonna Egle's delectable pasta dish, reinvented here as "Nonna Sophia's Pasta").

Thanks also to my wonderful beta readers for their comments on the manuscript: Robin McDuff, Nancy Lundblad, Patrice Maginns, and most especially Erin Byrne, whose detailed critique of my early efforts proved invaluable. *E grazie mille* to Shirley Tessler, for her assistance in editing the recipes, and to all my recipe tasters, Renée Almatierra, Rosanna Roa, Tom Ellison, Larry Friedman,

Robin McDuff, Shirley Tessler, Avron Barr, Patrice Boyles, and Enda Brennan.

I am also once again deeply indebted to Erin Niumata of Folio Literary Management; to Matt Martz, Jenny Chen, Sarah Poppe, Chelsey Emmelhainz, and everyone else at Crooked Lane Books; to Hiro Kimura for his gorgeous covers; and to my incomparable editor, Nike Power.

And finally, massive thanks to my fellow mystery writers and bloggers at Chicks on the Case, who always have my back: Ellen Byron, Marla Cooper, Vickie Fee, Kellye Garrett, Cynthia Kuhn, and Lisa Q. Mathews.